The Selected Stories
of Siegfried Lenz

The Selected Stories of Siegfried Lenz

EDITED AND TRANSLATED BY BREON MITCHELL

A NEW DIRECTIONS BOOK

The translations in this book were selected from Siegfried Lenz, *Die Erzählungen 1949–1984,* and published by arrangement with Hoffmann and Campe Verlag, Hamburg. The translator gratefully acknowledges the support of the National Endowment for the Arts in preparing this collection.

Manufactured in the United States of America
New Directions Books are published on acid-free paper.
First published clothbound by New Directions in 1989
Published simultaneously in Canada by Penguin Books Canada Ltd.

Library of Congress Cataloging-in-Publication Data

Lenz, Siegfried, 1926–
    The selected stories of Siegfried Lenz.

    Translation of selections from: Die Erzählungen.
    1. Lenz, Siegfried, 1926–   —Translations,
English.   I.   Mitchell, Breon.   II.   Title.
PT2623.E583A26   1989   833'.914   89-13120
ISBN 0-8112-1092-8 (alk. paper)

New Directions Books are published for James Laughlin
by New Directions Publishing Corporation,
80 Eighth Avenue, New York 10011

CONTENTS

Tales of Our Times

Tales from the Village

SULEYKEN

CONTENTS

The Selected Stories
of Siegfried Lenz

Tales of Our Times

THE LAUGHINGSTOCK

 The wind was right. Atoq's scent didn't carry to the dogs lying snowed-in near the cabin. Unnoticed, he walked past the battered, empty meat racks. When his father, the great hunter, was still alive, the racks had always been full, but now they stood battered and empty before the cabin. There was no blubber in the hollow of the side platform, the furs on the sleeping platform were worn through, and the translucent sheets of seal intestine at the windows were torn.

Atoq walked unnoticed past the sleeping dogs. He strode across the gray, dead plain and heard the frost popping on the lakes and knew that cracks were appearing in the new ice. He strode across the plain until he reached the great Fern Mountain. Then he turned to look back, and saw that his departure was still unnoted.

The worst hunter in Cumberland had set out in secret to hunt. He left the dogs sleeping and pushed the sled himself. He laid his gun across the sled and opened his parka.

He listened, but there was nothing to hear. No one in the village knew that he was on his way. They were lying on their platforms, unaware that he had set out in secret to dispel their scorn. He thought of the scores of satirical songs about Atoq, the hunter with the empty racks. This time he would return with a loaded sled. He would not come back until he had enough meat for both racks. He set out in secret because they would have laughed at him as he left. The laughter would have angered him, and that might have ruined the hunt. This time he would silence their ridicule, and eliminate his name, once and for all, from their songs of scorn. He had arranged everything for this day.

Atoq glided slowly across Fern Mountain. He looked down at the rifle lying on his empty sled, and he pictured it no longer below him upon his return; instead he saw it high atop the meat, at eye-level. Atoq was confident this time.

A faint birdcall drifted toward him. He turned his head and saw a ptarmigan: red lids and a brown back. The ptarmigan ducked behind a snowdrift as Atoq approached. He was on his way to his father's old hunting ground, to the mountain valley where the black musk ox grazed. It was a long journey, and he didn't want to lose any time. He thought of the huge, black musk oxen, grazing peacefully, and he recalled their powerful flanks and their cunning. He remembered his father's arrows whirring through the air, how they lodged vibrating in their chests. Atoq had brought his father's bow, and his harpoon too, although he thought he wouldn't need it. He had his high-caliber rifle, and that would be enough. Atoq, the worst hunter in Cumberland, sang as he crossed the dead plain. He still had his right foot on the sled's runner. He hadn't switched feet because he knew that he went faster pushing off with his left foot. They were long, powerful thrusts, and the sled glided smoothly over the plain.

He thought of the terror that seized the animals each time one of them was hit and crumpled to the ground. He saw his father again, the great hunter, creeping soundlessly across the morass, damp from the icy water, unseen, his bow and arrow in his teeth. He saw the old man creeping within bow range. Then the arrow flew, an animal crumpled, and the herd scattered. Atoq thought of these things and, as the sled glided over the plain, he thought of his own misfortune, the bad luck that always dogged him on the hunt. He had a good eye, his hand was steady, but whenever he set out on a hunt the wind was wrong, or the animals were too nervous, or the surface of the tundra crumbled beneath his feet and he couldn't stalk them properly. So he was often forced to return home without any meat, where he was greeted by scathing ridicule, his name ringing forth in their songs as a joke. Now he had set out in secret to redeem his name.

Atoq traveled across the plain for eight hours. Then, through the mist, he saw the weathered glacier. He glided over rolling hills, past gray boulders, toward the glacier, until he reached the valley and his father's dilapidated hunter's hut. His father had used whale ribs for the frame, covering the roof with moss and sod. Storms had beat about the hut and caved in the roof. Only the whale ribs remained standing, broad and pale gray, forming an almost perfect circle, a final testimony to the great hunter. Atoq placed the sled against the protective stone wall that encircled the hut to keep out the bears. He began to repair the wall and the hut. He fixed them up as best he could; he realized that he would be spending at least one night there. When he had finished the roof, he entered the hut, ate, and lay down.

Atoq couldn't stand it for long. He was seized by a great restlessness, a hunter's restlessness. He sensed game nearby. He slung his father's bow across his back, took the harpoon and line in one hand and his gun in the other, stepped out of the hut, and scanned the rocky slopes of the hills. He climbed up to a glacial moraine where he had once lain in wait with his father, but he found no game. He combed the area of the glacier and crossed the hills, and in the afternoon he found the animals in a narrow, foggy ravine. He saw there were five, the brown coat of an old bull and the black coats of two cows and their calves. The wind was right.

Atoq dropped to the ground, hid behind a boulder, and observed the animals. They moved about slowly, seldom lifting their heads. Suddenly the old bull disappeared in the mist, apparently moving further back into the ravine. Atoq decided to kill one of the cows first. He left his hiding place and crept closer to the animals. He would have to get closer to make certain of the first shot, since the drifting fog made it difficult to see, and the animals offered a poor target. They had turned and were following the old bull deeper into the ravine. Atoq stalked them slowly and cautiously, aware of the strength and cunning of the musk ox. Then he reached a pile of boulders that provided both a vantage point and protection from a frontal attack by the animals. He crouched down and aimed at one of the black cows.

The shot sent a dull echo reverberating through the ravine, but before the echo returned, Atoq knew he had missed. Just as he pulled the trigger, a snow hare had jumped out in front of him. It was so close that he was startled and jerked the gun barrel upward. He was totally taken aback and watched the hare scurry away in wild flight down the ravine before he turned to see the effect of his shot. Then he heard them thundering toward him, and lifting his gun for the second time, he shot at the lead animal, the one that would have reached him first, and saw it crash to earth in the midst of its rumbling charge, thrown to the ground by the force of the shot, rolling head over heels. But the others were still charging and would be on him before he could lift his gun a third time. This time he wouldn't run. He had seen how his father's dogs evaded charging oxen, and he was prepared. He quickly rolled behind a boulder as the enraged animals roared past. He laughed, and it was his father's laugh in the face of danger, the lonely laugh of a great hunter. He saw their long, sharp horns, their powerful necks, their beady, furious eyes, and laughed.

But suddenly he heard their rumbling attack coming from both directions, and looking back he saw the old bull, who had managed to get behind him. Atoq knew there was only one way out. He had to climb up the rocks before they were on him. He had to scale the smooth rock face. He threw his harpoon high onto a level ledge, gathered his strength for the great leap, and used the butt of his rifle to help him vault upward. The rifle butt was well braced, jammed solidly into a crevice, but as Atoq, in the very midst of his jump, tried to pull it after him, it proved to be stuck tight. It was so firmly wedged that the only way it would have come out was straight up, and Atoq was forced to release it in order to complete his jump. He reached the ledge, threw himself flat and looked down. He quickly lowered the harpoon line to the gun in hopes of passing it under the trigger or the bolt and lifting it up to him, but the line got caught on the barrel, and with a quick, short jerk the barrel was yanked backward, the butt sprang free from the crevice, and the gun flipped over and tumbled down the rocks. Atoq groaned as the rifle fell. Instinctively, he leaned out from the ledge, and would have leaped down had not the animals reached the bottom of the rocks at that very instant.

He heard the old bull snorting, saw its powerful neck and heaving flanks below him, then watched as the enraged animal trampled on the rifle, flung it against the cliff with its horns, and splintered the butt in its jaws. He watched without making a move, then grabbed the bow from his back, pulled out an arrow, and shot it from close range with all his strength into the side of the old bull. But the arrow struck a rib and didn't penetrate deep enough. Over half the arrow's shaft remained exposed, and the animal bit it off and trampled on it. Atoq took out another arrow, and this one shuddered deep into the animal's chest. But still the bull didn't fall. He rejoined the other animals standing on a rise on the opposite side of the rocks.

Keeping his eye on the animals, Atoq climbed down from the ledge. He had to have his rifle, and he wasn't going to leave the ravine without it. He jumped to the ground. But before he could bend over he heard them thundering toward him and scurried back up onto the ledge. They stood trembling beneath him. He heard them panting and pawing the ground. In order to save arrows, Atoq picked up stones and began throwing them at the animals, trying to drive them away. It worked. They withdrew to the rise and waited. He again climbed down to retrieve the gun, and this time he managed to. He grabbed the rifle by the barrel and returned safely. The butt was splintered, the barrel was bent, and the bolt was jammed. Atoq, the worst hunter in Cumberland, was still a laughingstock.

But he didn't give up. He had set out in secret to purge his name from their taunting songs. He had carefully prepared for this day. He had arranged everything, and Atoq, the hunter of misfortune, slung the rifle back down the rocks and laughed his father's bitter laugh. He peered into the ravine and saw, lying on the ground, the heavy black animal he had shot during the first charge. That was his kill, meat that now belonged to him, although he still didn't have a clear path to it. It would fill half his sled, enough for one meat rack, enough to give him new strength. The gun was worthless, but he still had the harpoon and the bow. He climbed down from the ledge to provoke the animals into charging again. They came thundering at him when they saw him on the ground, the old bull, with the arrow in its chest, leading the way. The hunter had eyes only for him. Atoq knew that the other animals would withdraw permanently if he killed the old bull. And so he devised a plan. He tied the end of the harpoon line around a corner of rock and lifted the harpoon high in the air. Aiming carefully and powerfully, he held the heavy shaft as if it were weightless. He dipped the sharp iron tip and cast the harpoon at the bull with all his might. It shot downward, and the iron point disappeared into the base of the animal's neck. The bull threw himself sideways, but neither stumbled nor collapsed. He raced back with the other animals toward the rise, shook himself, then pulled and chewed at the line, which, because it was made of elastic sealskin, remained intact. The bull reached the rise, but with the harpoon still in his back. And now Atoq took out an arrow. He placed the arrow in the bow, climbed down, and, standing upright, walked slowly toward the rise. He saw that the animals were bunched together with lowered heads, but he walked on. He continued straight toward them, and as they began to charge, he shot and hit the old bull in the throat. He struck the bull in mid-leap, and the animal collapsed at the base of the rise. Atoq could see that this arrow too had not been fatal. He must have broken a leg. Now he had won. He rolled behind a rock and let the other animals charge at empty air. Watching them pass by, he saw that they would not attack again. They left the ravine without turning about, and he was alone.

Atoq killed the old bull, and only then did he realize who was lying at his feet. It was the one they called Agdliartortoq, "he who keeps on getting bigger," hunted in vain for years, the largest and strongest animal of them all, spoken of with trembling awe. He had killed several of their people, and had proved too much for even Atoq's father, the great hunter.

Although the battle had tired Atoq, he set to work. He didn't want to leave the meat in the ravine overnight, and he loaded as much as he could on his back each time and carried it to the hut. He made several trips from the ravine to the hut without resting, even though he was extremely weary, and on the final trip he brought back the powerful, sharp horns of the bull, and the worthless rifle.

Atoq was at the end of his strength, but he was filled with certainty that his name would no longer be heard in songs of scorn. They would cease, he had confounded their laughter for all time. He threw the mighty horns in the hut, piled up the meat inside the wall, and covered it with large flat stones, stones his father had once used for the same purpose. They were heavy and hard to move, and by the time Atoq was finished night was falling.

The night was not deep. A dull light lay over the hut, and when Atoq looked out the peephole, he had the impression it was still day, a reluctant day beneath a dead sky. But he knew when he had started out, and what he had done, and he spread the furs on the floor of the hut, blocked up the entrance with stones, and lay down to sleep. He felt only the vague happiness of exhaustion. He curled up, put his head on his arm, and, breathing slowly and deeply, waited to fall asleep. But sleep didn't come. After a while he opened his eyes and felt behind him for the horns of the old bull. He touched them and then rolled onto his back. Looking out the peephole at the tiny section of the heavens, he thought of his father. He remembered that his father too had never been able to sleep after the hunt. Atoq would awake to find the old hunter crouching in a corner, waiting silently and impatiently for the morning light. He never dared speak to him, nor would his father have answered. Atoq remembered that.

Suddenly he heard the sound of crunching steps, then digging and scratching, followed immediately by the gnashing of teeth. He jumped up, grabbed his bow, and approached the peephole. Inside the wall, so near that he could almost touch it, was a polar bear, a huge, thin creature, whose coat had a greenish shimmer in the dull light. Atoq watched the bear lift a large piece of the old bull's shoulder and begin to chew greedily. The smell of the meat must have drawn it to the hut. Perhaps it knew the place from the days when Atoq's father kept his meat covered there. Atoq saw that it was an old female. But while he was watching the bear, he heard a loud scratching from the other side, and when he went to the opposite peephole, he discovered four bears trying to lift the flat stones. They had pushed their way in through a hole in the wall, a hole Atoq hadn't felt he needed to repair, since he didn't expect to spend many nights in the hut. The bears rolled the stones to the side and devoured the uncovered meat. Atoq ran from one peephole to the other, and saw that all was lost. The gun was no longer of any use to him. Had it still worked, he could have driven them away. He might even have dared to step outside the hut with it, but he could do nothing with the harpoon and the bow alone. The bears would tear him to bits. He placed an arrow in the bow, pointed it through the peephole, aimed, and shot. He aimed at the mother bear first, believing that the two young bears on the other side would leave with her. The arrow whistled through the hole and hit her in the neck, but without any real force. She bellowed in anger, dropped the piece of meat, looked around, then came so close to the peephole that Atoq was able to stab her with his knife. It wasn't a serious blow, but the bear was warned off. She left the piece of meat lying on the ground and trotted around to the other bears. Now they were positioned so that Atoq could not reach them with an arrow. The shaft of the arrow would have brushed against the side of the peep-hole and been deflected in its flight. The bears were keeping a close watch on the hut. They knew it was a source of danger, but they still weren't prepared to give up the meat. Soon they dragged their chunks of meat beyond the wall and continued eating. Atoq could hear the grinding of their teeth.

He hadn't brought all the meat to the hut, just the best pieces, and the ones he could carry most easily. The rest he had left behind in the ravine. He knew that by tomorrow very little would remain. The foxes would see to that, and the ravens, and even other bears, drawn by the smell. The meat that Atoq had covered at the hut had been just enough for his sled, would have loaded the sled high enough so that when he laid the rifle on top, it would have been at eye-level, just as he had pictured it. Hastily he tried to estimate how much meat he still had. He had counted five bears, and if they hadn't taken too much, there would still be some for him. Enough to fill at least one meat rack. He examined the stones from his peephole. He could see only two that hadn't been overturned, two small flat stones near the entrance. Whether or not he would continue to be judged a laughing-stock depended on them. He had to prevent the bears from overturn-ing those last two stones. He was willing to do anything. He watched the bears shimmering greenishly in the dull light, watched their every move from the peephole. Atoq, the worst hunter in Cumberland.

And now he saw the mother bear, approaching suspiciously. He watched the small, black nose and the long, swaying neck. She drew near the entrance, coming toward the last stone covers. Atoq seized a stick and began to wrap a cloth around it. It was a torch-cloth he had laid out for the night, and when the torch was prepared, he ignited it. It flamed up strongly. He bent over in its light and opened the door a crack. Taking the harpoon and torch, he stepped outside the hut. The bear stood directly in front of him. She was a gigantic animal. She raised up immediately on her hind legs when she saw him, ready for battle. Atoq hurled the harpoon, but at that instant the bear dropped to the side and the harpoon merely grazed her thigh. The bear quickly raised up again to attack. She looked as if she wanted to crush Atoq. But Atoq threw his burning torch and struck her on the chest. She jumped back, fell on all fours, and disappeared behind the wall with a roar.

Now the other bears arrived. The burning torch couldn't keep them off. They came through the hole in the wall, and Atoq was forced to retreat into the hut and block off the entrance. He stood near the entrance, knife in hand. Suddenly he saw a stone move and fall inward, pushed from the outside. In the same instant a gray-white paw appeared in the opening. Atoq stabbed at it. He stabbed the paw with all his might. The knife went through it and struck stone on the other side. The bear jerked its paw back with a roar of rage. Atoq waited. He thought they would try to force their way into the hut. He was ready for anything, but the bears heeded the warning. They were either afraid or they had had enough. No more paws appeared in the opening. He closed it up again and looked through the peephole. The torch was still burning. It illuminated the snow and the area near the hut with a violet light, and in this light the bears shoved the last stone aside, dragged out the meat, and carried it away. Atoq stared fixedly as they lumbered off over the hill, a swaying line. He already felt the paralyzing derision, the inexorable judgment he had been unable to reverse, and he collapsed before the entrance.

When he awoke the light had changed. He stepped out of the hut and viewed with indifference the remains of the meat the bears had left behind. He pulled the sled from behind the wall, then gathered his rifle and bow and the splintered harpoon. Returning to the hut, he carried the horns of the old bull to the sled. He glided slowly over the hills, the hunter of misfortune, pushing the sled on at an easy pace. Silently and without grieving, he headed home beneath the dead sky. He had not been able to prove them wrong. They would continue to sing his name in songs of scorn. They knew by now he was out on a hunt, and a mocking reception surely awaited him. But he had to return. He had to wait for another chance.

He glided across the great Fern Mountain. From a distance he could see them, waiting for him at the entrance to the village, watching him. But Atoq did not slow down. He went right on, passing through the lane they had formed. Upon his sled lay the worthless rifle, and the splintered harpoon, and the old bull's horns. He passed between the rows, the defeated hunter of Cumberland. He stared at the path before him. And those who watched him come, and looked upon his sled, said nothing. They were silent.

THE GREAT WILDENBERG

 The letter brought new hope. It was brief, dictated with polite indifference, and carried no salutation. It showed no particular personal involvement, and certainly was not intended, even between the lines, or by some involuntary turn of phrase, to encourage me in the belief that my chances were good. Although I reread the letter several times, searching for phrases I feared I might have overlooked the first time through in my excitement, and in spite of the fact that try as I might I could read nothing particularly favorable into it, I believed I was justified in placing some hope in it, for it was an invitation, or a suggestion at any rate, to come to the factory and introduce myself.

I folded the letter and placed it in my billfold, so I would have it on hand if I needed it, and rode out to the factory. It was a wire factory, a long, low building. It was already dark when I arrived, and snow was falling. I walked along in the lee of a high, brick wall, on a sidewalk illuminated by electric arc lamps. I met no one. Rails were embedded in the pavement of the street, shining dully, the snow melting as it touched them. The tracks led me to an entranceway. They left the street in a sharp curve, ran under a chain-link gate, and disappeared within a dark garage. Next to the gate there was a wooden porter's lodge with one dim lightbulb hanging from the ceiling.

In the glow of the lightbulb I could see the porter, a morose old man sitting at a dilapidated wooden table, observing me. A coal fire burned at his back. I approached the lodge, and the porter placed his ear against the window, waiting for me to speak. I said nothing.

Annoyed, he pushed open a little window in front of me. I felt a stream of stale, sweet air flow outward. The porter was apparently worried that too much air might escape from his room, and he asked impatiently:

"What do you want? Have you got an appointment?"

I said that I had been asked to come, and that if he wanted me to, I could show him the letter. The letter had been signed by a man named Wildenberg.

When I mentioned this name, the porter glanced at his watch, then looked at me, troubled and slightly scornful. He seemed to have forgotten his anger, and now felt only a sort of professional pity for me.

"Isn't Mr. Wildenberg in?" I asked.

"He's almost always in," said the porter. "He hardly ever goes away. But you won't be able to speak to him today."

And then he told me how difficult it was to get to see Wildenberg. He told me about all the burdens borne by this great man, who reached his decisions in silent loneliness behind distant doors. There was no point, even if I had been asked to come, in trying to approach him at this hour. He said I should come again tomorrow, shrugged his shoulders with a sigh and added that was the only advice he could give me, and that I would do well to follow it.

I took the porter's advice and went back home. The next morning, at the first break of dawn, I set off again for the factory. The arc lamps were still burning, it was cold, and the smell of cabbage came from the factory canteen. The porter seemed to have been expecting me, and greeted me affably. He motioned for me to stay outside, remained on the telephone for a fairly long time, and finally told me in a pleased and eager tone that he had succeeded in getting me on track. I could proceed without further ado to Doctor Setzki's office, the doctor's secretary was expecting me.

The secretary was thin and energetic. She offered me a cup of freshly brewed tea, then excused herself to get back to some pressing task. I took the tea as a good sign. The offer made me so confident about the state of my affairs that I tried to give the secretary one of my two cigarettes, but she refused it. I didn't light up either, since Doctor Setzki might come out of his office at any moment. I heard noises behind his door, a rustling and murmuring.

Outside it was growing brighter, the arc lamps faded, and the secretary asked me if she could turn off the lights in the room. I gave a long and complicated reply in hopes of drawing her into a conversation, because I was embarrassed for her sake that Dr. Setzki was keeping me waiting so long. But the young woman didn't respond to my remarks, and immediately hid herself again behind the security of her typewriter.

Dr. Setzki finally came out. Unexpectedly young, he excused himself for having made me wait so long, and led me through a corridor. He placed most of the blame for his tardiness on the fact that Wildenberg, the great and lonely laborer, never left anyone in peace, but was instead constantly asking questions, checking and rechecking things, and thus prevented anyone else from sticking to a precise daily schedule. I felt a twinge of fear at the prospect of sitting opposite Wildenberg within a few seconds. Sweat broke out on my palms, and I longed to return to the secretary's room.

Dr. Setzki took me through an office and into a room in which there was nothing but a desk and two chairs. He asked me to sit down on one of the chairs and wait for Dr. Petersen, who, he said, was Wildenberg's right-hand man, and could open all remaining doors to the great man. He showed himself informed concerning my situation, spoke with great admiration of Wildenberg's talent for finding people, and finally took his leave, having placed his hand briefly on my shoulder. When I was alone, I thought over what he had said, and the tone in which it had been uttered. The admiration with which he had spoken of Wildenberg seemed to me now to have been tinged with concealed irony.

The secretary came into the room to do something and told me that Dr. Petersen was in a conference. She couldn't say when he would be finished, but she thought it wouldn't be too long; such conferences were a great strain. She laughed knowingly and left me to myself.

The secretary was right. I had waited for just ten minutes when Dr. Petersen arrived, a tall man with watery eyes. He begged me not to rise, and we talked about my application. Wildenberg still had it, he said, having kept it himself in spite of his tremendous work load, and I would certainly oblige the great man if I didn't mention it any further, and kept my visit with him as short as possible.

"I'm certain," said Dr. Petersen, "that the more succinctly you express yourself the better Mr. Wildenberg's mood will be. People like him prefer everything brief and to the point." Then he asked me to follow him, knocked on a door, and a voice called out, "Come in." He made one last hasty gesture urging me to keep all his advice in mind, and showed me in. I heard the door close behind me.

"Come on," said a weak, friendly voice, "come over here to me."

I looked into the corner from which the voice had come and saw a small man with a sorrowful smile sitting behind an enormous desk. He waved his rimless pince-nez forlornly, gave me his small, arthritic hand, and shyly asked me to take a seat.

After I had seated myself, he began to talk. He told me the entire history of the factory, and whenever he paused and I got up to go, he would beg me fervently to stay. Each time when I sat down again, he thanked me profusely, complained about his loneliness, and wiped off the top of his totally clear desk with his delicate arm. I became restless in light of the advice I had received, but his need to express himself seemed genuine, and I stayed.

I stayed with him for several hours. Before I took my leave, I asked him about my application. He smiled sadly and assured me that he had never seen it. It was true, he said, that he was given something to sign once in a while, but only so that he wouldn't feel so lonely, for it was immediately whisked away from him again. And he advised me in a whisper to try Dr. Setzki, who was more likely to have it, and who could be reached through the porter. That was how things were.

I said goodbye to the great Wildenberg, and when I was already at the door, he came skipping after me, tugged at my sleeve, and asked me to come and see him again soon. I promised I would.

A FRIEND OF THE GOVERNMENT

▬§ They had issued weekend invitations to journalists for an on-the-spot look at the strength of the people's support for the government. They wanted to prove to us that none of the things being written about that troubled region was in fact true: no one was being tortured, there was no poverty, and above all, there was no raging desire for independence. So they invited us most civilly, and a very polite, perfectly dressed official met us behind the opera building and led us to the government bus. The smell of varnish and leather surrounded us, soft music was playing, and as the bus pulled out, the official took a microphone from its clip, scraped across the silvery mesh with his fingernail, and welcomed us again in a soft voice. Modestly mentioning his own name—"My name is Garek," he said—he pointed out the various beauties of the capital city, gave us the names and total number of public parks, and explained to us how the government had constructed the model housing development lying atop a chalky hill, already dazzling in the morning sun.

Outside the capital the road branched off, and we moved away from the sea toward the country's interior, past rock-strewn fields, past brown slopes; we came to a deep ravine and drove along its bottom until we came to a bridge which crossed a dry riverbed. A young soldier was standing on the bridge, holding a lightweight submachine gun with tender carelessness. He waved to us cheerfully as we passed him on the bridge. Two more young soldiers were standing in the dried-out riverbed among the white, polished stones, and Garek said that we were passing through a favorite training area.

Up a series of switchbacks, across a hot plain. A fine chalk dust pressed in through the open windows, burning our eyes; the taste of chalk was on our lips. We took off our jackets. Garek was the only one who kept his jacket on. He was still holding the microphone in his hand, explaining in a soft voice the government's carefully worked-out plans for cultivating these lifeless fields. I saw that the man sitting next to me had closed his eyes and was leaning his head back; his lips were dry and pale with chalk; the veins of his hands, which were resting on the chrome-plated metal armrests, stood out bluely. I thought of nudging him in the side, since now and then a glance from Garek's melancholy eyes would come our way through the rearview mirror. But while I was still thinking about it, Garek stood up and came back down the narrow aisle, smiling and distributing straw hats and ice-cold drinks in wax-paper cartons.

Around noon we passed through a village. The windows were nailed shut with boards from wooden crates, the shabby fences of dry woven branches were riddled with holes and had been forced apart here and there by the wind which came off the plain. No clothes were hanging out to dry on the flat rooftops. The well was covered over; no dogs barked in our wake; we didn't see a single face anywhere. The bus passed through without reducing speed, drawing after it a gray banner of chalk dust, like a flag of surrender.

Garek came back down the narrow aisle again, distributing sandwiches, politely raising our spirits and promising that it wouldn't be long before we reached our goal. The countryside turned hilly and rust red; now it was dotted with large rocks interspersed with small colorless bushes. The road dropped away, and we passed through a tunnel-like trench. The semicircles of the blasting holes cast slanting shadows across the ragged walls of rock. Inside the bus the heavy heat struck us like a blow. Then the road widened, and we saw the valley carved out by the river, and the village at the river's edge.

Garek gave us a signal that we had arrived and it was time to stir ourselves. We put our jackets back on, the bus slowed down, and we stopped on a clay-encrusted square in front of a neatly whitewashed hut. Its chalk surface was so bright that it hurt our eyes as we descended. We stepped into the shadow of the bus, flicking our cigarettes aside. We squinted at the hut and waited for Garek, who had disappeared inside.

It was a few minutes before he returned, but then he came out, bringing with him a man none of us had ever seen before.

"This is Bela Bonzo," Garek said, motioning toward the man. "Mr. Bonzo was just doing some work in the house, but he would be glad to answer any questions you might have."

We looked with frank curiosity at Bonzo, who bore up under our scrutiny, while inclining his head slightly. His face was old and dust-gray; his neck was furrowed with deep, dark lines; his upper lip was swollen. Bonzo, who had just been caught by surprise doing some work in the house, had neatly combed hair, and the traces of dried blood on his old, thin neck bore witness to a rough and thorough job of shaving. He was wearing a fresh cotton shirt and cotton trousers which were too short for him, coming barely to his ankles; his feet were encased in new, yellowish boots of untanned leather, like those worn by recruits in training.

We said hello to Bela Bonzo, each of us shook hands with him, and then he nodded and led us into his house. He invited us to go ahead of him, and we stepped into a cool hall in which an old woman awaited us. We couldn't see her face, just her shawl glowing in the dim light. She offered us strange fruit the size of our fists, fruit with a juicy flesh which shimmered redly, so that at first I had the feeling I was biting into a freshly opened wound.

We went back out into the clay-encrusted square. Barefoot children were now standing beside the bus. They were watching Bonzo with a sharp attentiveness which was almost overpowering, neither moving nor speaking to one another as they did so. None of them even glanced at us. Bonzo smiled with a pleased look of mysterious self-satisfaction.

"Don't you have any children?" Pottgiesser asked.

It was the first question, and Bonzo said with a smirk:

"Oh yes, I have a son. We're trying to forget him right now. He rebelled against the government. He was lazy, he was a good-for-nothing, and because he wanted to be a big man he joined the saboteurs, the ones causing trouble everywhere. They're fighting the government because they think they can run things better." Bonzo said all this firmly and with a soft insistence. While he was speaking, I noticed that his front teeth were missing.

"Perhaps they really would run things better," said Pottgiesser. Garek smiled in amusement at this question, and Bonzo said:

"All governments are a burden we have to bear, some are lighter, some heavier. We know this government, all we know about the other side is their promises."

The children exchanged glances.

"In any case the great promise is that of independence," said Bleiguth.

"You can't eat independence," Bonzo said with a smile. "What good is independence to us if our country is reduced to poverty. This government has protected our overseas exports. They've built highways, hospitals, and schools. They've cultivated the land and plan on cultivating even more. And they've given us the right to vote."

A movement ran through the children; they held hands with one another and took an involuntary step forward. Bonzo inclined his head and smiled with his pleased look of mysterious self-satisfaction, and when he raised his head, his gaze sought out Garek, who was standing discreetly behind us.

"After all," Bonzo said without being asked, "independence requires a certain level of maturity. We probably wouldn't know what to do with independence if we had it. For a people, too, there is such a thing as an age of majority. We haven't reached that age yet. And I support the government, because they don't leave us to our own devices while we're still underage. I'm very thankful to them, if you really want to know."

Garek retreated to the bus. Bonzo watched him carefully, waiting until the heavy door of the bus fell closed and we were standing alone on the dry clay square. We were by ourselves now, and the radio reporter Finke turned to Bonzo and questioned him rapidly: "How is it really? Quick, we're all alone." Bonzo swallowed, looked at Finke with an expression of surprised consternation, and said slowly: "I don't understand your question."

"We can speak frankly now," Finke said hurriedly.

"Speak frankly," Bonzo replied with slow caution and gave a broad grin, so that the gap in his front teeth was visible.

"What I said was frank enough: we are friends of the government, my wife and I. Everything we've achieved, we've achieved with their help. We're grateful to them for that. You know how rare it is to have anything to be grateful to a government for—we're grateful. And my neighbor is grateful too, and so are those children over there and every person in the village. Knock on any door, you'll see how grateful everyone is to the government around here."

Suddenly Gum, a pale young journalist, stepped up to Bonzo and whispered: "I have reliable information that your son has been captured and is being tortured in a prison in the capital city. What do you say to that?"

Bonzo closed his eyes; chalk dust coated his lids. He answered with a repressed smile: "I don't have a son, and therefore he can't be tortured. We support the government, you hear? I'm a friend of the government."

He lighted a crooked, hand-rolled cigarette, inhaled sharply, and looked over toward the door of the bus, which now opened. Garek came back and asked how things were going. Bonzo rocked back and forth from his heels to his toes. He looked sincerely relieved as Garek rejoined us, and he answered our subsequent questions cheerfully and at length, from time to time letting the smoke escape with a hiss through the open gap in his teeth.

When a man with a scythe came by, Bonzo called him over. The man approached with shuffling feet, took his scythe from his shoulder, and listened as Bonzo asked him the same questions we had just been raising. The man shook his head indignantly: he supported the government passionately, and Bonzo received each of his avowals in quiet triumph. Then the men shook hands in front of us, as if to seal their common bond with the government.

We said goodbye as well, each of us shook hands with Bonzo—I was the last to do so, but as I took his raw, cracked hand, I felt a small ball of paper between our palms. I pulled it away slowly, with curved fingers, walked back and pushed it down into my pocket. Bela Bonzo stood there taking quick, short puffs on his cigarette. He called his wife outside, and together with the man with the scythe, they watched the departing bus while the children climbed a hill covered with rocks and those small, colorless bushes.

We didn't go back the same way, but instead continued across the hot plain until we reached a railroad embankment paralleled by a road made of sand and gravel. During this trip I kept my hand in my pocket, and in my hand was the little ball of paper. Its center was so hard that I couldn't dent it with my fingernail, no matter how strongly I pressed. I didn't dare take the paper ball out, because

Garek's melancholy gaze reached us from time to time through the rearview mirror. A startling shadow flitted past us overhead across the dead land; only then did we hear the sound of the propellers and see the airplane flying low over the railway embankment in the direction of the capital city. It turned when it reached the horizon, roared past us again, and then stayed with us.

I thought about Bela Bonzo, held the ball of paper with its solid core in my hand, and felt my palm becoming moist. An object appeared at the end of the railroad embankment, and as it drew nearer we could see that it was a railway handcar with young soldiers sitting on it. They greeted us with friendly waves of their submachine guns. I took the paper ball out cautiously, and without looking at it, transferred it quickly into my small watch pocket, the only pocket I could button. I thought again of Bela Bonzo, the government's friend: I saw again his yellowish boots of untanned leather, the dreamy self-satisfaction of his face, and the dark gap in his teeth when he began to speak. No one among us doubted that we had found in him a true friend of the government.

We drove along the sea back to the capital. The wind carried the drawn-out caressing sighs of the water to us as it beat against the base of the rocky cliffs. We got out at the opera house, and Garek bade us a polite farewell. I walked back to my hotel alone, took the elevator up to my room, went into the toilet, and opened the ball of paper secretly entrusted to me by the friend of the government: the paper was blank, no sign or word was written upon it, but wrapped within lay a broken, nicotine-stained front tooth, and I knew whose tooth it was.

ESKIMO LAMPS,
or The Trials and Tribulations
of a Specialist

⊷ The architects thought of everything for my institute, even the view: a free sweep across the Alster River, past the salt-white sails in our harbor, to the ferry-boat shelters, the sailing clubs, and the perfect insurance buildings in which all the mishaps of Hamburg are indemnified with ease and efficiency.

After the former Hassebrouk-Villa had been converted into our institute, we had everything we needed to make our work easier. My students and I breathed a sigh of relief when we left the run-down attic at the university, where we had been forced to spend so many years. Now we were rewarded by being allowed to move into a building that fulfilled our every need. We were pampered with grants at a level appropriate to our institute, allowing us to be more expansive in our research work. With the view of the Alster out our window, and a neighborhood of quiet, melancholy villas about us, we eagerly pursued our important mission. I would still be pursuing it today, if I hadn't made a trip from which I returned in complete disillusionment.

Since coming back from that trip I haven't had the strength to begin again where I left off. A deep dejection, and a feeling of bitterness so strong it leaves a metallic taste in my mouth, keep me from appreciating the functional beauty of my institute and prevent me from taking up my work again—at any rate with my old self-assurance. After all, at the very least, the trip has destroyed my life's work.

I admit that it was supposed to have the exact opposite effect. When the Kingfisher Shipping Line opened a new service to Greenland and invited a scientist to accompany the maiden voyage free of charge, I thought I was going to experience a brilliant confirmation of my academic work, the crowning moment of my career. I wasn't surprised that they chose me. My institute had long been known as a center of Greenland Studies, or at least of one important area of Greenland Studies, namely the lamps and lamp-wicks of the Torngasuk Eskimos.

I had devoted myself to this project for fifteen years, bringing in colleagues and founding an institute. Because we pursued our goals with productive energy, we soon were rewarded by various signs of success, including inquiries from all around the world, and a visit by the English anthropologist Bancroft. Anyone anywhere on earth who was interested in the lamps and lamp-wicks of the Torngasuk Eskimos had to take account of our work. It seemed to us only natural that several doctoral dissertations were dedicated to our institute, and that the research team of Rink and Blau declared in the foreword to their standard reference work, *The Domestic Culture of the Eskimos* (Oslo, 1956, 2 vols.), that they could never have completed their book without our help. We alone possessed all the pertinent secondary literature on the subject, as well as the only complete collection of Torngasuk lamps and lamp-wicks in the world, a collection I may modestly lay claim to having both founded and developed. Our collection included a rich profusion of flat wicks and free-standing round wicks, wicks made of cotton, linen, or sealskin, woven wicks and twisted wicks, even unsaturated wicks with interesting defects.

But our collection of lamps was even more universal and extensive than our holdings in wicks. It ranged from early vessels with an opening for whale oil to modern suction or pressure lamps, and from tiny elliptical ornamental lights to large convector heating lamps. Every lighting device ever used or still in use by the Torngasuk Eskimos was present in multiple examples in our institute's exhibition hall, including precious flame blowers which were only employed during communal tobacco rites.

Still, I was not satisfied. It was my ambition to include in the collection not only every existing type of lamp and wick, but also interesting variations of each type, with particularly successful or unsuccessful examples, as well as lamps that burned poorly, were misshapen, damaged, or flawed. In this way I hoped to create a complete panorama of lamp culture.

And so I wrote my middle man in Umiuki, M-Whan, as I had so often over the past years. For it is to M-Whan—whose name simply means "man who eats raw flesh"—that I owe the entire collection that has made our institute what it is today. M-Whan was always ready to help out on a dollar basis. He shipped us huge crates, with his list of expenses enclosed, and promised to continue combing eastern Greenland, wherever the Torngasuks had settled, in search of lamps and wicks.

Correspondence with Raw Flesheater was by no means regular. Sometimes we had to wait half a year for an answer while we pictured him toiling across snowy, wind-swept plains on our behalf. At other times we would receive two laconic telegrams at once, asking us for an advance, not so much for himself as to oil the wheels of commerce with the owner of a rare earthenware lamp. And occasionally the delivery firm's truck would arrive at the institute with three man-sized crates at the same time.

Although he never held to any deadline, and his expenses had gone up substantially of late—which he explained by the rising price of intestinal lining for the windows, and the cost of domino and board games to while away the long and lonely winter nights—we stuck by him. For with the friendly cunning and quick native intelligence of his tribe, he had immediately understood the needs of my institute. Of course I informed him immediately of our expanded activities, which led, by return voyage, to the arrival in our harbor of fourteen crates on a Danish ship.

In one of the crates I found a photograph of M-Whan with a warm dedication to me. An American missionary had taken the photo while passing through. It showed Raw Flesheater in a kayak, smiling, wrapped in a reindeerskin coat, with his whalebone harpoon raised high. Later I received a second photograph which showed him in a sealskin summer jacket, eating berries and roots, as well as a dark mass which we finally determined to be the contents of a reindeer's stomach. I had both photos framed and mounted in the institute's exhibition hall.

I worked together with M-Whan for sixteen years, developing our collection, but also developing a friendship with this member of a poor and simple people who call themselves the Innuit, which simply means "human beings."

Now as *The Seal*, the flagship of the Kingfisher Line, cast off its hawsers to open the service to Greenland, I was hoping for two things from the trip: I expected my hypothesis of a general decline in the lamp culture of the Torngasuk Eskimos between 1789 and 1812 to be confirmed, and I awaited impatiently the opportunity to meet our buyer, Raw Flesheater. I wished to strengthen in person our long-standing epistolary friendship. I was carrying a certificate of appreciation from the institute in my luggage. I planned to give it to him in recognition of his services, along with several gifts I thought appropriate for a trapper and seal hunter, including a pocket knife with a corkscrew, a handy-sized ax, and a storm lantern.

The Seal was a solid ship with reinforced ribs. The Faroe Islands came into sight and disappeared aft, and, four hours ahead of schedule, we entered the straits of Scoresby, blinded by the unbearable brightness of the glaciers. As we were dropping anchor a seaplane shot over the ice, circled around us, and touched down in a spray of water.

A launch picked up the pilot, came alongside *The Seal*, received passengers, mail, and luggage, and carried us all to the landing dock. I sat beside the pilot on the crossing, an athletic man in his fifties, who wore an English flannel suit beneath his shabby aviation outfit. He seemed so strangely familiar that I looked him boldly in the face. He bore my scrutiny with the natural politeness of his race, and nodded goodbye to me as we disembarked.

Two bundled-up women struggled silently over my luggage, settled things equally silently, and led me to a hotel where a muffled porter appeared, took my luggage, and drove the women away. I asked him whether it was very cold for this time of year, and he replied with an old saying: "Anadyr, Anadyr, Angekok"—which may be roughly translated as "The ptarmigan's eyes are always red." The implication was that it never did get too warm there.

He led me to my room to the subdued strains of "The River Kwai March," which issued from a loudspeaker. I soon discovered where M-Whan lived, and at the same time learned that he was not at home, but that they were expecting his return at any time. They gave me his address, Gyndefasa Glacier, whereupon I rented a dogsled and set out impatiently to see him, ready to share for a few days the simple igloo life of my scientific supplier. If necessary, I was even prepared to bash seals with him.

We approached the glacier across a dazzling, snow-covered scree, and as the sled rounded a rocky outcropping, I saw a spacious country home with an attached garage, and a long landing dock with a shed on poles beside it for a seaplane. I relaxed the reins in confusion, and the dogs pulled at a slower pace. Slowly and bewilderedly we pulled up to the wrought-iron gate.

My arrival had already been noted. A woman with tiny feet, her hair pulled back and oiled with butter, and wearing a close-fitting Italian dress, received me warmly and led me into the house. Her face was broad and flat, her skull displayed the typical pyramid form of the Torngasuk Eskimo. She gave me her name with a smile: M-Whun, which can be roughly translated as "woman who eats raw flesh."

She didn't ask why I'd come, but instead offered me my favorite whiskey and turned on the indirect lighting. We sat and drank whiskey and looked out at the fjord. I complimented her on the Scandinavian furniture and the efficient lighting. She nodded and said that she had recently acquired a small electric generator of their own for the house. She was planning to surprise her husband with it when he returned from Florida.

"Unga, Unga, Pöki," she said, which translates into "An old sled dog tires more quickly." By which she meant that her husband had needed a vacation. After a moment she got up with a sad smile and said that she had to return to her duties. She invited me to come along. We passed through the house and entered a spacious workshop in which a dozen industrious young Torngasuk girls were at work. They greeted us shyly as we entered. Their efficient hands hammered, ground, polished, and twisted. One girl assembled, another packed, a third nailed the crates shut. They worked away steadily.

I nodded to them appreciatively. Then I saw my name, which one of the girls had just written in black ink on an address label. Now their work began to interest me even more. And I saw that their busy hands were turning out lamps and wicks: antique vessels for whale oil, imaginative ornamental lights, designed without pause by a pretty girl, flat wicks and round wicks and twisted wicks, with interesting defects being worked in. One little midget's only job was dipping the lamps in mud. A yellow-skinned girl threw completed vessels at the wall, then skillfully glued the pieces together. An underaged worker did nothing but saturate sealskin wicks. And then everything went into the waiting crates addressed to my institute.

Raw Flesheater Woman pointed to the workshop contentedly. "In the begining we only needed two girls," she said, "but there's a big demand now, and we'll soon have to expand."

"Have you produced all the lamps and wicks here?" I asked, and she replied: "The shelduck builds the nest it needs," by which she meant to confirm the justice of her rise in society.

Watching them, I understood where my institute's funds had gone. I had no doubt that the institute's entire collection had been produced in this domestic factory. In my despair I no longer had the heart to attempt to confirm my hypothesis that there must have been a general decline in the Torngasuk lamp culture between 1789 and 1812.

In my haste and despondence I left the country home by Gyndefasa Glacier without ever meeting Raw Flesheater, taking nothing with me but well-founded grief, and a bitterness that still remains as I contemplate the salt-white sails on the Alster. What should I do? Our budget has just been increased again, and now I've received word that four more crates of Torngasuk lamps and wicks have arrived at the harbor. In any case we must open the crates. Who knows? There may be an interesting piece in the shipment.

THE DICTATOR'S SON

﹏§ My father, Gongo Gora, whose official title is Father of the People and of the Mountains, quickly recognized his own abilities in me. At age fifteen he had already named me Deputy Commander-in-Chief of the Air Force, and soon thereafter I became a voting member of the Academy of Arts. On my sixteenth birthday he appointed me editor-in-chief of the government newspaper *Przcd Domdom,* which can be roughly translated as "joyful awakening." Although these various posts gave me a good deal to do, my father insisted that I also complete my high school degree. In order to lighten the burden of my school days, he promised that once I had passed my exams he would reward me accordingly. By accordingly it seems he meant the post of Minister for Power and Energy.

But now I will never receive nor enjoy this promised reward. The abilities I inherited from my father, and which he recognized in me at such an early age, will never be utilized in any higher-level national office. I won't even be named First Secretary of the Unions, for according to our encyclopedias and standard reference works I am already dead, one of the dearly departed of our nation. The record shows that I lost my life in action at age seventeen fighting a rebellious band of Ostralniki, and a new edition adds that my death occurred just before my final exams. As compensation for my loss a group of Ostralniki prisoners, described in the official state encyclopedia as "Ostralniki scum," were shot to death. I wasn't able to attend my own state funeral, but I could hear the funeral oration through the walls of the private cell in which my father, Gongo Gora, had personally incarcerated me. I heard as well the tortured sobs of my mother, Sinaida, and the threatening cries of the people, lamenting my death and demanding the rapid elimination of all Ostralniki.

No, the likelihood that I will be able to guide our nation toward happiness from some appropriate government position has distinctly diminished, if not wholly disappeared. When I ask myself today, on my eighteenth birthday, where things went wrong, what mistakes I must have made, mistakes my father prudently prevented me from regretting in public, I keep coming back to the name of my teacher, Alfred Uhl. He is, so to speak, the first link in a chain of errors which led to my present situation. Yes, everything started with Uhl, a consumptive, lanky man with yellow skin, who taught me history in a classroom filled mostly with the offspring of government officials, generals, and deserving artists. He was the author of my father's official biography, the editor of our textbook on national history, and had been named Honorary President of the Historical Society for his services. It was also his duty to edit our *Who's Who?*, a task which was still unfinished after twelve years, since the list of persons to be included changed constantly during typesetting.

Alfred Uhl was a fanatic disciple of my father. I still remember the morning he strode into our classroom and, embittered by an abortive Ostralniki assassination attempt, shook his fist out the window. He paced back and forth in silent exasperation, murmuring to himself from time to time, "Jackals, jackals." But then, unexpectedly, a glow of satisfaction spread over his yellow face. Politely, he asked us to take out our pens and paper. With indulgent care he revealed to us what it was he wanted. We were to carry out a written assignment, and he announced the theme triumphantly. As a response to the assassination attempt, we were to list all the titles granted my father by the people, the press, the academies, and the congresses. Shaking his fist in repressed rage at the window, he said, "For the past two months those jackals have taken liberties they've never dared to before. We know that a new leader is responsible for their most recent actions, a wretched mercenary to whom they've given the nickname Ostral-Wdinje, or Lucky Bug. Now we'll give these insects the answer they deserve." He nodded to us encouragingly, and I saw the boy next to me listing my father's titles effortlessly, from "Father of the People" through "Luminary of Rattan Chemistry," "Marker of Inland Shipping," and "Helpful Friend of all Nonswimmers," to "Crystal Ball of Progress." He came up with forty-eight names.

When the assignments were handed in and Alfred Uhl had leafed rapidly through them, I knew what was coming. Shaken, he called me up front and asked me cautiously why I alone had turned in a blank notebook. I said nothing, and as he gently continued to probe, I thought back on the confrontation with my father the previous night, at the end of which he had given me a thorough beating. The point at issue was his favorite liquor, Butor Glim, a fine cognac captured from the Ostralniki, the last bottle of which I had consumed in the company of the prima ballerina of our State Opera House. As I recalled that scene in a cold rage, Uhl continued to question me softly but insistently. When he received no answer, he assigned me the list of my father's titles as homework. I opposed this for various reasons, but because I hesitated to reveal those reasons to Alfred Uhl, and because I knew that he would certainly ask me for my homework the next day, I considered it to my advantage not to have to face him again. So that same afternoon, in my role as editor-in-chief of the government newspaper *Przcd Domdom* ("Joyful Awakening"), I wrote an article attacking certain outmoded methods of instruction on the part of older teachers. The article had its effect, and within a very few hours Uhl had been named Director of the State Lumber Mill, far away in the blue forests of Pumbal. In line with my pet plan, I turned over a few of the newly freed positions to a classmate, Gregor G. Gum, whom I had long counted among my trusted friends.

Since the whole of our nation was holding its breath in the face of the Ostralniki and their new leader Ostral "Lucky Bug" Wdinje, my article and its results were soon forgotten. Whenever anything happened—when crops dried up, when trees fell prey to bark beetles, when the true number of pigs was concealed from the official government census bureau, or when a car came to a halt with a broken axle—the Ostralniki were always blamed. And since the population was crying out for revenge, the general staff of the Air Force decided to do something about it.

Marshall Tibor Tutras, a good-natured man with swollen feet and a receding chin, to whom my father had granted the title "Cloud-Controller First Class," called a secret meeting. As Deputy Commander,

I sat at his right hand. After citing my father's name and various Air Force titles, he suggested sending several squadrons on a demonstration flight over the uncultivated karst and burned-out areas infested by the Ostralniki. As he explained to the appreciative nods of the officers present, "Since these jackals have found a new leader in Ostral 'Lucky Bug' Wdinje, their actions have become increasingly violent and cruel. They operate safely in areas our troops have just left, or are still trying to secure. They act almost as if they have agents at the highest levels of our staff. Therefore I suggest a punitive raid to frighten them off, with a few bombing runs at individual targets. I recommend we restore justice with the new napalm bombs." The officers nodded with the required enthusiasm. I was the only one who smiled, as I had been smiling throughout Tibor Tutras's entire speech. Shocked and disturbed, he asked me if I disagreed with him. He pointed out that my father had in fact made the same suggestion in the last cabinet meeting. I responded that such a raid wouldn't even be worth the fuel it took to get there, and continued with raised voice: "The squadrons belong to the people, and the people don't like to see them used without tangible results." The officers nodded, and Tibor Tutras too began to nod in an attitude of pained reflection. I was ready just to forget his suggestion when he pointed out that he was supposed to report to my father that weekend. So I was forced to act quickly. Instead of spending the night with Nadwina Chleb, the prima ballerina of our State Opera House, I wrote a lead article for the government newspaper *Przcd Domdom* ("Joyful Awakening"). Since I had carefully thought out the objections to the highest officer in the Air Force, Tibor Tutras never reached the point of having to report to my father. By the next weekend I had managed to get him transferred as an Air Force attaché to Santiago, Chile.

Since I don't have any particular love of flying, I passed up the opportunity to step into Marshall Tutras's job myself. But because his post was indisputedly a so-called key position in the government, I saw to it that it was filled by yet another classmate of mine, Boleslaw Schmidt, who was familiar with my pet plan.

It began with my history teacher, Alfred Uhl, continued with Marshall Tibor Tutras, and within a few weeks I had managed to fire a whole series of people from important posts and replace them with classmates of mine who knew what was happening—mostly sons of government officials, generals, and deserving artists. Things were made even easier by the fact that my father continued to make speeches in which he stressed that the old guard was getting tired, dangerously tired. In most cases, then, it took only a lead article in the government newspaper, with at most an occasional follow-up story, to replace the members of the old guard with my trusty classmates. The Minister of Popular Enlightenment hung on with particular tenacity, until we managed to convict him of having secret contacts with the Ostralniki. We had him shot that spring.

My father proved to be quite open to my activities. He dealt with me in a friendly manner, freely offering me the Ostralniki cognac, Butor Glim, which had been recovered from the dead bodies of the enemy. When I had finally filled all the key positions in the government with classmates I could trust, my father said to me: "A revolution that thinks of itself in historical terms is worthless. Revolution must be continual." I seconded that idea heartily, and pointed out the degree to which I had brought new blood into the highest offices. My father stroked my hair in dreamy gratitude.

Thus arrived that bright day my father set out for Luhuk, in a wild and barren region where the largest power station in modern history was to be officially dedicated. My father wanted to deliver the dedication speech himself, and to march across the dam at the head of the entire corps of diplomats, in spite of my mother Sinaida's warning that the area around Luhuk was infested with pockets of Ostralniki. Yes, he was determined to stand on top of the dam until he heard the thunder of the turbines beneath his feet. "Power," he said, "loves power."

I preferred to remain at home, for I had no reason to doubt the integrity of Ludi van der Wisse, to whom I had given the post of Director of the Bureau of Engineering, and who had promised me that the bomb would go off at the precise moment at which my father and the majority of the diplomatic corps would be awaiting the thunder of the turbines. So I was content to lie on the couch with Nadwina, and while she did my math exercises for me, I rolled cigarettes for us from captured, spicy Ostralniki tobacco, which would surely compare quite favorably with Virginia Gold. From time to time I had Nadwina massage my forehead as well, since I had stayed away from the dedication of the power station under the pretense of suffering from a pounding headache.

We entertained each other until twilight silently fell, and I heard the voices of the newsboys in the street, calling out a special edition. I kissed Nadwina in a burst of joy, ran down, and tore a newspaper from the hand of an old woman. Then I shut myself in my father's study, pulled the curtains closed, and began to read in breathless anticipation. "Bestial Attack by the Ostralniki" ran the headline, and I clapped my hands for joy. I had to smoke a cigarette to settle down before I could continue. But then I stopped in shock. My glance fell upon a photo in which I saw myself, grotesquely twisted, lying on the rocky ground. I saw my bloodstained face, my torn uniform, my charred hands, and in the background the monumental remains of the exploded dam, with the pent-up waters pouring over the rubble in foaming torrents. Dazedly I read the caption. It said that the jackals had blown up the dam in a dastardly attack, and that I alone was responsible for the fact that no lives had been lost. "Having received information about the bomb," the caption ran in part, "his son first warned those present, and then, while trying to remove the bomb, sacrificed his own life. Jürgen Gora did not die in vain."

I didn't bother to read the full text. My eyes returned again and again to the photograph of my corpse—a photograph so convincing that I saw nothing to object to. And while I sat there lost in thought, my father entered the study through a secret door I had forgotten to lock, rubbing his hands in good humor. He was not surprised to see me, and poured himself a water glass full of Butor Glim, Ostralniki cognac. With a gesture toward his desk, at which I was still sitting, he said to me: "That desk is a bit too large for you right now, Jürgen. Your school desk is still the right size." I understood what he was saying, but since I could think of no answer, I just looked at him silently. He took a drink from the water glass, came closer, and seeing the newspaper with the photograph, said with self-satisfaction: "It wasn't so easy to find a boy on short notice who looked so much like you that even your mother couldn't tell the difference. And we had to transform him into a corpse without anyone noticing. But as you see, we managed. After the trick you tried to pull on me, I had no choice."

"Ludi van der Wisse," I said disappointedly.

"Oh, Ludi isn't any worse than the rest of your classmates," my father said. "They were all my trusted agents. It was easy to win them over, because I did something you forgot to do in your indecent haste.

I provided them with unlimited pocket money from a private bank account. You just gave them jobs—that wasn't enough."

"The scoundrels," I said.

"Ah well," my father said with a contented sigh, "in a way I'm sorry this epoch of the surprises you prepared for me is over. What did your friends the Ostralniki call you? Ostral-Wdinje, 'Lucky Bug.' You're a dung beetle as far as I'm concerned. But I have to admit that you were the most skillful leader the Ostralniki ever came up with. However, as the photograph shows, you're dead now."

This time I wasn't embarrassed. In a low whisper, I asked: "And mother?"

"Your mother is changing into black right now. She doesn't know anything." Upon these words my father took a pistol from his pocket, released the safety, and waved me ahead. I walked in front of him, and he locked me into the private cell he had prepared for certain special situations. Although no office will benefit from my particular abilities for the time being, I'm not without the small comforts of life. And I do appreciate them. They demonstrate a father's pride in his son. And is not fatherly pride also an expression of love?

DOCTOR FUN

꿈§ Nothing causes me as many problems as providing amusement. That's been my means of livelihood for three years now. I draw my salary for attending to the human needs of my company's foreign clients. At the end of a hard day of negotiations the exhausted gentlemen are passed on to me, and it's up to me to utilize my particular talents to cheer them up, to put them in a good mood so that they will be relaxed and ready for the next round of negotiations. "Give me a man in a good mood and I'll give you a good contract," said my first director, summing up the assignment I've been at for three years now. Why anyone would think I was suitable for such an assignment I can't say. The crucial factor at any rate was my graduation as a Doctor of Law, and not so much my cheerful Hanseatic nature, although that was certainly taken into account as well.

I began, then, as a specialist for cheering up important clients, and I placed my abilities in the service of a firm that manufactured fish processing machinery: slicing machines, deboning machines, and first-class guillotines which decapitated fish with a newly developed curved blade. There was one model that could turn a six-foot tunafish into filets in four seconds with such swift and sure slices that we named it "Robespierre," without the least fear that we were promising more than we could deliver. The company also manufactured conveyor belts for fish, traps to catch and process the scraps, and replacement parts in impressive number. Since these were high-precision, high-quality machines, customers arrived from all over the world. No journey

35

seemed too long. They came from Japan, from Canada and Hawaii, from Morocco and the Black Sea coast to place their orders personally. And so in a manner of speaking it was my job, when the day's negotiations were over, to amuse the entire world.

On the whole I dare say I managed to do so quite well, to my company's benefit. Chinese and South Africans, Koreans and Norwegians, even a bundled-up man from Spitsbergen: I taught them all the enlivening power of good cheer, releasing the tensions inherent in all business transactions. Our evening strolls through the pleasure district produced such good moods that they could be regarded as massages of the spirit and the pocketbook respectively. Since I took national character into account, pressing the right button to produce the best mood in each case, I had little difficulty attending to their needs, or to use a more modern term, creating good will. I led our customers to pleasure by the shortest path. Humor was my métier, and I managed to provide amusement even for the spiritually insulated man from Spitsbergen. I threw myself into my work. I loved it, particularly after they had provided me with a very satisfactory raise.

But for some time now my love of work has been disturbed by moments of doubt, or if not doubt, at least a certain distrust. I'm afraid I've lost my confidence. But above all I now feel that I'm significantly underpaid, for I was never before aware of the risk I've been running, how much danger is involved. I've only come to this realization quite recently. And now I think I know what brought it home to me.

It's all the fault of Pachulka-Sbirr, a giant of a customer from a distant island in the Aleutian chain. I still remember the first time I saw him: a grim, sallow-faced man in a bearskin cap and heavily creased boots. And I still can hear his voice, which resembled what I thought the surf might sound like on his native shore. When he was turned over to me by the head office and entered my room grimly for the first time, I was somewhat startled, but I was soon confident that I would be able to loosen up Pachulka-Sbirr too. After warming him up with a glass of cherry brandy, I shoved the gloomy customer into a car and took him to our pleasure district, firmly convinced that my expertise in producing good moods would prove effective in his case as well.

We skipped the shooting galleries, where our Japanese customers generally began whistling happily, because I felt Pachulka-Sbirr would have to have something a little stronger to cheer him up, something more substantial, so to speak. We went straight to Fiete's bar, where three women did an artistic striptease at regular intervals. I knew the women well. They had often helped me with repressed Scandinavian customers who couldn't get their minds off business, making them bubble with joy. So I gave them a sign this time as well, and they promised to help.

The moment arrived: they stripped artistically and then, as is the custom at Fiete's, one of the guests was asked to play the role of a refined Paris and award one of them the apple. As had been arranged, Pachulka-Sbirr was selected. The giant customer walked to the middle of the room, received the apple, and stared at the nude women so darkly and threateningly that a note of fear appeared on their faces and they instinctively retreated a bit. Suddenly, in the uneasy silence, Pachulka-Sbirr shoved the apple in his mouth, and the crunching and grinding of his powerful jaws could be heard. He returned to our table amidst the speechless amazement of the crowd, sat down, and stared darkly before him.

I didn't give up. I knew how much I owed the company, and what I owed myself. I told him funny stories from my well-stocked store of jokes, all of them previously tested with great success on taciturn Finns, Irishmen, and laconic Faeroe Islanders. Pachulka-Sbirr listened grimly without reacting.

Irritated, I left Fiete's with him and crossed over to Max's. We found our reserved table and ordered a bottle of cherry brandy. I had always succeeded in getting grumpy Americans and even grumpier Alaskans in a good mood by the time we were at Max's, because Max offered a band that allowed guests to be the conductor. Americans and Alaskans are used to controlling large territories. The musical empire is a large territory, and as soon as our customers were allowed to conduct it, their business tensions were forgotten and they were filled with pure pleasure. Since the Aleutians aren't too far from Alaska, it seemed to me that I could show Pachulka-Sbirr a good time in the same way, and after I had quietly made the arrangements, he stamped up to the director's podium in his ever-present bearskin cap and heavily creased boots. He took up the baton. He cracked it in the air like a whip, at which the musicians spontaneously ducked. Then he inserted the baton between his shirt and skin and started leisurely scratching his back. I still don't know how it happened, but suddenly he pulled out the baton, broke it in two—evidently it hadn't been long enough to reach the spot he wanted—and flung it into the band. He returned to the table with a gloomy look on his face as the horn section gradually and fearfully reappeared.

I looked at Pachulka-Sbirr in desperation. No, I was not yet prepared to give up. My honor was at stake; a professional pride familiar to us all had been awakened in me. I made a vow not to take this customer back to his hotel until I had succeeded in cheering him up. I reminded myself that my colleagues in the factory referred to me as "Doctor Fun," and not without a note of respect. I wanted to prove myself worthy of the title. I decided to risk everything. I told him a joke that I had hitherto used only on a customer from Siberia, as a sort of last resort. Pachulka-Sbirr received it in stony silence. No matter how hard I tried, I couldn't wipe the gloomy look from his sallow face. A donkey ride, a visit to the house of mirrors, erotic films, and a few more bottles of cherry brandy: nothing seemed to lift his spirits.

I had saved Wanda for last. After everything else had failed, we went to Wanda, who bathed twice a night in a giant cup of champagne. All my remaining hopes were placed on Wanda. Her children and my children are schoolmates, and she and my wife exchange cuttings now and then for the flower-box in our window. Given this relatively intimate relationship, I found it easy to take her into my confidence and explain to her what was at stake. Wanda promised to help. As she looked about for a guest to assist her in emerging from her champagne bath, her choice fell with unforced naturalness on Pachulka-Sbirr. I thought victory was at hand, for Wanda had already helped me on a previous occasion, when I had to thaw out a particularly icy customer from Lake Baikal. Surely she could do it again! Yet to my amazement the attempt failed. Yes, I was amazed at what happened as Pachulka-Sbirr walked onto the stage and stood before the huge champagne glass in which Wanda was lolling about suggestively, unexpected as such behavior was for a refugee from the East. She smiled at him. She stretched out her arms to him. The audience applauded wildly. At which point Pachulka-Sbirr dropped to his knees, bent over the champagne glass, and began drinking noisily—with the result that Wanda soon found herself in an empty cup, no longer in

need of help. She looked at me helplessly, and I returned her gaze
with the same helpless feeling. I was ready to surrender.

But in the early hours of the morning I was offered an unexpected
opportunity. Pachulka-Sbirr wanted another look at the machines that
had brought him all this way. We drove to the factory and entered
the exhibition hall. We were alone, for the porter knew me and already knew him by now, and let us in. Lost in deep thought Pachulka-
Sbirr ran his hand over the machines, shook them, listened to them,
had me explain them to him again, taking notes all the while in a
pocket diary. Every machine interested him, but the one that interested him most was the "Robespierre" model that could cut a six-foot
tuna into filets in four seconds with the most fascinating blades. He
put his pocket diary away as we stood in front of the "Robespierre."
He began to inspect the high point of our efforts in detail. From time
to time he whistled in admiration, clicked his tongue, or puffed out
his cheeks. I could sense how he was being won over more and more
to this model. However, he seemed unable to bring himself to the
point of actually agreeing to buy our "Robespierre."

To make his decision easier, I got onto the machine and lay down
on the metal spring-cushioned chopping trough. He'll be able to decide more easily if he has a visual impression, I thought. I stretched
out and lay there like a tunafish four seconds away from being turned
into filets. I looked up at the tempered steel knives gleaming merrily
above my throat. They were extremely heavy and supported only by
narrow stays that could be moved aside by simply flipping a lever.
I lolled about smiling on the chopping trough to show Pachulka-Sbirr
what a pleasure it must be for a tunafish to lie on our model. Pachulka-
Sbirr did not return my smile. He just asked which lever had to be
pushed in order to activate the blades. As soon as I told him, I saw
the stays flash away from the blades. The knives came whizzing toward
me. But just short of my throat they stopped and bounced back grat-
ingly. The blade compressor had jammed. Trembling and scared to
death, I pulled myself out of the chopping trough. I looked into Pachulka-Sbirr's eyes. Yes, he was smiling happily. He was smiling, and
at that moment nothing else seemed important to me.

Today, of course, our "Robespierre" model has been even further
improved. The blade mechanism never jams, and I ask myself how

far I dare go when the next Pachulka-Sbirr comes to us from the Aleutian Islands. I learned from him the magnitude of the risk I constantly run, and that the professionals who provide for such amusement cannot be overpaid. I consider myself well aware of the danger now, for when I think about fun, I see the gleaming knives of tempered steel swaying merrily above me . . .

SIXTH BIRTHDAY

~§ Alfred got the advance. He didn't give it to me right away when he got home from work; he kept the money himself until the next morning and only then, when I'd gone to the door with him and he had kissed me goodbye like he used to, did he hand me the unsealed envelope. I spread the envelope open with two fingers and quickly saw that it was all in small bills. I wanted to give him one of them, but he shook his head with a smile, tapping his breast pocket as if alluding to some mystery, a secret horde of cash. I knew that he was lying, and I tried to stick a bill into the pocket of his jacket. He grabbed my hand, pushed it back, and said quietly: "Buy him a gift, Maria, the nicest one you can find. Ask him again what he wants, and then buy it for him. I'll get off work early."

I promised him I would, and I promised I wouldn't drink anything on that April eighteenth, the day we had chosen to celebrate Richard's sixth birthday. At first we had wanted to have the party early in May, after Alfred got his paycheck, but the doctor said the sooner the better, and so we surprised Richard on a Wednesday by saying that we would be having his birthday that Friday, and of course the boy got all excited and talked only about what he wanted, a list that grew and grew without a single thing ever being dropped. Sometimes it amazed me that he knew how to wish for all those things. I could never have thought of so many, I never know what to say when I'm asked what I want.

After Alfred left, I straightened up the apartment, took a shower, put on my blue dress and went into the kids' room where Jutta was standing at the foot of Richard's bed, silently imitating the movements of animals and making him guess what they were. Of course Jutta was trying to make him feel his inferiority by making sure her movements didn't give things away too directly, so that he wasn't getting anywhere identifying the animal she had in mind. I interrupted their game. I pulled Jutta to me and felt her strong, involuntary resistance, but without turning her loose I pulled her to the head of the bed. Everything about her betrayed an unusual alertness, an almost hostile watchfulness, and sometimes when I looked into her eleven-year-old face, I could see an age beyond her years. I held her very tight and heard Richard ask: "When does the birthday start?" and I heard myself answer: "This afternoon, when everyone's back." "Good," he said, "then just be sure there's a red telephone: I want that too. If I can't have that I don't want anything." I nodded and left everything open because I was sure that he had long since forgotten the things he had asked for first. I asked Jutta to stay with him and left to buy the things for the party.

The streetcar was overcrowded, but I had to take it because I'd already missed the bus, and a little old man with the face of a hedgehog and button eyes pushed me forward along the aisle. He was slobbering and sucking on a cigar that he never took out of his mouth, puffing small clouds of smoke onto the back of my neck, pressing his briefcase into my rear. The air was warm and stale. When the car pulled out it jerked so sharply that the people standing up were thrown against one another, and the old man propped himself up with his elbows on my hips. I had a hard time keeping my face out of a strong-smelling clump of damp feathers adorning the hat of the lady in front of me. My joints were swelling, my lips were burning. A bald-headed pleasure-lover on a poster pointed out the advantages of a mattress. I looked down at my hand and saw that it was trembling, and I knew why I wasn't up to this trip. Just one drink would have made it easier for me.

I stuck it out all the way, rode to the main station, then got off the streetcar and had just checked myself in the mirror of a candy machine, quickly, not displeased, when I felt a sprinkle of sand against my legs, yellow, artificial-looking sand thrown by a young worker. He was on his knees in his black Manchester workpants, laying tiles, cement-colored rhomboids, carefully tapping them into place. He smiled at me, quick and dirty, and went on with his work.

I crossed over to the big department store, watched myself approach in the large show windows, growing bigger, and then had to close my eyes in the stream of warm air which rushed out from the entrance. A well-dressed man with neatly combed hair approached me. I could hardly understand a word he said as I stared at his coated tongue. He directed me to the toy department. He held the door to the elevator for me, it took me up to the fourth floor, where the voices, steps, and movement confused me less, were more bearable. The light formed shining puddles on the floor of an immense room. A saleslady approached me slowly, looked me over condescendingly.

"May I help you?" she asked in a tone which sounded as if my arrival annoyed her, and I said: "I don't know yet. May I look around?" She nodded permission haughtily and returned in dignity to her colleague. She didn't deign to glance at me as I went past the racks with the balls, on to the doll section and toward the shelves with stuffed animals. The white envelope held eighty marks. I was determined to spend them all, and I knew that this was what Alfred wanted too.

I weakened for the first time when I saw the sheriff's outfit, with its holster, vest-jacket, and the golden star. It was what he wanted, yet I couldn't see him rounding up cattle thieves in it or chasing school-age bank robbers up the stairwell. Instead I saw Richard lying dressed up in bed, a very lightweight, motionless, and extremely apathetic sheriff, so weak from leukemia that he couldn't even raise his gun. I didn't buy the outfit. I held on tight to the counter and didn't buy it.

The saleswoman was watching me now. I called her over and asked her to show me a xylophone with gold and silver bars. Just for the sake of something to say, I asked her whether she thought it would be a suitable gift for a six-year-old who was fairly advanced for his age. Wordlessly, the saleswoman handed me the small wooden mallets so I could see what it sounded like. I tapped the bars with the mallets, listened to the cheerful tinkling, and couldn't decide whether to buy it. The saleswoman listlessly pointed out a kit for a model ship which would supposedly show Richard how to cut out pieces for the world's first atomic freighter and glue them together to scale, and again I didn't dare buy it. I saw the pasteboard model glued together, standing in his room, senseless and ownerless, just one more memory, and so I said no.

I knew what it would have taken to make it easier for me to buy something. The weakness came over me again, a small vague nausea. My skin was reacting against something, or needed something. I felt a familiar dizziness. The saleswoman turned away impatiently, and I looked up at the gallery of stuffed animals. All at once I had the distinct impression that they were shrinking back, cowering in fear that I would buy them.

Suddenly the saleswoman asked: "What about a model train? No boy's ever been disappointed with that." "As a matter of fact he even asked for one," I said, and the reprimanding smile of the saleswoman clearly implied: why didn't you say so in the first place? She led me to a flat table on which a model train was mounted, pressed a button without enthusiasm, and the train was set in motion, signals went up and down, and little lights came on. But I had already lost interest: the train cost over two hundred marks. And I thought about the fact that in six to nine months, if the doctor was right, the whole thing would be packed away in a box in the attic in permanent twilight, consigned to undisturbed oblivion. There was a cheaper model, for seventy-two marks. I don't remember why I didn't buy it.

I thought about Richard and how innocently he had gone along with the suggestion to celebrate his birthday on the eighteenth of April, even though it actually fell on September second. He hadn't hesitated, or wondered why, or shown any signs of mistrust. When we said, this Friday is your birthday, he had simply counted the days off eagerly on his fingers, then looked up and nodded as if to confirm the date. Jutta was the only one who knew what was happening. We hadn't told her why we were advancing the birthday by several months, saying only that it had to be that way, and she was ready to go along with it all and not say anything.

Suddenly I began to think I wasn't going to be able to decide on anything at all, and I thought about calling Alfred at his office in the translation bureau and asking him to come over. The outfits, musical instruments, model kits and trains—they all seemed wrong to me as gifts, meaningless, unsuitable for someone in our boy's state. Something kept me from buying the things Richard himself had asked for, a feeling, a sharp sense of distrust, as if we might give ourselves away by buying the wrong thing. Since Alfred was planning on taking the afternoon off, I gave up the idea of asking him to come over now. I walked up and down the aisles, picking up things and putting them down, looking things over and constantly rejecting them, until I discovered a red telephone in a wooden box. I bought it without asking the price. The telephone came with a fifteen-foot, red-and-white braided cord, it was connected to batteries, and with it you could actually telephone from room to room. It cost forty-two marks.

I felt an unexpected sense of relief now that I had taken care of the first, and most important, gift. The painful tension receded, my skin seemed less sensitive, and it now seemed easy to pick out a coloring book, a box of watercolors and a game, "The Little Mountain-Climber." I paid while the gifts were being wrapped and received twelve marks in change. I decided to have a cup of coffee before going back.

There was a restaurant on the ninth floor of the department store. I took the elevator up and was surprised to see how crowded the restaurant was for this time of the morning, how many people were already eating hot meals. The only free table was in the middle of the room. I sat down and waited to have my order taken. I looked over the drinks on the menu, but then began to feel that everyone was staring at me. What was the matter, what did they want? What was I doing that was so interesting? All the people around me—dumpy little women, old men, even children—were looking me over, not with a smile or sympathetically, but almost with repugnance, intrigued and repelled at the same time. I could neither explain nor escape their interest, I had to swallow, my face was burning. Then the waiter came and I heard myself say: "Coffee and a cognac." I heard him repeat the order indifferently, then I lifted the bag with the gifts onto my lap and began to go through it just to have something to do, although the others couldn't know that.

The stares became more insistent and the interest more pointed when the waiter served me the coffee and cognac from a plastic tray. What did they want with me? I reached out for the cup, my hand trembled, but I couldn't pull it back. I drank the hot coffee in small sips, set the cup down, and looked at the glass of cognac. Near the rim of the glass the soft swirl of the cognac had left a trace like a slowly receding oil slick. I didn't touch the glass.

I paid and left, took the elevator down, checked my face in the mirror of an advertisement, and could see no reason why I had excited so much attention. On the way home in the bus no one paid any attention to me, and when I got back Jutta didn't notice anything either, but simply greeted me in her skeptical and silently questioning way. She took the shopping bag from me and disappeared with it into the kitchen. I could soon hear the rustling of paper, then a suppressed cry which revealed that she was in the process of unpacking the gifts for Richard. She thought they were just right. She was so pleased with them that she asked if she could have the same things for her own birthday, including the dice-game "The Little Mountain-Climber."

I promised her she could, and then we fixed lunch together.

Alfred came right on time. He had bought something on his own, a pocket flashlight with a rubber rim, which Jutta immediately added to the other gifts. He kissed me at the door like he used to. He seemed to be able to tell that I had kept my promise, at any rate he didn't ask. There was a lot in the way he acted and seemed that reminded me of how things used to be, and that helped me in many ways to measure up to this day, this sixth birthday.

After lunch Richard got dressed and was banished from the bedroom. Alfred stayed with him while Jutta and I prepared for the party. We made a lantern out of the lamp, draped streamers across the room, set the table, and arranged a half-circle of flower blossoms at Richard's place. Jutta stood around and watched me prepare, and all at once she said: "Maybe he won't be happy." "Why shouldn't he be happy?" I said. "When he realizes that today isn't really his birthday." "He counted it up himself," I said, "so he's not going to object." "But it's the wrong day," she said, "he's really supposed to wait until September." "He can't wait," I said. "What about us?" she asked. "We're doing what he wants to do," I said, "we're celebrating his birthday."

I could see that Jutta wasn't satisfied with our decision, that she had reservations about it and would have preferred not to join the party— not because she didn't want to give Richard his day, but because we were refusing to celebrate it on the right date. I had to ask her, even warn her, to play along with us. After that I felt so dizzy that I had to go into the bathroom and run water over my wrists. I checked to see that my secret store was still in its hiding place, but I didn't touch anything.

Before the party began, Jutta lighted the candles. Then we brought Richard and Alfred in, and to the delighted laughter of the boy, Alfred had to eat a flower in front of us because of a bet he had lost. He ate it twisting and turning about gaily in mock suffering, while Richard clapped his hands. Then came the gifts. Richard was led to a chair where he tore into the wrappings, working wordlessly, not looking up, hastily and seriously moving from one gift to the next without ever lingering over what he had just unwrapped. He placed each gift on the floor with a satisfied nod, quickly but carefully, and finally he unwrapped the red telephone. Now he looked around for the first time. He sat down on the floor, put the receiver to his ear, listened, motioned to us to keep totally still, made a face, smiled, and said: "I hear him. I can hear him good." "What's he saying?" Alfred asked. "He's fine," said Richard.

Alfred bent over, took the receiver, listened, and said: "He says we should try the birthday cake now, he'll call again when we've eaten." Richard listened for a brief moment and confirmed the message. "I want to hear him too," Jutta said. "Not now," Richard said, "he's gone. He's not saying anything now." He made an impatient movement, keeping her from lifting the receiver, and we sat down at the table. We ate applecake and drank coffee, and Alfred winked at me like he used to do. "I'll unwind the cord and take it from here into the kitchen, and then we can talk," he said. "Don't have to," Richard said, "I can hear him like this. I hear everything he says." "You don't hear anything at all," said Jutta, "the telephone has to be hooked up first. And someone has to talk to you." "Somebody talked to me," Richard said, "he said he was fine." He was seized by a secret excitement, refused to eat, and waited impatiently for us to finish so he could get back to his telephone.

Alfred and he unwound the red-and-white cord, it reached across the hall into the kitchen, and we didn't get a chance to carry the dishes out. We were not allowed to move or talk while the connection was being tested. Both doors were closed, and those talking on the telephone were lying on the floor in the kitchen and the bedroom. They talked loudly enough to have heard one another through four doors. Alfred handed me the receiver with a smile, stayed crouched beside me, and while I shouted to Richard to inquire about the weather where he was, Alfred supported me and held me tight. Then I felt the pressure in my stomach again, I let him take over talking, got up and went out into the hall. I opened the door to the kids' room cautiously, just opened it without going in, and leaned against the wall. "Let me too," Jutta said, "please, let me do it once." Richard didn't answer, and I heard Jutta insisting: "Please, Richard, it's my turn now. You can use my things . . ." "Get away!" said Richard, "Leave me alone!" "All right," Jutta said, "then I'll tell you something you don't know: it's not even your birthday today! It's not! It's not! Your birthday's in September!" I didn't go in to them, and I didn't wait for Richard's reply. The nausea was so overwhelming that I went into the bathroom, and without even bothering to lock the door, took just one swallow and put the bottle back immediately. I stepped into the hall and heard Richard's voice roaring in pleasure on the phone, lost in the game. I wiped my mouth and lighted a cigarette as Alfred came out of the kitchen with a smile. He came up to me on tiptoe, was about to whisper something. But then he didn't, he just walked on past, as if he didn't see me at all.

AN ACCEPTABLE LEVEL OF PAIN

⌇ৡ We're not even finished cleaning up the room, the two of us from Interrogation, when the adjutant appears. The adjutant asks Eric to report, listens carefully, much more carefully and attentively than he usually does, looks us over with skeptical curiosity, as if he doesn't trust us, isn't satisfied with just a frontal view, walks around us, very slowly around us, and checks us out from behind as well, so that it soon becomes clear to Eric and me that this is not going to be one of your ordinary days. The adjutant has never spent this much time on us.

The slow movements, the attentiveness, the thick greasy layer of distrust all tell us one thing: he's got something on his mind, and he proves it to us by the way he's inspecting the tools we're forced to fall back on now and again. Silently, with bowed head, he walks over to the stretching board, takes a meditative look at the rocker and the bench of nails, nods silently at the rubber hoses, ropes, and electric cables, devotes his attention to the clamps and leather belts, all of which present themselves in perfectly disciplined order. The adjutant doesn't say a word, he doesn't even nod. He moves about stiffly, hesitantly, something is bothering him. We expect something from him, in fact we expect something specific—let's just call it appreciation. Eric has earned that for the highly successful ironing board he developed all on his own. But the adjutant just checks everything over carefully, taking care not to touch anything, and then goes out again without a word.

We look at one another, start to relax, and are just about to begin trying to figure out what the visit was all about when the chief of staff appears. The chief of staff asks Eric to report. He too looks at us more carefully and attentively than usual, walks around us, has us finish our report while he's standing behind us. Finally he orders us to hold our hands out. We hold our hands out. The chief of staff turns our palms up and begins to read them. The readings tell him what he needs to know. He smiles cautiously, his mistrust seems to be partially overcome. The chief of staff has seen something in our palms. He pushes them down gently and looks around. Perhaps he'll even have a word of praise for Eric's ironing board. The chief of staff turns indecisively to our tools as the general's orderly appears with two woolen blankets, a bottle of cognac, and cigarettes. The orderly winks at us, he's known for his winks. He places the woolen blankets carefully on the stretching board, sets the cognac on the rocker, and puts the cigarettes in plain sight nearby. Eric looks at him in confusion, and you can tell what he wants to ask, but doesn't dare. The orderly straightens his uniform and stands at attention by the door, forcing us all to stare at it in anticipation. We can't help ourselves.

We watch the door. Unlike the adjutant, the chief of staff has been running his hands over our tools, perhaps without even thinking. Now he comes forward and watches the door too. It's no longer necessary to tell us who we're waiting for.

All at once the chief of staff sighs, as unlikely as that sounds. He sighs and shrugs his shoulders and indicates to Eric that something is bothering him. You can tell that he wants to let Eric know what's troubling him, and is trying to find the right tone to take. The chief of staff is looking for an appropriate way to take him into his confidence. He keeps hesitating. Then he tells us what we already know: glancing first at the general's orderly, he says that the general himself will be appearing soon, and that we should prepare ourselves to receive him.

We stare at the door. The general has never once been in the interrogation room, we only know him from newspapers and newsreels, but we know him so well that we will recognize him easily. His chief of staff nods thoughtfully. He informs us that the general has a special reason for coming here: back home, some distance away, the chief of staff says that people are getting stirred up about the means used to interrogate prisoners. He claims there's even active resistance. Signatures are being gathered to protest the method of interrogating prisoners. The chief of staff pauses for a moment and inspects the backs of his hands. His silence is not intended as a rebuke. Then he speaks quietly, his eyes lowered: the general wants to silence his critics back home, he wants to show them personally that they're wrong. To prove that the methods used in interrogating prisoners are reasonable and acceptable, he's coming here himself to let those methods be used on him. He wants to undergo interrogation under normal conditions, a test to prove to everyone that the procedures are both necessary and tolerable. It will serve as an example, a humane experiment, so to speak.

He goes over to the rocker meditatively, lifts the bottle of cognac, and reads the label. He finds nothing to object to in the brand. He orders Eric to put away the shovels and brooms. He strokes the woolen blankets brought in by the orderly. He's not interested in whether or not we have anything to say about the general's plan. As Eric is putting the shovels and brooms away in the locker, you can see the damp circles of sweat at his armpits, and his hands are trembling noticeably. Eric keeps licking his thumbs like he always does when he's excited, polishing them on his hips. Eric's heavy, cube-shaped head begins to nod slowly and rhythmically.

Suddenly the orderly jerks the door open, apparently he can hear his master's step before others do. He stands at attention and holds the door open. We stand at attention too, and the chief of staff salutes. The general walks in just like he walks in the newsreels, looking like the photographs that appear every day in the newspapers. He comes in tired and listless, a small, worn-out man, his face spotty, his dark eyes sunken. In defeat he has won the respect of his enemies, in victory he has become a legend in his own time. How narrow-chested he is! His shoulders are slight, his neck stringy, you can see the cervical bones through his uniform. Absent-mindedly he lifts a small dry hand to his cap in salute. He walks across the interrogation room, turns around with a jerk, and looks evenly at his adjutant and a man in civilian clothes who have followed him in. The general is dressed only in a khaki shirt and cotton trousers. He's wearing light cloth slippers and a single medal with a yellowish tinge. He takes off his cap. He closes his eyes, then turns to Eric and asks if he knows what he is to do, and if he's ready.

Eric gives a pained smile. He knows a little but he doesn't know that much, he's heard some things that he can't believe, maybe what he is being asked to do should be done by someone else, and so on. Eric explains that he's not up to the task. Eric makes every effort to appear helpless, overstrained, unsuitable. Eric confesses that he's not the man to carry out a test interrogation, and certainly not one on his own general. He can understand the point, Eric says, but even so he's just not up to it.

The general has his orderly pour him a glass of cognac, takes a sip, opens his shirt at the chest, and stands in silent expectation. Eric polishes his thumbs on his hips. The adjutant, the chief of staff, and the civilian go over to the window, lean against it, forming an audience. I have the impression that all of Eric's previous experience is of no use to him now. The general stands there silently, no, that's not exactly true—once he says something, to himself: I need to prove this, let's get started. Eric looks around helplessly, assailed from every side by quietly insistent stares. He twists around in embarrassment, wheels about, waggles his head, stretches his arms out. It's no good, Eric says dejectedly, I can't do it, what am I supposed to be finding out?

The general nods, he can see that this is a point of legitimate difficulty, and he decides that the interrogation will concern the redeployment of enemy forces in the hill country to the west. Eric takes a step backward, a step which expresses perplexity and refusal, at which point the chief of staff slowly repeats what the general has just said. Now get going, the adjutant says. The civilian is silent.

All at once Eric looks directly at the general, a long look, much too long it seems to me. They scrutinize each other, probe each other, then Eric motions to me and I know what the gesture means: I offer the general a cigarette and light it for him. The general doesn't smile, he smokes rapidly, as if he's been needing a cigarette for quite a while. Eric submissively asks the general if he would care to take a seat, pointing to an ordinary chair. Since it doesn't have an authentic ring to it, the request finds no response, and Eric has to repeat it more directly and forcefully. He simply says: Sit down there. The general wants to know whether Eric uses the polite or familiar form of address in interrogating prisoners. Of course he uses the familiar form he says—when you get that close to someone you can't help but be familiar. Then do the same with me the general says. Eric shakes his head in consternation and gives me another sign, at which, as always, I take the lighted cigarette away from the general. The adjutant likes that. You can tell the adjutant is amused, he taps the civilian on the forearm. Eric thinks it over, ducks his head between his shoulders, thinks it over carefully, and then he laughs aloud, throws up his arms, his face twisted, and lets them fall weakly to his sides again. Eric, the picture of perfect helplessness.

Then the general gets up from the chair Eric had him on and stands there without speaking, not demanding anything or giving any orders, just standing there, small and worn-out, silently forcing Eric to look into his deep-set eyes. And all at once Eric, presumably to his own surprise, yells out: Sit! Sit down, you! The general sits down. He crosses his short legs. He waves off the glass of cognac the orderly holds out in his direction and calmly watches Eric, who draws near to him hunched over in what seems a purposeful manner. Now let's have a little talk, you and me, Eric says, and steps behind the general with his arms crossed.

The civilian takes a notebook from his pocket, pulls out a pencil, and moves a short distance away from the adjutant, who still seems amused, as if he is watching to see what Charlie Chaplin is going to do with his cane. I keep my eyes on Eric, who nods to me. That's my signal to stand directly in front of the general: that's my place. The general and I regard each other in silence. Eric asks the questions from behind. But first he speaks in generalities, confirming a few facts: it's all over for you now, son, the fighting, the fear, the whole mess—over and done with. You're alive, Eric says, and you should be thankful for that. You can show your thanks by telling us what you know.

I search the general's face, his eyes are closed, he's fallen asleep. No, he's just listening with his eyes closed, as Eric, bending low over him, gives him some friendly advice: make it easy on yourself, son, tell us what you know about the troop movements in those hills to the west, where we caught you. You were being transferred to a new regiment, weren't you? What was the number of that regiment? The general remains silent. Everyone's that way at first, Eric says, in the beginning. Pure joy makes them forget everything they knew, but we help them remember, we've always been able to help them remember. You just have to concentrate.

Eric gives me a sign, and I ask the general to stand up. I take him over to the rocker. I ask him to sit down in it, and he does so without a word. In the background, over by the window, someone groans. It's the chief of staff. I strap the general tightly into the rocker for his own safety, and at a signal from Eric I point out to him politely that he is to lift his right index finger if things get too uncomfortable. What follows now, Eric says to the civilian, is intended to sharpen concentration and aid the memory. Then he takes the general by his delicate shoulders and pulls him over backward, holds him way over backward and can actually be heard begging his pardon, then releases him so that the rocker suddenly hurls the general's bound body forward toward the wall. He sees the wall coming and jerks his head sideways, making use of what free play the straps allow, but he doesn't smash against the wall, the swing of the rocker stops him ten centimeters short. And now he whips back and forth, again and again, in calculated rhythm, a carefully measured oscillation. Anyone fastened to the rocker has the inescapable feeling that he is coming closer and closer to the wall, so that if not now, surely next time his face will be smashed against it. The general jerks his head aside each time. He makes no protest. His right finger remains motionless.

Eric places his foot on the rocker, keeps it moving. He asks: Do you remember? Now do you remember the number of your regiment? No? Not yet? But maybe you know some other numbers, eh? Sorry, Eric says, turning to the window in shock at having fallen into the familiar form of address with the general, but those at the window encourage him to keep it up. The civilian is, predictably, the only one who has a question. The civilian wants to know if every prisoner who's brought in for interrogation has the chance to interrupt the questioning by raising his right finger. Eric lets me answer this one, and I say quite clearly: yes, and then at the given signal I release the general from the rocker.

He staggers dizzily. It seems the small delicate man hasn't come to himself yet. His body is trembling, and he's moaning softly. His orderly starts to float over again with a glass of cognac. The adjutant holds him back. The adjutant takes the cognac and downs it himself—distractedly of course, that should be mentioned. Eric himself makes sure that the general doesn't get a cigarette. Eric has long since fetched the clamps. He's working now as usual, with short puffs. The clamps are snapped around the thin wrists of the general and hold him fast under the shower. The memory shower. Which regiments, Eric asks, and pokes the general in the back to get him going. Which troops are being transferred? What's their objective? The general can't remember anything, he's totally lost his memory, so I turn on the shower because I know that Eric is about to give me the signal.

The general is wet. The cloth of his uniform is turning black, sticking to his body. The thin body twists about. The general looks like a poor bedraggled bird in the rain. Predictably, the civilian asks what temperature the water is, seems satisfied with the answer, and makes a careful entry in his notebook. In order to revive the general's memory, I let it rain down briefly a few more times, but without success. Although Eric punctuates his questions with the flat side of a ruler, he receives no answer.

I know that any moment Eric is going to start screaming, and now he does, he's screaming at the general, shaking him, so that I'm starting to get a little worried, and I even hear the chief of staff calling out from the window: hey watch it now! when fortunately Eric settles down again, smiles, and points triumphantly at the general's right finger, which hasn't moved, hasn't stopped things. Come on now, Eric says, out with it, what is the number of the regiment, why do you want to keep it to yourself, you're only hurting yourself.

I know now that it's time for the business with the cigarette and the rubber hose, but as I light the cigarette, Eric signals me sharply, shakes his head with pity for me, and frees the general from his bonds.

Eric shoves the general over to the stretching board. I force the delicate, thoroughly soaked man down onto it. I tie him to the board with cable wire—he's small enough to stretch all sorts of ways. His face is expressionless, his lips are trembling. He lies there without protesting. I listen to him breathing and have no doubt that Eric will get anything he wants out of him. We'll know everything about troop movements in the western hill country before the various commanding officers have heard a thing.

Eric turns the wheel, and the wooden blocks slide into place. The little body in the wet clothes stretches tight. The general's lips purse. This is all part of the process of reviving the memory, Eric says. We watch tensely as the bound body begins to be stretched, thrusts itself upward and falls back, and finally responds to the steady pull with nothing but a moan. We don't have to keep our eye on the right finger—the chief of staff by the window is taking care of that—we can now devote ourselves to the interrogation itself. I want to pass the leather belt over to Eric, but he warns me with a glance, and I hang it back on the hook. I lean down over the general. He is fully conscious. Eric begins whispering his questions, tightens the ropes, asks, tightens still further, asks again—until the general screams out and bites his lips. He doesn't raise his finger. Just give us the number of the regiment and then everything will stop, Eric says, just that one little number. Tell us what you know, Eric says, and turns the wheel again. More than one person would have started talking after that many turns. The general says nothing. He takes the pain and says nothing.

We can understand the unease from the window area, we can see why the orderly keeps wanting to bring a full glass of cognac to his general, but since this is supposed to be a normal interrogation, we can't permit the considerable strengthening offered by the cognac. The civilian is now writing rapidly, feigning indifference. The adjutant is smoking; only the chief of staff seems to be suffering. I look at Eric in amazement and ask myself: how can he stay so calm when he's not getting any results? Is he placing all his hopes on the ironing board, where, when the time comes, everyone starts talking? No one has ever managed to stay silent on the ironing board. I mean to tell you, everybody suddenly regains their memory. Does Eric want to let it go as far as the ironing board?

Eric gives me a sign, and I untie the general, set him back on his feet, and have to catch him to hold him up. I'm surprised at how light he is. I take him by the arm and lead him over to the ironing board that Eric himself developed. I tie him down again and point out to him that, like everyone who has come before him, he can bring the interrogation to a halt at any time just by raising his right index finger. I check to make sure that he understands. He understands, nods weakly. He keeps his eyes closed and shivers from the chill of another pain as yet unknown.

Eric hunches over. Eric suddenly screams out, and even I'm startled. The number, he screams, I want to hear the number of your regiment. The general says nothing. Eric takes the preheated iron out of its holder, lifts it high above the delicate body, and forces the general to look at it. Eric tests the heat of the iron by lightly tapping two moistened fingers against its hot surface, receiving in confirmation a moist hiss. Then he slowly lowers the iron, brushes it lightly over a thigh, watches the steam rise and says: we're going to dry you out, we're going to iron you dry. We can't let you leave here in a wet uniform. Eric goes to work. The general beats his heels, his shoulders are jerking. He holds his breath. He wants to say something, now, now he's going to say something, no, he's just swallowing, tightens the muscles of his neck. He digs wildly at the table with his hands, but he doesn't raise his right finger.

Then I notice that he's opened his eyes and is staring at Eric with a look that's more skeptical than questioning, and which contains a touch of contempt as well. Eric, hesitating, seems helpless and at a loss. He puts the iron back in its holder. He shakes his head, demoralized. He doesn't understand how this has happened, and tiredly orders me to free the general from his fetters.

I untie him, set him back on his feet, and let him regain his balance on his own, while the adjutant and the chief of staff take the liberty of congratulating him on successfully passing the test—they actually congratulate him. The orderly approaches with the glass of cognac and cigarettes and places a woolen blanket around the general's trembling shoulders. Eric sits on a stool at a loss and polishes his thumbs on his hips. Yes, the general is saying to the civilian, it's an acceptable level of pain, I hope that I've demonstrated that.

I knock as always on the door of the medic's room, knocking out of habit, and the red-haired medic appears as usual with the finger splints and the bandages. He has only splints and bandages with him, is taken aback when he enters the room, and turns to leave, but then I point toward the general. The medic goes up to him without a word and starts to put a splint on his right index finger. You can see why the civilian is surprised and asks: what are you up to? And you can't blame the medic for answering, quite normally: I'm putting a splint on his right index finger. Everything's all right, the general says, nothing's broken: we've answered our critics.

Now of course the medic would do well to stop looking so astonished.

THE EXAM

ᴥᔄ See, there's Jan Stasny stepping onto the escalator of the new sub-way station, and in the course of his steady descent he turns and waves up to his wife and former fellow student, standing in the window of their apartment in a green sweater. Waving back, she makes a fist with her right thumb inside and shakes it, so that from below it looks as if she's rapping at the window. He understands her gesture. The stocky man with the blue-black hair and the Kalmuck eyes knows what she's wishing him as he heads toward his final oral exam in his black suit, bearing beneath his arm his college briefcase, empty now except for cigarettes and a blank pad of paper. He smiles, appears confident as he descends, manages to give her a last quick soothing gesture, traced in the air with a fluttering hand, like a drowning man whose head has already disappeared beneath the waters: don't worry, everything will be all right, you don't have to worry. And so it begins.

As she's turning away from the window, she realizes that her ges-tures have been seen and that someone is responding. There, on the extended platform arm of the service truck, high up beneath the street-lights, where they're replacing the fluorescent tubes, two men are stand-ing bare-chested, waving to her and inviting her to jump down and join them on the red-and-white platform. The heat shimmers up from the asphalt, trembles above the metal of the streetlamps. Come on, we'll get right up close to the window if you want, we'll catch you. She affects a studied nonchalance, steps back, closes her eyes against the sun reflected from the bright front of the buildings across the way. Was that the doorbell?

Hello, Mother, yes, Jan's already gone, things are underway. Here, give me your purse, you can start right here in the living room. But rest a while first. Her mother slips past the exhibition posters of modern photography, takes off her hat, and places it on one of the white-enamel homemade brick-and-board bookcases. She passes her hand over a female tailor's dummy on which an admiral's uniform has been painted. Did you do this, Senta? I gave it to Jan for his birthday. She sees the little round table, covered with books and lecture notes faithfully recorded, the stained teacups in which lemon slices are turning brown. We listened to Jan go through things again yesterday afternoon, Mother, and last night. Charles says that Jan will make summa cum laude, no problem. By this evening it will all be over.

With exaggerated caution her mother makes a detour around the record player which is standing on the hard coconut-fiber runners used throughout the apartment. These same runners continue into the next room, which is separated from the living room by a curtain that's just a bit too short. On the homemade table beside the couch a loud necktie chokes a candy glass filled with brightly colored glass marbles. A travel alarm clock presses down upon an opened book. Senta lights a cigarette, rolls up the bedclothes, pushes and stuffs them into a bedchest, and smooths down the cover over the couch. Have you smoked all the cigarettes? Charles was here, and Heiner, we studied away into the night. From now on things will be different.

Her tight green sweater is matted beneath her arms, darkened with perspiration, the seat of the trousers over her slim firm bottom has been worn smooth on the shapeless leather cushions, which are coming apart here and there at the seams, about to spew forth. Her mother sees this, while Senta, the cigarette between her lips, works at a controlled angle over the couch, barefoot, not bothered by the rough coconut fiber. Believe it or not, Mom, I haven't been to the hairdresser in four months.

Where did this come from, her mother asks. On a shelf on the wall, amidst stuffed animals, sea shells picked up on the beach, and brass bells from a horse's harness, stands a wood carving in three colors, carefully and effectively painted. It is the Holy Family, a narrow-eyed Joseph, a broad-cheeked Mary, listening in bewilderment to an elderly child Jesus who is reading something to his parents and who clearly has Jan's features: the sharp profile, the quietly insistent look, and the soft mouth that belies those looks. Oh, that? Jan's favorite uncle was here. He used to make a living with them you know, in Suwalki, and now he's doing it again. He's sold over eighty in Hamburg. He calls that our royalty, because he used Jan as a model.

Her mother pulls the rust-red curtain aside—this is still Senta's room then: the blocky wardrobe that seems to be at home anywhere, the couch squeezed in between the wardrobe and the windowsill, the floating mobile, fishes of various sizes swimming hopelessly after one another, the transistor radio, and on the wall Marcel Marceau, about to set a butterfly free. She examines the room in a manner which betrays neither acceptance nor mental reservations. Nor is it curiosity that leads the tall, fair-skinned, freckled woman past the bookcases and couches, but at most a desire to note, simply for herself, any changes which might have occurred. But there's a distance.

I brought flowers for you, Senta, she says to the wardrobe that once belonged to her own mother. Senta, pulling the green sweater over her head, approaches barefoot. We only have one vase, Mom, I think it's in the bathroom. I'm sorry, I've got a horrendous list of things to do: the hairdresser and reserving the table, and shopping for the others coming this evening. And taking a bath. Can you put them in something?

Senta puts on a skirt and blouse, fishes out a pair of high-heeled shoes, combs her hair energetically in front of the big mirror with her head tilted. No, Mom, I'm not sorry I gave up studying, if Jan passes the exam that's plenty for both of us. You know he's like everyone in his home country. They do things very deliberately, and they're down to earth. They plan ahead for the next few years, and when they say first one thing and then the other, they stick to that order.

She rushes into the adjoining room with a little cry. The cigarette has fallen from the ashtray, and the glowing tip has burned another indelible scar into the homemade nightstand. Senta is so angry that she takes the cigarette into the kitchen and holds it under a stream of water. There is a brief hiss, the paper blackens, the blackness runs up to the filter, and the wet cigarette is flung into the full garbage pail. Senta turns to her mother, who has entered with her purse and now places it on the kitchen table. Standing behind her mother, she places her hands around her upper arms, squeezes, then squeezes again more tightly, as if she wants to compress her broad upper body. I'm sorry, so much depends on this, everything is coming together today, it's like the eye of a needle. As soon as we've forced our way through things will be better. In a way it's *my* exam too. I understand, says her mother. Now don't worry about me. I'll soon find my way about here, things haven't changed that much in four months. Make yourself a drink, Mom. Sure.

There's the cloth handbag, there are the sunglasses on the shelf, now just a band, a velvet band to hold my hair back. Does the mirror second that? Senta squeezes a short colorless worm from a tube of moisturizer, rubs it between her palms, and applies it in strong strokes to her forehead and cheeks. She juts her chin forward, grimacing, piranha-like, sucks in her upper lip with her lower one, need a bit of carmine there, so she pouts her lips, rounds them, draws the lipstick from the corner of her mouth to the middle of her lip, smacks her lips drily, bares her teeth, takes the precaution of placing a paper tissue between her lips, presses them together, and leaves an imprint on it. Now just dab the beads of perspiration off the nose, wipe the neck. Is it true, Mom, that it's over a hundred degrees out? Well, I'm off now, bye.

It's so cool in the stairwell. The coolness rises from the mopped linoleum, which seems to retain the moisture. A flight below her she sees a hand on the railing and a blue sleeve. The hand clasps its way higher and higher, reaches the landing, and soon Senta recognizes a shoulder with a leather strap cutting into it. Just a moment, Mr. Paustian, I'm coming.

Just a postcard for you today, Mrs. Stasny. That's all? That's it. Tomorrow, Mr. Paustian, you'll see tomorrow. A birthday? An exam: my husband is taking his oral exam today. Well, congratulations. It probably started just about now. Oh I see.

It's Jan's favorite uncle crossing his fingers in advance for the exam. He's already carving on a piece of wood from which he hopes to "redeem" a special figure for the candidate, as a gift, which of course he won't be able to deliver himself because of his rheumatism. He will entrust it to the mail. She puts the card in her purse, skips down the stairs with the purse swinging from her arm, and who does she encounter in the entrance hall but the ill-tempered old scarecrow towing her two-wheeled shopping cart behind her and not saying hello this time either, seemingly surprised to be greeted at all. This makes no difference to Senta, since over the past fourteen months she's grown used to not being greeted by her next-door neighbor. She steps out into the sunshine, closes her eyes, and hears Charles asking—or a voice that could be Charles's: What can you tell us about Wieland's concept of humanitarianism? At the same time she feels the suction as the hot side of the streetcar passes before her, sweeping the dust from the tracks. The list.

Senta crosses a main street; a wealth of carefully controlled bodily movements may be observed: a quick start with the body bent slightly forward, hesitating steps from the hips, rapid strides in safety, a swaying pause to let a truck go by, a final spring to reach the sidewalk. Furniture–Marquardt, Tea–Müller, Flowers–Preisler: now they're putting their names after the products they sell. What if someone named Pocks sells chicken?

The Dutch Oven is the name of the pub, and a worn cellar stairway leads down into it. Senta opens the door, then pulls a brown felt curtain aside. This is where Jan wants to celebrate with her, in one of these cool niches, where the walls are covered with photos of famous chefs who either got their start here and moved rapidly upward, or returned here to play out the final stages of their careers. Each table has its own little electric buzzer. What would you like?

An old waiter with gray eyes and a fleshy face points out to her that they don't start serving until twelve-thirty. She's already read that, she just wants to reconfirm what her husband has already arranged with the manager: a table for two for Stasny. One moment please. The waiter brings the reservation book, places it on the table, bends over it and, breathing softly but heavily, begins to read. He wears orthopedic shoes. Little red dots begin to rise and fall before Senta's eyes, forming a spiral. Stasny, you say? Yes, there's a reservation in that name. We'd like to be a bit to ourselves, Senta says, we have something we want to celebrate. Of course. Number four. The waiter looks her over with frank indifference, she has trouble looking him in the eye. Although she hasn't planned to, she says: it's a little celebration for an exam. We've reserved number four, the waiter says, and follows her along the windowless hallway, past the office, from which the manager now emerges to ask if everything is all right. The waiter reports to him and looks at Senta, and finally does ask after all: is the exam in medicine? Germanic Studies, says Senta. Oh, yes.

She climbs the stairs to the street, the sun hits her in the face. What can you tell me about the place of natural science in Büchner's works? Did someone call her name? Sit, Senta, the man in riding boots says as he disappears into the travel agency, and the German shepherd sits where he has tied her, panting as she eyes the stage hands who are carrying props from the side door of the theater and loading them onto a truck. The theater troupe is going on the road, or maybe the stage decorations are just being loaned out. To what play could these delicate pieces of white furniture belong, and this sparsely wooded forest with nothing German about it?

Senta wipes the perspiration from her upper lip with a pocket tissue. As she walks, she takes from her purse the net shopping bag she's rolled into a ball and reads the specials scrawled on the windows in white chalk. Bulgarian raspberries, chicken parts, new potatoes. She stops, and shows how many unexpected reasons there are for stopping: startled, she twists around, lifts her right foot, looks at the heel, puts her foot out in front of her, and makes a small circling motion. Then she walks ahead and into the shop. Good afternoon, Mrs. Stasny.

They both say it, Delicatessen–Grützner and Delicatessen–Son. Soon they will be offering her sample slices of sausage and cheese on greasy knifeblades, but first comes the manifestation of their friendly interest in her personal affairs, and that means that both of them, from the bottom of their hearts, so to speak, express their hope that Mr. and Mrs. Stasny's vacation wasn't spoiled by bad weather. To which Senta replies that she and her husband haven't gone anywhere yet. The weather on the vacation to come they meant of course. Where'd I put that slip of paper? She knows that she wrote everything down and stuck the piece of paper in her purse—it doesn't matter, I can remember it all. Heiner and Charles only drink beer, Jan likes whiskey and soda—a bottle of good whiskey, please.

We probably have to have some champagne, let's say three bottles. No, it's not a family reunion, my husband is taking his exams just now. Thank you, but he hasn't passed yet. The heat doesn't bother him so much. Dear Mrs. Stasny, the Delicatessen–Son says, we will do this celebration up right for you. Having allowed himself this sentence, and having discovered that eight people are to be involved in properly honoring Jan Stasny, he takes the liberty of making suggestions. Pretzel sticks, for example, people like something to nibble on. Or here, how about a jar of gherkins.

Senta shakes her head. You don't have a lavish party for an exam, you know, and it probably won't last too long, maybe an hour and a half. She looks at the trays with herring salad, mayonnaise, and rendered lard in which the crackling is embedded like spots of rust. Cellophane bags of chicken parts lie squashed together. Yellowish flaps of fat shimmer in the pale pinkness. Here's pickled herring in a cloudy brine; the flesh looks flaky, seems to be dissolving away at the edges. A carved ham makes its bid for attention, sweating smoked sausages puff up boldly, draw the eye. A little cheese, perhaps? Sure.

Senta takes on her lost look—that's what Jan calls it when her eyelids come together, her mouth opens, and she places her outspread hand on her neck. An inexplicable pressure, a mysterious congestion arise. Senta tries to counteract this stress attack by swallowing and wetting her lips to remove the sour taste. I beg your pardon? She hasn't understood the question. She was thinking about how Jan, in his headstrong planning mode, had reserved a hotel room for them tonight—she hadn't been able to talk him out of it—and how after the brief celebration for the exam they would be leaving their friends and going to the hotel. And a package of salted almonds, please. More recently, in the last few days, she had noticed how much she was looking forward to it herself, not just for its own sake, but because the exam would be behind them then. She had found out long ago that it would be a special trial for him because of the few grammatical mistakes he still made in speaking.

The Delicatessen–Son, hair oiled and combed flat, band-aids on two finger tips, gathers up her purchases, then follows her gaze eagerly to the shelves and showcases. Some mixed pickles? Or paprika? Maybe some olives, they always put on a good show. Thanks. Olives. Where in the world does he get those phrases? When Senta asks if she can pick up her purchases on her way back, he shoves one shoulder forward and says, of course, but most assuredly, Mrs. Stasny, see you soon then. His gaze follows her out as if he's trying to think of something to apologize for.

Cross the street quickly, it's still green. Senta is the only person crossing in front of the waiting cars, besieged by the heat. Feeling everyone's eyes upon her, she changes her gait and skips forward, speeding up awkwardly. She can't walk right with everybody watching. She smiles into a windshield turned opaque by the bright reflection and hops up onto the curb just as the light turns red. They had both been students for the first three months, then Jan started saying one of them should give up studying. She knew what that meant. Standing in front of a shop that makes picture frames and mirrors, looking into the window in which all sorts of frames await faces and landscapes, she recalls how much Jan enjoyed the ritual of coming home at first—he wanted her to be there waiting to greet him, to ask how things had gone that day. She could see how much pleasure it gave him to report on what he'd done while he was away. Then we had Sturm und Drang with Jäger. Today we read "Shearing the Sheeps," you know, or is it, "Shearing the Sheep," without an s? The hairdresser's shop is next to the art glass factory. The same name on both businesses. Maybe they're brothers, maybe they manage to work together, hand in hand, Senta thinks, and is immediately greeted as she enters by an ill-tempered voice telling her to leave the door open. She waits at the desk, listens in the direction of the booths in which electric lights are burning; Senta has an appointment. She has to tell that to the young woman in a very short, faded white smock, who steps backward out of a booth and says: we can only take people with appointments. Just a shampoo and set, and shorten it a bit. Take a seat, please.

Senta watches the young hairdresser in the mirror as she works on the broad-necked woman with a flushed face, notes the peevish manipulation of the comb and rollers, the way she keeps looking herself over in the mirror whenever she tells Senta to look up. The hairdresser has nothing on under the faded uniform of her smock except a brassiere and panties. Why does she do that, Senta thinks, why does she bleach silver strands into her thick, brown hair? Now their gazes meet in the mirror, measure each other, an inquiring and mutual appraisal. Then the hairdresser reaches into a drawer: would you like a magazine?

Senta leafs through the magazine while the hairdresser works straddle-legged behind her, pressing a small, soft stomach against her elbows from the side, combing her hair, trimming her curls. Neither one has any desire to talk to the other. Instead each seems intent on indicating her own superiority by a stubborn silence. They've sized each other up, and they both want to let the other feel their dislike, but not all too clearly of course. Suddenly tired, surrounded by insistently pleasant smells, Senta closes her eyes. Little red dots drift through the darkness, like gently floating embers. What's the magazine claiming? That a television at the foot of the bed improves a marriage. Lean over further, please, right over the sink, thank you. American researchers have proved that watching television together in bed can restore happiness to endangered marriages. The hairdresser lifts Senta's hair over forward into the wash basin and says in a bored tone: close your eyes. Now she's staring at my neck, Senta thinks, and feels a sharp burning pressure in her stomach, as if she had swallowed a sip of hot coffee too quickly. She can't relax.

The rust-red curtain that divides her room from what they call the big room won't close completely. She sees the image offered to her from her bed over the last few weeks: Jan sitting at the little round table, only halfway into the sharp circle of the lamplight, reading, smoking, writing down a few sentences from time to time, sentences she knows are copied word for word. If I write it down I remember it, Jan said, explaining his method. He had agreed that she would quiz him until she got tired, and as soon as he decided she was tired, he took her into her room, smoked a cigarette by her bed, aired out the room, and returned to his work. How did he manage to drink whiskey and soda while he did it? Scientists have discovered that variety shows and love stories are particularly good for patching up marriages in trouble. Moreover, statistics offer triumphant proof that married couples who watch television in bed are blessed with a higher birth rate.

You can sit up now. A warm hand towel is laid on Senta's face. She feels the hairdresser's fingers through the cloth as they glide over her chin and cheeks. Then she gathers the damp hair into a fold of the hand towel and predries it. If only they spare him Gothic and Old High German, or if I could only answer for him if they start in on the vowel shift series. Now the owner comes in. She's finished breakfast in her private room in the back, relaxed for a bit, and before finding her way back to her own personal customer, now suffering beneath a hair-dryer, she sails past all the other booths to see how everything is going: yes, hello, Mrs. Stasny.

Senta answers while the young hairdresser sullenly continues to work on her, and all at once they're discussing the day's main event. No, it's probably not over yet, they're probably still in the middle of things. What's that? I don't really know if everything will be finished after the exam. In any case, congratulations, says the owner. Thank you, Senta says quickly.

What was that story Jan's favorite uncle told? The most famous exam on the American West Coast was taken in a prison cell. An elderly man who had once committed double homicide, killing both his parents because they hadn't allowed him to study the behavior of nocturnal birds, took a final exam in ornithology, under unusual security precautions, before an examination board from the University of California. He passed with highest honors, apparently taking care to avoid embarrassing the professors who examined him. The night following the examination he hanged himself.

Senta closes her eyes, notes the careless skill with which the young hairdresser handles her hair, feels the pleasant pressure of the foreign fingertips upon her scalp. A shy male voice offers something, repeats the offer. Postcards. A man is standing there with thinning hair and the shifty eyes of a habitual drunk, offering picture postcards. Don't need any, says the hairdresser, but the man has long since recognized Senta as an easy mark and waits for her to answer. I'll take six, Senta says. She sees that they are shopworn, perhaps stolen somewhere, but they can still be used if necessary. So, six cards to spread the news about passing the exam, if things turn out right.

The hairdresser seems noticeably cooler, almost as if the purchase were aimed at her, a form of protest, a call to battle. She doesn't even glance into the mirror. That's it. Now under the dryer please. Afterward, Senta sticks the postcards into her purse and gives the hairdresser a tip which the latter accepts indifferently, although with perhaps a hint of a smile. She pays the owner at the counter. Does the celebration start soon, Mrs. Stasny? Yes, pretty soon now, but I still have a lot to do to get ready.

Before stepping out onto the sidewalk, Senta shoves and pats her hair skillfully back into its normal position and wipes the perspiration from her nose. She'll make the final necessary adjustments to her hairdo when she gets home. A hot breeze is blowing through the streets, popping and snapping the awnings above the store windows.

Her skirt lifts and catches between her thighs. Cover yourself, my little one, says a familiar voice, camouflage yourself or the sharks will get you. Oh, Charles.

And Charles, thin-chested, bearded, a giant who seems to enjoy bearing the sorrows of the world, offers her a bite of the melon he's just taken from a vegetable stand. The only thing that refreshes me, Senta, he says, and at that moment he appears to be eyeless behind his nickel-plated frames. No thank you. Your old man is probably sweating now, says Charles. In these latitudes you should take your exams in February, like me. But don't you worry. All you really have to do is give first-class answers to stupid questions, and our Jan will. I've already predicted that for you.

Charles slouches along beside her with slumped shoulders, bites aggressively into the slice of melon, and reminds Senta that neither of them were ever able to catch Jan out while quizzing him. You'll see. Your old man will produce the exam of the year. Senta tries to stay in the narrow shadows of the shops. Don't you feel well? You can help me carry home the beer you'll be drinking later. Do I have to?

And so to Delicatessen–Grützner, who has packed everything that will make the party a party in two cardboard boxes. Senta is left only with the net shopping bag, which has never seemed as heavy as it does today. Her shoulder and elbow ache, and the reinforced grip of the net burns into her palm. Not so fast, Charles, Senta says. She stops and leans up against a bicycle stand, then pushes out her lower lip and blows across her face. Okay, let's go.

Side by side they cross the street, and in the hallway of the building Senta sits down on the stairs and tells Charles to just leave the boxes there. But since he has a good grip on them, as he says, he takes them up and puts them in front of the door. She hears him slowly descending. You really seem in pretty bad shape, he says, and adds, shall I take the bag on up? She shakes her head, pulls herself upright on the railing, motions with a smile for Charles to lower his head, and kisses him on the cheek. Thanks, see you soon. He watches Senta as she climbs the stairs, waits until she has reached the first landing, then they wave again.

She has to turn the key twice in the lock, so her mother must have left already. There's a note lying on the kitchen table. She lies down on the couch, lights a cigarette, rereads the note, and watches the cigarette smoke as it is swept away at right angles by the draft. Still lying down, she removes her skirt, lifts it high with one foot, and in a carefully controlled motion, flings it onto a leather cushion. This wheezing sound, like air escaping in short bursts from a tube. Senta listens to the sound, clears her throat, coughs, and stands up.

Can you give me examples of the form in which the classical motif of the golden chain reappears in literature? Senta goes into the bathroom, undresses, pulls down a blue-and-white showercap from the shower-head. Jan laughed the first time he saw her in it, and he still laughs every time she puts it on. Do you know what you look like? Like a seal disguised as a hussar. She pushes her hair carefully under the cap, turns on the shower, watches the tiles on the wall begin to shimmer under the sharply etched hatchwork of the streaming water, which rises in a cloud as the spray strikes the bottom. The cigarette has fallen from the edge of the soap tray, and the water carries it to the drain, separating the paper and washing away the strands of tobacco. Senta steps under the stream and raises her arms. Was that the doorbell? She puts on her bathrobe, goes to the door, and opens it. A bouquet of flowers is lying on the doormat, with a letter for Jan pinned to it.

Now it's time. Senta dresses in front of the large mirror on the wardrobe, smoking, trying to remember where she read a description not long ago of a young girl gazing at herself in the mirror. She feels as if she's imitating someone else. She combs and arranges her hair, and puts on a new headband. Now, in her bright green dress, slender and long-legged, she steps up to the mirror, hesitating between doubt and understanding, like the young girl in the novel just before she leaves for court to testify against her former teacher. I've got to eat something, maybe an apple, so long as it doesn't smear anything. She turns on the transistor radio, listens to the final bars of "Up, Up and Away," carries the radio into the kitchen, and begins unpacking the boxes and shopping bag.

All at once she stops, steps into the hallway still holding two bottles, and, watching the keyhole, realizes that a key is being cautiously inserted into the lock. It must be Jan.

She runs back into the kitchen and turns up the music. She hasn't heard him coming, she wants to be caught completely by surprise. Yes? Jan? How did it go? Yes or no? Why aren't you saying anything?

Jan enters, pushes by her without a look, his jacket under his arm, tosses his briefcase on the kitchen table. Come on, tell me. He doesn't open up, his face reveals nothing, the dark, Kalmuck eyes betray nothing, there's nothing to be gathered from his gestures. How is she to interpret the calm with which he opens the cupboard and removes two glasses. What does his stubborn silence mean as he fills the glasses with whiskey and soda? Jan, you did pass didn't you? He pushes a glass into Senta's hand, steps back, lifts his glass to hers, stands there against the unbearable brightness, and breathes out with a sigh. So, here's to what lies behind us. You passed? she asks again. With honors! he says.

Jan drinks with his head back, eyes closed. Senta brings the glass to her lips, sees how badly she's shaking, and sets it down quickly without a sip. And now you can congratulate me, Jan says. She presses against his stocky body, won't let him go, holding him in an embrace made awkward by his stance. From in front it almost looks as if she's strangling him. She presses him against the edge of the kitchen table, kissing him. Jan holds his glass out to the side. I'm so happy, Jan, I'm so happy. Flowers have already arrived for you. He loosens her fingers from his neck, brings them forward, and finally smiles. Everything ready for the party? Everything, says Senta. Then come, first let me tell you how it all went.

They sit on the bulging leather cushions in front of the little round table. They've emptied and refilled their glasses and are holding hands as if they have to endure something together. You should have seen Jäger, Jan says. He didn't make things easy for me, he started out with his favorite subject, German literary criticism. Lessing? asks Senta. Schlegel, says Jan, or Lessing, right. You know, Schlegel's discussion of Lessing's essay "On the Nature of Criticism." I handled that one all right. Aren't you feeling well?

Senta puts out her cigarette, stands up abruptly, and goes to the open window. She presses her hands to her stomach. Senta? Yes, she says, yes. Her eyes are full of tears, as if she's been holding her face into a cold wind. It's nothing, Jan, I just had trouble catching my breath for a moment. Drink something. He hands her his glass. She takes a swallow, sits down, and looks at him inquiringly. And Baroque poetry? That never came up. But guess what old man Pörschke tried to get me with, after I'd done such a good job for Jäger. Well? In the

Classical period, he wanted me to describe the Classical ideal of art, and I launched out into Sturm und Drang, longings for Nature and Sensibility, you know, and how it was all superseded. I had no idea that Pörschke only wanted to hear three words. You wrote them down when he was lecturing back then, but I didn't think of them, I got stuck on beauty as harmony between sensual desire and the law of reason, but that wasn't it. And suddenly I remembered what you said to me while you were rinsing me off under the shower, do you remember? Restraint, regularity, rule. You're really pale, Senta.

Senta jumps up, runs to the toilet, locks the door from the inside, kneels down, lays her arms on the rim of the bowl, and vomits. A sudden pain in the back of her head, a tense pain gripping her temples keeps her pinned to her knees, her eyes fill with tears, the pressure diminishes. She stands up in the dark and turns on the light. She looks in the mirror over the little drainpipe and feels the urge to be sick again. The dizziness is so overpowering that she clutches the drainpipe with one hand while she washes her face with the other. Senta, Jan yells in, what's wrong? Not answering, she rinses her mouth, then opens the door. You're swaying, Senta, do you have a fever?

Supporting her, Jan leads her slowly to the couch. He lays her down and puts her legs up. I'm sorry, Jan, I'm so sorry. Just lie there for a few minutes, he says, and it'll pass. It's going to come again, Jan, I can feel it. What is it? I feel so awful.

Jan stands in front of the couch, smoking, a glass in one hand. He sees how an attack of shivering roughens her skin, and hears her labored breathing. You can't get sick on us, he says, not today of all days, you're not going to be a wet blanket. I'm so sorry, Jan. He sits down on the edge of the couch, puts his glass aside, lays his hand on her trembling shoulder, and suddenly sees something in her face he's never seen before, an expression of painful relief or submission, and he passes his hand gently, almost pointedly, over Senta's face, as if to wipe it away.

They'll be here soon, Senta. I'm so sorry, Jan, but I can't, I can't do it. Shall I call it all off then? You can see I can't, Jan. She turns and looks at him in silence. After a while he stands up, gets his jacket from the kitchen, and goes to the door. Then he waves to her and leaves.

FANTASY

✒ It certainly spoke in Dieter Klimke's favor that even outside in the rain, while heading for the Serbian pub near the railroad station, we continued talking about the reading he had given that evening. Gregor had drawn his overcoat around his head as protection against the cool rain, and hunching over as he walked along ahead of me, he repeated his views on Klimke's first performance at our writers conference. I had trouble understanding him because he was talking into his overcoat and kept turning his head to peer into side streets where he hoped to rediscover the pub he had first noticed as we were passing by on the bus. He walked along as though moving through heavy surf, in the gigantic, floppy shoes he made his grown-up sons break in for him.

Take it from me, old boy, he said, you've let Klimke put one over on you, you and the others. The only thing he had to offer was clever tricks, a few samples of a skilled balancing act.

I called up the image of Dieter Klimke, a gentle, bony man, with a touch of the priest about him. He had put on a black tie for his performance, and read his short stories in a monotone from a manuscript which shimmered beneath the reading lamp, now light green, now bluish, now pale rose.

No, Gregor, I said, Klimke is no sleight-of-hand artist. He showed more than just a strikingly powerful imagination. He also demonstrated the laws governing fantasy. Gregor mumbled something into his overcoat, and then took my arm and said: fantasy—yes, but a fantasy without any power to bind. I'm sorry, old boy, but I just can't get excited about stories in which people walk through walls. Or horses talk. Or figures step out of picture frames and sit down at the table to eat. They don't offer any recognizable reality. What do you mean by reality, I asked. The force of gravity, he said, that pulls fantasy back to earth. Gravity may perhaps keep us humble, I said, but it doesn't disprove the imaginary. Didn't you see how Klimke wove the fantastic right into the general order of things, so that it ceased to seem strange?

Well, old boy, I must say that a talking horse will always seem strange to me, even if it talks in my hometown twang. Even in a lifeless, artificial landscape, I asked? A landscape like Klimke's, without a blade of grass, a drop of water, or a single tree? What's that got to do with it? Gregor asked. I responded that Klimke's talking horse was standing upon a surface which seemed to be made of metal. In a distorted, enchanted setting. No wind. No sky. A place, it seemed to me, in which a horse might well speak. At any rate, I heard a horse speak, or at least I heard a man talking who was dressed up as a horse. You need a slivovitz, old boy, said Gregor, in fact you need a double. And if you want to know what I really think about the Dieter Klimke affair, I think it's a case of the magician's tricks of the trade, that's what it is.

Something else strikes me, I said. And what's that? Fantasy is not an independent realm. It doesn't exist in isolation from reality, it's a part of reality. It penetrates everywhere . . . And crashes to earth at the pull of gravity, said Gregor, interrupting me.

He stopped suddenly, lifted his head out of his wrap, and looked around to get his bearings. There's the entrance to the railway station, the dark box behind it is the market hall, so it must be right around here, in one of these little side streets. I suggested we go into some other pub, one of the many wine cellars we had already passed, but he wouldn't give up. He pulled me past filthy façades, plastered with defaced election posters: politicians adorned with long canine teeth, with their eyes gouged out, or with obscenity-filled cartoon balloons issuing from their mouths.

After all the readings we've heard today, I'd really like to have something Serbian, said Gregor.

Glancing behind us, I noticed a tall man following us through the darkness, a gliding shadow who paused whenever we did, and then sped up when we moved on. So there was nothing left but to go around a corner and let him walk into our trap. Gregor placed his two hundred pounds across his path, while I came up from behind and asked him if he had some business he'd like to discuss with us. Pleasure, he said, in case you gentlemen are looking for pleasure, I can lead you to it. Beat it! Gregor said, stepping aside. We watched him go. He kept turning around to look back at us. I give up, old boy, Gregor said. I'm for going into that pub on the corner.

An algae-choked aquarium glowed in the ground-level window of the pub. Spindly, ornamental fish darted out from beneath aquatic plants, confronting one another with bulging eyes. The tavern was called The Last Anchor, and the owner called himself Boss Rusche-wey. Gregor tapped the sign and said: there's a name would never occur to us, old boy, sounds like an overstrained imagination.

He pulled open the door and stepped in ahead of me. It was a respectable, dimly lit pub, with tables bolted to the floor. There was a sturdy counter, and the bar behind it was adorned with photographs, stiff, dust-covered pennants, and tarnished loving cups. The stocky host returned our greeting sullenly, as if our appearance had forced him into unwelcome action. We had free choice of tables, or almost free, since only the one in the corner by the slot-machines was occupied. I left it up to Gregor to pick a table. I don't care where we sit, I said—and then I felt him stop short in surprise. He groped at me with one hand, while he pointed with the other to a niche near the aquarium. Look who's sitting there, old boy. Over a steaming cup of tea, a long cigarette dangling from his lips, sat Dieter Klimke, smiling as if we had caught him in the act. He stood up, and although he didn't invite us to sit with him, we took off our coats, pulled two chairs up to his table, and accepted his cigarettes.

Did you just drop in too? Gregor asked. Klimke nodded. I couldn't take being in the spotlight, he said, and all the discussions: it's my first writers conference, and I'm really not used to listening either. I live alone, in an old gatehouse next to a closed-down factory.

Your reading went very well, I said. He looked at me in disbelief, remembering all the objections raised by Gregor and the others. So I added: there's no unanimous victory among writers. Believe me, if

Kafka or Dostoevsky had been reading today, they wouldn't have come
off any better than you did.

The host approached to take our orders. He noted them in silence
and returned jerkily to the bar, a clumsy, wound-up doll. Why are
writers like that? asked Dieter Klimke, and Gregor responded, they're
all one-man parties. Each one is a prisoner of his own platform.

One of the corner slot-machines started spitting out what appeared
to be a jackpot, raining clumps of coins into the cup. But the player
just calmly gathered them up and fed them anew into the machine.
He was not the only one unmoved by this success. The woman in the
light trench coat was similarly indifferent. She didn't even look up
from her glass, but simply sat there lost in her pain, smoking rapidly,
feeling for the fresh band-aid above her cheekbone. She seems to have
calmed down, Klimke said. Just a moment ago, when she started to
take a drink, her hand was shaking so badly I thought she wouldn't
manage it.

The host brought us beer and a double slivovitz. We ordered another round and drank a toast. Dieter Klimke stuck to his tea. He
smiled grimly, inspecting Gregor out of the corner of his eye as if
he expected something from him, a new objection to his reading or
one of his avowals of faith in the power of gravity. At last he turned
to Gregor himself and said, you weren't pleased with my texts. That's
right, said Gregor. If I understood you rightly, said Klimke, you called
my works "arbitrary figments of the imagination." Something like
that, said Gregor, texts that don't commit you to anything aren't confirmed by reality. And why don't my texts commit you to anything?
asked Klimke. Take a man who can walk through walls, said Gregor,
the man in your second story. Love affairs mean nothing to a man
like that, he doesn't get sick, presumably he can thumb his nose at
death. We can't compare ourselves to him, he doesn't reinforce any
of our own experiences, and therefore he's of no interest to me.

It's that simple, is it? asked Klimke with a smile. And Gregor, pulling his turtleneck sweater down over his massive body said, yes, it's
that simple. When someone's hat blows off, I laugh at his bad luck.
That's something that could happen to anyone. But when a man
walks through walls I lose interest, because he's done something none
of the rest of us can.

No, Gregor, I said, that seems too simple to me. You're basing your argument on the fact that we can't walk through walls. You're relying solely on the common image we have of a wall, plastered bricks and mortar that our bodies can't pass through. That's the given concept. We take that as "solid fact." But this common concept is at some point influenced by what we perceive. And sense perceptions can take on different meanings. They follow a necessity of their own. They can change our concepts.

But they can't make a wall permeable, said Gregor. No, I said, but you can conceive a man in such a way that you would have to grant him the ability to walk through walls.

Gregor tipped his glass and looked at me in feigned concern. For me, old boy, the only power of proof lies in the realm of reality. Or call it the power of gravity. Fantasy always runs aground on it, and will continue to do so in any future borderline case. Dieter Klimke shook his head in hesitant protest, and then said softly, fantasy, for me it has its own powers of proof. And its own reality. But there's no way to disprove it, said Gregor, and what can't be disproved isn't real.

Dieter Klimke straightened up and looked into the corner at the slot-machines, and we followed his gaze. The young man, wearing a checkered sports shirt and a tight leather jacket, took the woman's purse and emptied it onto the table. The contents included, among other things, the pinion feather of a good-sized bird. Rummaging among keys, I.D. cards, and lipsticks, he gathered up the coins. The woman simply stared vacantly at her glass, pressing her hands together under the table. She was perhaps ten or twelve years older than he was, with very bright eyes and hard but regular features. Apparently she had a standing order with the host, because from time to time he would refill her glass.

Something's going on over there, said Klimke, something's simmering. The same old thing, said Gregor, either a break-up or a reconciliation. No, said Klimke, I don't think so. It's a more complicated case, ruled by special conditions. At any rate they don't strike me as normal customers.

It seemed that the woman was trying to reach a decision, and that the more she drank, the harder it was for her to make up her mind. Something is ending, I said, and the longer she sits, the harder it is for her to be done with it.

We could have a go at it, said Gregor, since you put so much faith in fantasy. We could try to tell their story, their story so far . . . what's already happened . . . what brought them here . . . What do you think? Each of us gives a version. And what's that supposed to prove, I asked. Not one of our fantasies is real, said Gregor. You're wrong there, said Klimke, sometimes we have to invent the truth. Well, let's invent it then, said Gregor, examining the pair with narrowed eyes, let's try to put them in a story. He gestured to Klimke to start, but Klimke waved him off. The one who had the idea ought to go first, he said.

While the host was bringing a new round of drinks, Gregor stared at the slot-machines in the corner. His pudgy fingers drummed on the ashtray, his chin moved rhythmically in a chewing motion, and when the woman suddenly left for the women's room, he turned to us and said quietly, there's just one story that you can tell about them. It's the same old story, and if you want to know how I see it . . . what binds those two together or no longer binds them . . .

All right. Take the woman—to me she's Belinda. I see her helping her children with their homework in a quiet, cheerful home beneath the protective branches of soaring beech trees. They are tractable, well-dressed children, a blond boy and a dark-haired girl, or perhaps the other way around. They compete for their mother's favor, shoving their notebooks at her by turns, hoping for even a passing word of praise. Belinda is sitting so that she can look out the window. In the background is a moderately busy river, closer in are steep cliffs with exposed trees, then a winding ribbon of sandy road, and finally a reed-brown woven fence around the property that keeps others from seeing in. The children are hastily filling in pictures with crayons. Something of their mother's unease seems to have communicated itself to them. Then Belinda jumps up, goes to the window, and waves to the taxi that is slowly approaching along the sandy road. She throws on a light-colored trench coat lying nearby. As she leaves she both praises and admonishes the children, that looks very nice. But you have to keep practicing. I'll be back soon.

She's hardly out of the room when the children rush to the window and watch her run to the taxi. She says something hurriedly to the driver, who takes off his cap as he opens the door for her. He's a plump man with a shapeless body, unexpectedly polite and talkative. In the rearview mirror he sees the woman turn to look back at the children in the window. Nice place you have here, he says, and such nice children.

Yes, Belinda says. She grasps the strap and closes her eyes, more in resignation in the face of the driver's compulsive chattiness than from bodily fatigue. He feels compelled to tell her which families live in which roomy, cream-colored houses, and what sort of businesses they're in. He's matter of fact, and not at all disparaging, when he glances at a passing house and says, the Brusbargs, on the hill there, they owe everything to their sauces. That is, the grandfather had the idea of putting sauces in packages. I mean that powder that you make sauce out of. At first the whole family filled the packages at home. Then came the factory.

Belinda opens her purse in a sudden rush of fear, rummages about, finds the letter she is looking for, reads the name of the recipient— Thomas Niebuhr—and sticks the letter in her coat pocket. Look, says the driver, pointing to the city hospital, I was in there just two weeks ago. Nothing serious, I hope, Belinda responds mechanically. Ruptured navel, says the driver, seeking her eyes in the rearview mirror. Everything just pushed out, ma'am. I'd been hauling things long distance for eighteen years, you know, and I always loaded the trailers myself. Frozen sides of beef from Argentina, you know, each one about two hundred fifty pounds. The hard part is bending over with the load. No belly button can take that.

Please, says Belinda, I don't feel well. She rubs her temples gently and then buries herself in her coat. Sure, I see, says the driver, no harm meant, it's all a question of nerves you know. But now I wanted to ask—to get to this garden colony you want, we could either go by way of Helmholtzstrasse or Leistikowsteig—which would you like? I don't know, says Belinda, just make it fast. She lowers her head to escape the looks of reassurance from the rearview mirror, frank and even gentle looks, and because she hopes it will allow her to sink into silence, she says as if it's her last word, you can wait for me there. I'll be going straight back.

They drive across a bridge and then along the river to the garden colony. It's divided into streets and lanes all named after local flora. No one lives here now but Greeks and Yugoslavs, says the driver, and Belinda, startled, says, no, no, not just Greeks. She gives the driver directions in a low voice. She has him stop in a lane named for colts-foot, gets out quickly, runs across mushy garden plots to a wooden cottage with windows made opaque by dust and grime. The taxi driver notices that she doesn't knock, just jerks open the door, which seems to be warped. She steps in. You can furnish the room on your own. At your disposal are a sagging sofa, two old-fashioned, oversized easy chairs, and a propane gas stove. By the window stands a large-sized writing table completely covered with manuscripts, books, clay fig-urines, a transistor radio, and a typewriter. Next to the stove is a wash basin, and standing over it the young man, bare-chested, groaning as he works the soap into his hair. Now he raises his head, squints through burning lather, and says, it's you.

Belinda takes the letter from her pocket, turns off the transistor radio, shoves some books off a chair, and sits down. She says, this will only take a moment, Thomas, the taxi's waiting outside, I've got to hurry back. I knew it, says the young man as he rinses out his hair with warm water, I can't expect anything better on a day like this. He dries his hair on a hand towel, measures the woman with a quick glance, notices the letter in her hand, and approaches slowly. Read it to me, he says, nothing can go worse for me today. A glorious day of being shat on. Why, asks Belinda, what happened? Just call it a burial day, says the young man, nodding at the letter. So what else do I have to bury today? Read it to me. Was your application returned again? the woman asks, and the young man replies, it was, by the fifth com-pany. Returned, registered mail and insured, stating that my dossier was impressive, so impressive that the firm preferred not to hire me. Fine, and two hours ago I received notice. I have to move out of here—presumably some Yugoslavs will be moving into Villa Belinda soon—with their families.

I'm sorry to hear that, Thomas, she says. I have faith in your abili-ties anyway. Thomas laughs bitterly, pulls on a checkered shirt, and throws his close-fitting leather jacket over his shoulders. A cigarette in the corner of his mouth, he combs his hair carefully before a mag-nifying barber's mirror. He asks, and you, Belinda? Why don't you read me the letter? I'm really ready for things today.

The woman looks down at the floor, at the worn-out carpet. She says softly, Christian is being transferred, to the West. I'm going along, Thomas, I'm going with him. Is that the whole surprise, asks Thomas, and then, with forced irony, after all, he's your husband, and your duty is to follow him wherever he goes. Do you already have your tickets? Don't talk like that, says Belinda. I—this is the last time, Thomas, I can't visit you anymore. Well, says the young man, at least an era of suspicion will be over for him.

He turns and takes the letter from her, thinks it over, taps it lightly against the back of his hand, then tosses it with unexpected decisiveness onto the writing table. He says, farewell letters should be read in private, shouldn't they? I'm saving it for later, as the crowning conclusion to my day. Belinda stares at him at a loss. She asks, is that all? Is that all you have to say to me? And he replies, shrugging his shoulders, never hold up someone who's going on a trip. I know that from long experience. And then, after glancing through the window at the waiting taxi and the bulky driver leaning against the hood, can you take me along? Just a little way? Into the city? The woman presses her lips together, still waiting for something, but she can't quite say what. Then she quickly rises, nods, and goes to the door. They get into the taxi. The driver asks, home again?

Yes, says the woman, but this time go by way of the railroad station. Is it all right with you, Thomas, if we stop near the railroad station? Fine with me, says the young man, and slides closer to her, reaching for her hand. They sit together in silence, and as they are crossing the bridge, he puts his arm around her and draws her to him, while the driver, because he is oddly offended by or dislikes the new passenger, not only suppresses his urge to talk, but also refuses to look into the rearview mirror. A gentle rain darkens the cobblestones. The driver turns on his lights. He hears the passengers whispering in the back seat, and the woman asks unexpectedly, would it be possible, please, to go back again? To the garden colony? asks the driver. Yes, to Coltsfoot Lane, I forgot something. It's all the same to me, says the driver. He turns off onto a side street, checks the meter, and speeds up through a traffic light that's still green. It turns yellow just as they enter the intersection.

It was green. Nevertheless the other car hits them on Belinda's side, tearing off the rear mud-guard and spinning the taxi around once on its axis, sending it into a lamppost. It's not Thomas, but the driver, who manages to open the door and pull Belinda out. He looks at her carefully. Are you all right? He sees that Belinda is bleeding above

the cheekbone, and while the driver of the other car approaches, ges-
ticulating and threatening in time-honored fashion, the driver calmly
opens his first-aid kit and hands the woman a band-aid, which the
young man applies for her. Quick, says the woman to Thomas, get
me away from here. Before the police come. But he'll need us as
witnesses, whispers the young man. I can't, she says, you've got to get
me out of here. She looks across the street, ready to take off, as the
taxi driver steps up to them. He's already holding a notebook, and
asks, you saw that the light was green, didn't you? The other driver's
sticking to his claim that the light was green before he started into
the intersection. We had green, says the young man decisively, and
we'll be happy to testify to that anytime. Thanks, says the driver, and
hands his notebook to Thomas, asking him to write down his name
and address. Must I? asks Belinda, as the driver gestures to her as
well. She writes down a name and address, closes the notebook, and
hands it back. But surely we don't have to stay here now, she says, and
the young man adds, we're really pressed for time. With these words
he hands the driver a banknote he's taken from the woman's purse.

Taking advantage of the increasingly intense argument between the
two drivers, they hurriedly cross the street, walk through an archway,
and reach Theaterstrasse, which leads to the railroad station. They
cross this street, not by common agreement, but simply because the
woman thinks they should, and the young man follows her. But
then she stops abruptly before a pub with an illuminated aquarium in the ground-level window. She leans against the young man.
What's wrong, he asks, what's the matter, Belinda? He'll find me
again, she says, my God, he'll come to our house. I put down another
name and address in his notebook. But that won't help. He picked
me up at our house. You wrote down a false name? asks the young
man, and Belinda replies, my God, I'm getting sick. Let's go in here,
Thomas, just for a moment. Let's have something to drink. My God,
I feel sick.

Gregor lifted his glass, gesturing toward the couple in the corner,
regretfully, as if it were their fault he couldn't invent a better story
about them. Look at them, old boy, he said to me. Note the indifferent
attitude of the young man, apparently he's switched machines, and the
dull despair of the woman, who's probably given up on finding a way

out. None of this offers anything unusual. We can assume an honest banality, and by the way I'd like to say that I have a great deal of respect for the banal. Dieter Klimke shook his head and smiled. I could tell that he had long since discovered other motives and relationships, but he chose not to respond to Gregor.

When the host brought us a new round of drinks, Gregor asked, what did you do to get all those pennants and trophies? Fish, said the host, I've been named The Fisher King on several occasions. They give prizes for everything, for the biggest fish, for the most valuable fish, for the heaviest total catch. And for the biggest one that got away? asked Gregor, at which the host waved him off and returned to the bar.

Since both of them now turned to me with a challenging and expectant look, I took up the couple by the slot-machines again, interrogating them silently, interpreting their behavior, letting their mutual indifference tell its own story. It was precisely that indifference, and my sudden realization that the couple shared certain physical features, that suggested a different assumption: the two must be siblings. Well, asked Gregor, what do you think? Brother and sister, I said, I have to assume they're brother and sister.

Having established this, I was immediately forced to review the relationships revealed by the couple in the corner. Couldn't the pained expression on the woman's face be the result of a discovery which had condemned her to a final helplessness? Might the so-called indifference of the young man conceal the desire to forget, and might the obsessive gambling at the slot-machines result from a need to distract himself from the discovery he shared with his sister? Other questions led to other possibilities, and then I began to seek a setting where their story might have begun, and a reason why they might be here together. Well, asked Gregor, how did this brother and sister get here? And what's their prehistory?

All right, listen, I said. Imagine a tidy little widow's apartment. It's afternoon. They're sitting at a coffee table, the pastries have been pillaged. The mother, who has trouble walking, is sitting on the mignonette-green sofa. Karen and Herbert, whom they call Hebbi, are sitting on two chairs facing her. They've appeared for their mother's sixty-fifth birthday. Mechanically, the mother urges them to have another piece of pastry. They both decline with a sigh, and look at each other in amusement as their mother takes another tart and begins to chew on it in melancholy pleasure. Look at all the flowers you got, Mama, says Karen. Too bad I don't have enough vases, says the mother, you can give me some for my next birthday.

The doorbell rings. Hebbi gets up to answer it, but his mother calls him back, cheerfully at first, then more emphatically. Although walking is hard for her, she insists on going to the door herself. Today I'm handling everything, she says, acting curious, and giving the impression she doesn't want her expectations cut short by anyone. She shuffles past the table and goes into the hall. The brother and sister wink at each other, then listen as she removes the chain from the door and opens it. They hear an explosive burst of best wishes for her sixty-fifth birthday, then the mother's gentle attempts to talk someone inside for pastry. Finally a cheerful refusal. Later perhaps, Mrs. Krogmann, when your guests are gone. She comes back in with a bouquet of flowers, and Karen thinks she hears a note of disappointment in her mother's voice as she says, just a neighbor, Mrs. Unertl. She's a receptionist, whatever that means.

Karen puts the flowers in a plastic pail and sticks the greeting card among the blossoms, while Hebbi lights a cigarette and enjoys himself looking over the sideboard which is crowded with mortars and pestles, photographs, dust-gathering immortelles, and a heavy model-train engine on a marble base, not to mention letter-openers, hand mirrors, and a worn silver-plated brush. He shoves the immortelles aside to reveal the largest of the photos, enclosed in a shell-studded frame, and regards it for a while with well-meaning skepticism. It shows a small, agile man with dark, dreamy eyes, who has set his railway uniform cap at a jaunty angle.

There's our little genius, says Hebbi, too bad he can't be here with us. Don't talk like that, says his mother, don't talk about your father like that. You mean he wasn't a genius? asks Hebbi in pretended astonishment. Karen speaks up, put him away and stop annoying him. After eleven years you should leave him in peace. Surely I have the right to admire him even after eleven years, says Hebbi. I really considered him the family genius. Nobody had as many ideas as he did, sharp ideas. You might at least honor his memory, says Karen, and Hebbi replies, aren't I doing that? When I mention his genius, I'm honoring his memory. And, speaking to the photograph: you were all right, little Paul Krogmann, you dreamed more boldly than most men. You just forgot to provide an insurance policy for your boldness. What do you know about life, says the mother, and turns back quietly to her pastry. Exactly, says Hebbi, all I have to do is compare myself with him, and then I recognize my shortcomings. What do you mean? asks his sister. Well, just think about all the things he tried, the courage he demonstrated, as a small-time locomotive engineer, starting up businesses. First the firm that planted trees that would grow quickly. For two marks you could be a member and own a tree. Or his disposable shirts: wear them once and into the wastebasket. Or his tinctures for physical deformities. Oh, yes, and his factory that made anti-insomnia magnets. Just let somebody try to equal any of that. Stop talking like that, says Karen, Papa paid for it. Sure, says Hebbi, he paid for it all with Mama's savings. That's not what I mean, says Karen, I'm talking about the accident that killed him.

Hebbi replaces the picture, tilts his head, and imitates the jaunty smile of the locomotive engineer. He says softly, no one could ever figure out how a man with his experience could run through that signal. His locomotive was the first and only car to tumble down the slope into the river. If you don't stop you're going to put a damper on the whole birthday, says Karen. The mother shrugs. What does he know about life? And then she asks Karen to fill the liquor glasses. Before drinking, she turns again to Hebbi. I hope you're able to do what he did. I hope you'll leave your widow a pension as good as mine. I have him to thank for the fact that I can't complain. And she nods in confirmation. No one will ever destroy her belief in this. No one will ever change her belief that this provision beyond his death was the final crucial act of her husband, making up for everything.

Brother and sister carry the dishes into the kitchen and place them in the sink. Seeing that it's time to leave, they decide to walk part way together. But break it to her gently, says Karen, that we're not staying for supper. The mother sits stolidly, imperturbable, in a dullness no message can transform, and when Hebbi says, Mom, Karen and I have to go now, she proffers her hand more in relief than in regret. The brother and sister caress her as they would a familiar monument, give her a glancing kiss, and wave one last time as they leave. When the door closes, the mother glances up at the clock on the sideboard.

As the brother and sister descend the stairs of the apartment building, Hebbi describes his experiences on the job. You won't believe it, Karen, but it's true. There's something about me. No matter what I do, bosses always come to me with better positions, more money, more responsibility. When I was washing windows, they wanted to make me foreman after two weeks. I'd barely arrived in the transportation firm when they offered to make me head of the packing department. And now it's happened again. I'm supposed to oversee all messages at the radio station. Are you going to do it? asks Karen. Me? Do you think I've got rocks in my head? One step up the career ladder and your days of ease are over. No more peace. No more innocence.

On the ground floor a baby buggy is blocking the basement entrance. Hebbi puts a foot in it and balances himself by placing his hand on his sister's shoulder. What I'd like to do most, Karen, is have you push me along, all my life. Like you used to.

Stepping onto the street, they face the traffic island in front of the branch railroad station and take each other's hand to hurry across the streetcar tracks. Protected from the wind by the glassed-in waiting area, they light cigarettes. Looking up, Hebbi gazes along the ramp of the loading dock, the packed carts and trolleys, then past the telephone booth. Suddenly Karen feels him stiffen. He remains motionless, crouching slightly.

What is it, Hebbi? What's the matter? There, he says hesitantly, by the telephone booth. That man. The man giving flowers to a kid. That's Father. You don't really believe that? It's him, Karen. The man bending over to the kid . . . giving her money now. But Father's dead, says Karen. Do you see where she's taking the flowers? asks Hebbi. They're meant for Mother.

The child nods at the man's instructions, then skips across the street and over the tracks, hesitates for a moment, and looks at the coins in her hand. She carries the flowers into the apartment building. It's Father, Karen, it's got to be him. You're seeing things, Hebbi. Then come on, come along and see for yourself.

He grasps her trenchcoat belt and pulls her to the loading dock, just as the small man quickly strides past and enters a passageway to a covered area from which the railway platforms can be reached. A dark billed cap like the ones worn by railroad officials or harbor workers recedes in rhythm with the steps, past the sandwich shop, the newsstand, to the city line platform. Hurry, says Hebbi, we mustn't lose him. They run, and get onto the same train as the little man. They get out at each stop to check that he's still in the next compartment. That's all they want, because before they speak to him they want to know more about him.

He gets off at the main railroad station, but now he's acting more reserved, taking his time. He saunters to a flower stall, but not to buy flowers. Instead he places himself at an angle to a mirror and watches the people behind him, particularly the brother and sister. He noticed them as they kept passing by the window of his compartment on the train. His alertness, his calm caution, seem to Hebbi an additional confirmation of his suspicions. It's him, he whispered, that's Father, Karen.

Abruptly, the little man turns and strides energetically, almost in flight, to the exit. He disappears between the waiting taxis, reappears at the illuminated entrance to a hotel, and turns into a dark side street. Now he's running, as are the brother and sister. Hebbi is in front. He can tell the little man has recognized who's behind him. His movements in flight become ludicrous. The long overcoat interferes with his legs, the large cap seems to sit back on his coat collar. He stops in front of an advertising sign and pulls open a door. A shaft of light falls onto the sidewalk. It quickly darkens, and he's gone.

The brother and sister draw nearer, approach the display window of a pet shop. The only person in sight is the salesman, a slender, rather solemn-looking man in a gray smock. They glance at the stock—pigmy rabbits, Guinea pigs, budgerigars tumbling and tumbling—and enter. Hebbi asks, did a man just come in here? The salesman bows to them in surprise and gentle remonstrance, a man? He hasn't seen any man, but he would like to know what he can do for them.

Karen, somewhat upset, is dragging her brother out of the shop when they hear a noise from the storeroom. Probably falling boxes, but Hebbi wordlessly jerks a curtain aside and pulls his sister into a dimly lit room. Parrots sound an alarm, marmosets whose sleep has been disturbed race around in their cages, baring their teeth.

There, Hebbi shouts, the door to the courtyard. They cross the storeroom and run into the inner courtyard, where a back door is just closing. He must have escaped through there. They stand pressed together in the hallway and listen, their heads tilted upward. They hear steps fading away and the increasingly faint sounds of panting, then the distant sound of a key in a lock. A door closes, and they bound up the stairs.

Either the fourth or fifth floor, Hebbi whispers. She moves his hand from her coat sleeve, leans against the wall, and tries to catch her breath. Simultaneously, she gestures that she's had enough. That's it, Hebbi, she says, I'm not going any further. You're seeing things.

But it's him, Karen, it's Father. You know he's been dead for eleven years. His body—it was never found after the accident. Then why is he running away from us? Let's ask him, says Hebbi determinedly, and pulls her toward the fourth floor, where he presses the glowing light switch. He reads the nameplates to himself, listens at the doors, and then motions his sister to draw near. Here, Karen, P. Ballhausen, that could be it. Children's voices are coming from the other apartments. Ring the bell. You ring it, says Karen.

The bell appears to be stuck, it rings continuously, until it's pushed again. When they hear footsteps approaching, Karen instinctively ducks behind her brother. A chain is removed, and the door opens slowly.

Hello, Father, says Hebbi. The little man with the dark, dreamy eyes looks at them, not unkindly, but at a loss. He stands before them with his jacket open, in house slippers, and with a bread knife in his hand. We followed you, Father, Karen and I. Perplexed, the man shrugs and says with a smile, I'm sorry, but there must be some misunderstanding. Please, don't pretend with us, Father, says Hebbi, I was just looking at your photo today. At least let us come in. Now the man shakes his head in amused surprise. The things that happen to me, he says, and then, please, you're welcome to come in if you want to.

They enter the apartment and pass a stack of brand-new, empty birdcages, straight from the factory. A freshly cut loaf of bread lies on the kitchen table, and bundles of animal magazines are scattered about the sparsely furnished living room. We discovered you by accident, Father, when you were giving the little girl flowers for Mother. We followed you. Why don't you stop playing hide-and-seek? The little man reflects, begs their pardon for the bread knife in his hand, and says with a smile, that would be quite a surprise, to suddenly have two full-grown children, but I have to disappoint you. My name is on the door, I own a pet shop, people have known me for years around here. Unfortunately I'm not the one you're looking for. How many years have you lived here? asks Hebbi. Too many, says the man, shrugging his shoulders.

The brother and sister exchange glances. Karen is urging him impatiently to leave the apartment, and is already heading for the hall. I'm sorry, says Hebbi in a subdued tone, but not yet completely convinced, we must have made a mistake. He walks toward the hall and the man follows, accompanying him to the door. As they leave, the brother and sister turn to say goodbye, but a bit too abruptly, and Karen bumps into the stack of empty birdcages. The upper cages topple off, and one of them grazes her cheekbone. They both apologize, but the man downplays the mishap. It's no problem, he says, then sees a trace of blood on Karen's cheek. He insists on a band-aid, or at least giving her one to take along. He leads them into the kitchen and takes a cigar box which serves as a first-aid kit from the kitchen drawer. While he's finding a band-aid, Hebbi sets up a framed photograph that seems to have fallen over. It's an old photo. It's of his mother.

Karen, Hebbi cries out, look here, look at this. Karen applies the band-aid and turns to her brother. Isn't that Mother? Yes, Hebbi says, that's a picture of Mother, and to the little man, this is no misunderstanding, this picture. It's a picture of our mother. Is it? asks the man. Then, after a moment's hesitation, it belongs to my roommate, he put that photo there. What's his name? asks Hebbi, and the man thinks a moment. Well, we have the same first name, Paul. His last name is Zech. Can we speak to him? Of course, of course, he'll be home in about two hours.

Karen takes her brother's hand and asks him to come along. You're a little pale, says the man, but it's not a serious wound. He leads them to the door.

The brother and sister descend the stairs in silence. Karen is no longer steady on her feet. She sinks onto the bottom step, groans, and covers her face. That was him, Hebbi says in triumph, that was Father.

So what, the young woman asks despairingly, what good does that do you? What good does it do either one of us?

I'll be back up there in two hours, says Hebbi threateningly, I just wonder what new story he'll have. But I'll pin him down, you can count on that. I'll pin him down. Why, asks Karen, what's the point? She takes her hands from her face. Don't you understand why he's done it? Don't you see that it's part of some voluntary penance? What is it you expect? Come on, Karen, come on little sister, says Hebbi, let's go to that little pub next door. We'll have something to drink. And two hours from now I'll dash up there just long enough to ask one single question. Then I'll take you home.

Gregor grinned at me, shook his head, even if only in partial disapproval, and said, typical, that's just typical of you, old boy. You leave everything hanging, because you consider neat endings an insult to the reader. He toasted me, stroked his beard, and gazed over at the couple by the slot-machines as if he could understand or learn something just by looking. Brother and sister? Do you really think so? We can ask them, I said, one of us, you should do it, Gregor, go over and ask them. It's too soon, said Gregor, first our colleague Klimke has to tell his story.

Klimke ordered another lemon tea. He avoided looking into the corner where the woman was salvaging the contents of her purse, considering each item carefully, as if she were trying to determine where the various things came from before replacing them. The only thing she kept out was the dark gray pinion feather, with which she was stroking the rim of her glass.

Gregor looked at Klimke in encouragement. Well? What have you come up with? But you've got to start off with what we all see. I don't know whether it's possible to start from that, Klimke said. Sure, the image is there, it has a certain inertia of its own, but the image doesn't remain itself for long. All too soon our imagination gives it a meaning. Presumably we perceive that meaning simultaneously with the image, but it's a meaning we've given it ourselves. Gregor listened to him skeptically, interrupted, and said, you can't get out of it with a theory. You've got to start somewhere, from some given assumption. That's what I'm doing, said Klimke, and talking past us, his eye on the pennants and trophies, he explained that it was the bird feather that seized his imagination most strongly, the gray pinion—you know, the one the young man spilled onto the table with all the other contents of the purse. Tell the story, Gregor said implacably. And, after shifting about uncertainly, Dieter Klimke said, is that enough?— to tell a story? What counts is to enlarge upon and justify it. And then he offered us his account, which he made quite clear was only a draft:

There goes Sophia sweeping across the marketplace, happy as can be. A basket and shopping bag swing from her hands as proof of her contentment. She walks like someone who knows she has a small but tangible advantage and enjoys expressing it in cheerful, superfluous action. She's purchased autumn, the yellows and the fading green, the sweet pith at the pear's brown core, the aromatic, earthy sharpness of the celery stocks, all at bargain prices, to carry back to her newly occupied apartment, in a boldly designed but comfortable tower known as "Tall Tom." The dealers behind their brightly colored stands and cases greet her affably, rubbing their hands together beneath their aprons to warm them up so they won't make a mistake counting change.

At the edge of the marketplace, where the canvas sides of the booths flap in the gusty autumn winds, a merchant calls her over to his stand, although he must see that she's already on her way home, happily encumbered. A man of indeterminate age, in a worn black suit, a broadbrimmed hat above his emaciated face, he bids her stop and indicates his special offering with outspread hands: mounds of cherries. Sophia, who loves to go to market, has never seen him before at the stands, this foreign-looking man with all the rings on his fingers. With a single gesture he compels her gaze downward toward the fruit, already but a summer memory. She stares in wonder at the dark morellos, the sour wild cherries, and the perfumed mahalebs, their flesh still pulsating with the heat of summer, and without asking the price, or where they've come from in such a season, she has the merchant weigh what he deems the right amount to fill a small rose-colored basket, and receives it from ringed fingers. And, as she pays distractedly, the strange merchant smiles and thrusts the quill of a gray pinion feather into the top layer of cherries in her basket. The tender skins burst, juice runs up the quill, pulpy fruit-flesh moistens the unscathed cherries. Sophia leaves the feather where it is and, somewhat pensive now, carries her spoils, well worth the price, to her apartment tower.

In her sensible, spotless kitchen, before the array of electrical servants, she unpacks her bag and basket, whistling all the while. She samples the sweating, smoked Hungarian sausage attentively, follows that up with a taste of the cheese she purchased, and finally, after everything has been put safely away, she washes a handful of cherries and eats them while lounging in her most comfortable chair. She lets the fruit burst on her tongue between teeth and gums and tries to lengthen the moment of invigorating pleasure. Picking up the feather, she twirls it slowly, strokes her knee and the gleaming trim on the kitchen cupboard, and later, contentedly going about her business, she accidently brushes the feather against the kitchen wall.

Sophia stops in shock. The part of the wall just brushed so fleetingly and lightly begins to move, the stone softens, visibly melts into a reddish-brown mass, tongues flow down silently like dripping wax and fall before her eyes upon the lacquered floor, not hot, not bubbling, but cool. No matter how closely Sophia inspects it, the feather reveals nothing. Looking up, she slowly approaches the melted hole in the wall in dreamy confusion, and looks into her neighbors' kitchen. There she sees the Töpfles, the delicate teacher of physics and his beautiful, surly wife. Mr. Töpfle is wearing a blue-and-white gym suit. A leash runs from his neck to his wife's spotted hands. He paws the ground, he snorts and dances before the artificial barriers set up in a circle on the floor: footstools, stacks of books, kitchen chairs. The woman in her dressing gown strokes him lazily and cracks her short whip. Mr. Töpfle springs forward, trots, clears the first barrier cleanly, then the second. He looks at his wife in an obvious plea for praise, but she tugs sharply at the leash and focuses his attention on the next obstacle. Mr. Töpfle balks. It takes a light blow across the calves to get the physics teacher up and over the kitchen stool. The double jump posed by the stack of books and the chair, however, simply isn't to his taste. He keeps shying away, snorting and blowing, taking new runs at it. Finally the whip drives him to jump, he falls, loses his nickel-plated glasses, and his wife releases the leash in keen disappointment. She hits him once with the whip, steps to the table, and pours herself a cup of coffee. Sophia doesn't seem up to watching any further and covers the hole, first with her hand, and later with a piece of wallpaper.

Not knowing what to do, she starts to prepare for her trip to the office. She works distractedly on her face in the mirror, uses the nose-drops that help her, takes some tissues, throws her coat over her shoulders, and finally, after a moment's thought, picks up the feather. She goes down to the underground parking lot, walks to her small blue car, and then slows down abruptly and stares at the annoying curbstone. She looks at it thoughtfully. It always makes her think in terms of centimeters, forcing her into tiring maneuvers. She bends over quickly and strokes the stone a single time—not really believing she has a right to expect anything—and recoils in fright as this stone too begins to drizzle, to melt, to run like cheese on a hot day. All she can do is get into her car and speed off, in the hopes that no one has seen her—and, by the way, with the feather carefully tucked in her purse.

In the outer office she controls she finds no better hiding place for her purse than the bottom drawer of her business desk, on which sit several phones, an intercom system, and in and out baskets. The boss, who has long regarded her in silent admiration, greets her in his usual good mood with a handshake, and, in the best of spirits, asks all about her vacation. He informs Sophia that he's brought in a new person while she was away: Miss Driessel from personnel, who, starting today, will be working side by side with Sophia in the outer office, to relieve her of some of the burden. As if on cue, Irmtraud Driessel appears, self-confident, a young woman Sophia would bet uses more water than normal while washing her face mornings. The boss introduces them to one another. Miss Driessel should be just a bit more hesitant, a bit more modest, about taking over her desk, after all, she's new here. At any rate she hasn't earned the right to test her swivel chair by whirling around so fast that her hair, in obedience to centrifugal force, flies straight outward. The boss, however, seems to find this carefree trial quite amusing, and, with a wink to Sophia, he asks Miss Driessel if she's ready to take dictation, expressing the hope that she'll prove to be equally "fresh" while at work.

Sophia's legitimate disappointment is now brought to bear upon the multicolored letters she slices open almost in rage. She skims them without interest and records them in the usual fashion before tossing them into the wastebasket with a flip of her wrist. Sophia thinks: that's how it always is. You've got to expect unpleasant surprises when you come back from a vacation. And she accompanies this reflection with vigorous nods.

The sound of muffled laughter through the padded door makes her prick up her ears. Is that any way to laugh during dictation? She jumps up and rushes to the door, but only to tear off the twenty-one days she's missed from the picture calendar, since no one else has while she was gone. Once more squeals of laughter, high-pitched at any rate, emanate from the boss's office. As longtime legitimate ruler of the outer office, Sophia takes out her purse in sovereign decisiveness, pulls the feather from it, and draws an energetic circle at a level with the picture calendar, in fact behind the lifted calendar—just the size of a coin. The wall sighs, the concrete softens and drips silently away. Through the resulting hole Sophia looks into the boss's office, sweeps the room slowly as she turns until she reaches the impressive, solid corner of the desk. Is that supposed to be dictation? Given the scene offered, no one will be surprised that she retreats from the peephole not only in disappointment, but deeply embittered, nor that she takes painful leave of her fondest illusions during the short journey back to her desk. The sheet of paper which she now inserts into the typewriter has no other choice—it can only be her request for transfer to another department.

From now on her relationship to the gray feather becomes more problematic. She often carries it in her hand, twirls it from time to time between her thumb and forefinger. Once Sophia forgets it in a café, but comes back a long way to get it. And one weekend, alone in her apartment in the tower, standing before the open window, she throws the feather out, watches it spin and float, until suddenly an updraft catches it and blows it back to her. She stretches out on the couch and reads her favorite book—*House of Air*—listening to her favorite music, using the feather as a bookmark. She continues until the little boy next door begins to squeal and shout, the son of an important actor, Kreuzer, who always greets her most politely. All it takes is a little stroke along the wall, a moment of anxious expectation, and she sees the boy through the slit that has been created. He's sitting on the floor, alone, surrounded by his toys, by cranes, bulldozers, locomotives, and cannons. The dolls of his apple-cheeked sister lie about in piles. Apparently she's been allowed to go out with her parents. He has scattered her dolls about, and is now undressing them with shouts of glee, blonde and brunette dolls, laying them naked on the floor. Then he happily winds up his bulldozers and tanks. He claps his hands whenever a tank or snowplow rams into a doll, crushes it, runs it over. He drums on the floor with joy as the locomotive shoves a little body along on the track. He even squeals as he twists the limbs off a few dolls, loads them onto a truck with his crane, and dumps them on the slope of the railroad embankment. He executes two large grinning dolls with his popgun. Shocked, Sophia wonders what the mother will say when she returns, Mrs. Kreuzer, who's already invited her over twice to see her rock collection.

Sophia hastily stuffs the crack with cotton wool, paces her apartment trying to decide what she should do, then quickly throws on her coat and goes down to the parking garage. With echoing steps she walks to her car, disappearing again and again in the shadow of the red cement columns, then reappearing in the indirect light. Just as she is stepping over the melted curbstone, Siebeck, who runs the garage, suddenly blocks her way.

He holds out his hand, grinning silently, demanding, certain she knows what he wants. But she doesn't understand his gesture, and he explains that he knows what she knows, that he needs the feather, just for a weekend, for a special purpose. In order to lend weight to his request, he points to the melted remains of the curbstone. Sophia hesitates, considers fleeing. He grabs the feather from her hand and rushes over in triumph to a waist-high concrete wall. He wants to test the feather immediately on the stone, to see how it conquers hardness. He strokes a corner, he rubs and tickles the concrete, but nothing moves, nothing dissolves—at which Siebeck, after a moment of indecision, forces the feather into Sophia's hand and guides it gently across the concrete. And now the wall begins to sink inward, to melt, the corner she's touched softens and flows down in viscous drops. Siebeck stands there looking like someone who's hatching new ideas in place of old ones. Then he nods as if he's settled on something. He's apparently found a solution. There's only one thing to do: Sophia has to come with him, since it seems the feather has the desired effect only when she's holding it.

He forces her into his car, affably, with decisive gentleness, and then they drive out to a white, floating restaurant on the river. They cross a swaying gangway, and Siebeck is greeted respectfully by several waiters and even more intimately by the host, who insists on leading them personally to a window table, and brings them a drink on the house by way of welcome. When Siebeck begs her pardon with unexpected formality, Sophia makes a soothing gesture. It's really quite cozy here, and besides they can probably guarantee that the sole is fresh.

Since the host is concerning himself personally with their needs, Siebeck deems it necessary to explain the origins of this solicitousness. He says that both he and the host are former students of sociology who met long ago at the university. And that's not all: in long conversations they discovered they shared a common contempt for a repressive, success-oriented society. They both threw in the academic towel at the same time and decided to engage in something socially relevant—namely this floating restaurant and the parking garage, respectively.

During the second bottle of wine—a fine Spätlese, Kröver Steffensberg—Siebeck explains to Sophia the rich meaning residing in her name, and although she knows most of this, she enjoys hearing his commentary, and is won over by the way he pronounces her name. Dancing together on the tiny dance floor, she feels the gentle undulating motion of the floating restaurant. She likes the controlled way Siebeck adjusts to her rhythm the moment she stumbles. She's quite happy to let him take her hand as he leads her back to the table, and thinks it very nice of him to order a second helping of her favorite dessert, vanilla ice-cream with rum and cherries.

He only mentions the feather once, in passing, deprecatingly. It's probably all just an illusion, he says, and acts surprised when Sophia contradicts him and maintains that the feather actually does soften any stone. He shakes his head in disbelief. He wants to know how many men have already told her that her nose wrinkles up when she smiles. And he also wants to know if she realizes that her eyes are two different colors. And her walk: does she know that she has a Windsor gait, that's slightly pigeon-toed? No one has ever said anything that specific about her walk, Sophia replies in amusement, probably because no one has ever observed her so closely before.

Unfortunately Sophia now sneezes several times—it must be the open

window and the proximity of the river—and since she only has a handkerchief with her, Siebeck goes to the host to get a package of tissues.
While the two men withdraw into the manager's room, Sophia goes
through her purse, doesn't seem to find what she's looking for, puts
everything back, the feather last of all—no, she changes her mind and
holds the feather between her fingers. She's obviously pondering something. Then she spears one of the maraschino cherries with the quill
end of the feather, pushes both the feather and the cherry into an
empty wine bottle, holds the bottle out the window with a smile, and
lets it fall into the river, unseen.

The host brings her the tissues in person. He closes the window
solicitously, backed up by Siebeck, and then he's stuck for words.
Not for long, however. He asks if what Mr. Siebeck has just told him
is really true, that there is this wonderful feather that can cause any
stone it touches to melt away. Might he be allowed to see it? Sophia
smiles; she smiles in triumph, and with a sense of relief which she
could best explain herself, she informs them that she's just freed herself from the "vile thing." Forcibly. Floop and gone. She expects to
see her smile returned by Siebeck, but to her astonishment he throws
open the window in an agitated rush, looks down at the river, whispers
something to the host, and dashes out—having given Sophia a look
of enraged reproach as he turned away. The host yells to some other
waiters, who run out after Siebeck.

There's no escaping it, Sophia has to assume that her pleasant evening is at an end. She doesn't feel like finishing her favorite dessert
now. Since she's been left so precipitously, she in turn leaves the restaurant herself, quickly and eyes forward. She pushes through the
narrow companionway, bumps painfully into something, but clenches
her teeth and ascends to the cloakroom. The old attendant who hands
her her coat has more than just a sewing kit, she has band-aids as well,
and she applies one to Sophia's cheekbone with clammy fingers. Sophia
pauses on the swaying gangway and looks down at the river. There
they are running along the riverbank, shouting to one another. It
looks as if they've found the bottle.

After a moment of indecision, Sophia crosses the street and strolls,
more and more slowly, past display windows and a wet and glistening
monument. She lifts her face to the rain. She stops. She leans against
a storefront grill. Are you ill? asks a passing woman, and Sophia holds

up her hand: I'm all right, thank you, I'm all right now. She hears someone running in the shadows and hurries in the direction of the railroad station. She flees from the running steps, paying no attention to the streets. She hears her name called out, urgently, once and then again, and now she stops in exhaustion and lets Siebeck approach. He has the feather in his hand. Without asking Sophia's permission, he puts it in her purse, takes her arm, and pulls her along with him. Naturally he has something to explain to her as well as something to propose. Around two hours from now, when the crowd lets up, she can expect to see his friend, the host at the floating restaurant. In the meantime, however—he points to the ground-level pub—they can talk things over here, in The Last Anchor.

And now they've talked things over, and it's just a matter of passing time until the host arrives as arranged. Sophia has listened to the proposal, an all too predictable proposal, and she realizes what having the feather means. She'll have to destroy it. A single match will suffice.

Dieter Klimke fell silent, and Gregor and I looked toward the slot-machines. The woman was just lighting a match. She held the tip of the feather over the flame. The light gray tip curled downward in a tiny jet of flame and immediately charred with a brief crackle. She threw the rest of the feather into the ashtray. Was she going to leave? She made an attempt to rise, trying to pull herself together for this one act, but things didn't go as she wished, and, in an apparent attempt to console herself in the face of this disappointment, she gave an order for another double and followed it with a gesture of disdain. Gregor ordered a double for us as well, and a hot lemon tea for Klimke.

His order was brief and to the point, for Gregor couldn't get the mismatched couple in the corner out of his mind. Presumably he was weighing relationships, checking for possible conflicts, was probably even looking for confirmation of Klimke's story, and suddenly he reached his conclusion. No, I just can't see anything to support your fantastic exposition. In any case, the woman's pain is not a result of having experienced too much. Now you're back in the same old rut, I said. Since you can't accept fantasy, you can't accept the force of its proof. Annoyed, Gregor looked down in front of him and threw a cigarette stub into the ashtray, raising a small cloud of ash. Fine, he said, and turned to Klimke, then please tell me what you meant by this story, briefly, in one sentence that I can apply to my own experience. To his experience of the force of gravity, I interjected.

Klimke shrugged his shoulders regretfully. He seemed to be begging our pardon for having put Gregor at such a loss, and in sincere embarrassment he said: I'm convinced that we can only reveal reality with the help of the fantastic. And what did I want to prove with my story? Just this: we need walls, all of us. But all that can only be of value if it's true for my lousy reality, said Gregor. I start from the assumption, said Klimke, that there is no more fundamental way to identify reality than by a demonstration in the realm of fantasy.

But we haven't gained anything, said Gregor. And looking at the slot-machines, he added: we've simply made three sketches. We've gained three truths that don't commit us to anything. We can sit here and tell stories as long as we like. The couple over there will keep their own story, and we'll never get any nearer to it, no matter how patiently we stretch our imaginations.

That's not what matters, said Klimke. What we are looking for with the help of fantasy is to find the boundaries of a model which would encompass all reality. Propositions of experience that are binding for us all.

But the only way you can tell that, Gregor said, is if you've heard the other side. I mean, in each case imagination has to be confirmed by reality. What we need now is the real story of these two, that's something that has yet to be told.

Klimke smiled, and then he rubbed his hands and said: I'll bet that something from our stories fits them—a mood, a hope, or an experience.

Go on, old boy, Gregor said to me, go over and take their confession. Beat the bushes. We should all go over together, I said. No, said Klimke, all three of us at once would be intimidating, a threat. You should really try it alone.

They looked at me encouragingly, urging me on, until I had no other choice but to stand up and walk over to the young man, of whom I already had a threefold image. He put a coin in the machine, won, and I congratulated him. Thanks, but that doesn't help me much, I'm still way behind. He seemed to think that I wanted to play, because he stepped aside with a gesture of invitation, leaving the slot-machine to me. While I was still trying to think of a way to start out, he had a question for me. Speaking softly, and nodding toward our table, he wanted to know if the heavyweight with the Santa Claus beard was by any chance Gregor Bromm, the writer. Yes, I said, that's him, and the young man replied: Bromm's my man, he's got it all together, I really liked his novel *Skin for Sale*. I nodded, hesitated, wanted to go on and didn't dare. Finally I asked him if The Last Anchor was his favorite pub. The young man shook his head. Favorite pub? He'd just dropped in by accident. Alone, I asked, and he replied, of course, alone. But the woman . . . I began, but seeing his narrow look of mistrust I didn't finish the sentence. I introduced myself to the lady, he said slowly, is there anything wrong with that? What do you want with us anyway?

I excused myself, walked back to our table, no doubt a bit too quickly, downed Gregor's drink, and broke the expectant silence: they've just met each other here for the first time. They looked at me for a moment dumbfounded. Then Klimke said: so what? I don't feel disproved in the least. In the realm of possibility we were right, and that's what really counts—for us.

———

Tales from the Village

&❧ S U L E Y K E N ❧&

THAT WAS UNCLE MANOAH

꿱 One market day not too long ago an itinerant barber showed up in Suleyken. He was a cheerful little man who trimmed people's hair under the open sky, in the midst of squealing pigs and hoarsely lowing cattle, surrounded by all the odors of a Masurian marketplace, the earthy smell of new potatoes and the stink of old cabbage, the sharp odor of crates and boards, of fish, oats, and turpentine, the soft chalky smell of gutted chickens, and the clear, clean scent of apples and carrots. Amidst all these noises and smells, in the filled and fertile air of a fine fall morning, the itinerant barber was at work on a tall, good-looking, black-haired fellow known as Handsome Alec, a fine figure of a man, albeit barefoot.

The barber hopped around him politely and energetically, chatting amiably while his scissors fluttered about Alec's ears like a merry swallow, snipping a bit here, a bit there, quickly and gently, and when he was finished, the barber opened a little bottle, as was his custom, and sprinkled a bit on Alec's jaw. The fragrance of Persian lilacs immediately welled outward in a large circle, and soon displaced all other odors in the marketplace. The Orient had vanquished Masuria. "Allow me to brush you off a bit," the barber said, and inserted a soft brush into Alec's collar, whisking the fine bristles gently against his skin, so that he bent forward slightly with pleasure. Then he snapped the barber's towel away with a practiced motion, said "Thank you very much," and awaited his fee.

Alec reached in his pocket, but instead of money he pulled out an old, dirty letter, unfolded it carefully, and asked the barber to read it. "It's a letter from my Uncle Manoah, who owns a barge," he said. "He just arrived today. Uncle Manoah's been working every known river and canal for the past thirty years, and now, as you can see from the letter, he's come home to die. Since I'm the sole heir to the barge, I'm sure you'll let me delay payment until this evening. I'll bring you the money when the market closes."

The barber read the letter carefully, with grateful devotion, as if he were being let in on a secret. He handed it back with a nod and walked with Alec to the sloping bank from which they could look out onto the river. There lay the barge, broad and black, carefully moored. In the stern they saw a tall, haggard man with bristly gray hair. That was Uncle Manoah. He was sitting on a crate, lost in thought, sipping coffee.

"I'll be happy to delay payment until this evening for the heir to that barge," said the barber. "Of course I can't wait any longer than that."

"No one has ever had any cause to doubt my uncle's word," said Alec. "By this evening the barge will be mine, and then everything will be taken care of."

The two men bowed to each other, and as the barber went back to his stool, Alec bore the fragrance of the Orient across the marketplace, strolling past carts and stands, exchanging greetings, and stepping aside whenever he thought it appropriate.

He paused in front of a talkative fisherwoman, leaned over the baskets of golden-yellow smoked whitefish, and, since he had made an impression on the woman and she didn't stop him, he picked one up, pulled off the skin, and sampled the warm, tasty dorsal flesh.

"These fish aren't bad," he said. "At the risk of being disappointed, I'll try a kilo, and make it a full one." The woman served him with alacrity, added two extra whitefish to the kilo, and handed Alec the packet. But instead of paying her, Alec took the letter out of his pocket again and had the perplexed woman read it. He walked with her over to the slope of the shore and pointed to his carefully moored inheritance. "You'll have your money this evening," he said, "and I'll have the barge."

At first the woman seemed satisfied, but then she suddenly got angry and asked who the man in the stern was.

"That man is no other than my Uncle Manoah," said Alec, "the man who's leaving me the barge. After thirty years on the river, he's come back here to die."

"But what guarantee do I have that God will allow him to?" the woman asked.

"That's not something you need to worry about," said Alec in gentle reproach. "The only reason Uncle Manoah came back was to die. He's as good as they come. He won't let me down."

With these words Alec calmed the fisherwoman and, putting the greasy packet under his arm, pushed up to an egg stand. Here he managed to buy a basket of eggs with his letter and the visible evidence of his inheritance floating on the river. At another stand he picked up a good-sized slab of smoked bacon, and after adding cheese, coffee, apples, and butter to the list, he walked down to the river and balanced his way across the narrow gangway onto the barge. He went up to Uncle Manoah at the back of the boat, bowed politely to him, and spread the things he had acquired at his feet.

"Please take whatever you feel like," he said with a wave. "The whitefish are good, the bacon's tolerably tempting, and the apples are nice and tart. Welcome home!"

"That's a fine welcome and an excellent idea," said Uncle Manoah. His voice sounded like a rusty buzz saw. He shoved his coffee cup aside with his foot and began eating. He ate every one of the whitefish, all the cheese, and the apples. Then he cooked the bacon, broke eight eggs into the pan, and continued eating while Alec sat quietly at his feet with an expression of submissive respect, ready to serve him in any way. After Uncle Manoah had eaten, they drank several cups of coffee, slowly and without exchanging a word. They sat together silently like birds, and noon came and went.

When the last cup of coffee was finished, Uncle Manoah said, "Well, Alec, here I am, as you can see."

"Here to stay," said Alec.

"Here to go," Uncle Manoah corrected him. "We'll have another cup of coffee when twilight falls, and when the moon comes up I'll be on my way. Then the barge is yours. You gave me a fine welcome, and you deserve a fine inheritance."

They sat together silently until twilight fell. Then Manoah brewed coffee for both of them. After they had finished with their coffee,

Manoah threw a bit of rigging and some rags into a corner and settled himself comfortably on them. He closed his mouth and let his breath buzz through his nose. It sounded as if two flies were lodged inside. Meanwhile Alec kept his eye on the slope. He didn't have to wait long before he saw the fisherwoman's silhouette, and then the barber's. Soon almost all his creditors had appeared, looking for their money. Alec tried to avoid this sight by taking refuge in pleasant childhood memories, but he couldn't quite manage it. The creditors were approaching inexorably, but the barge was not yet his, for Uncle Manoah was still alive, a fact which his buzzing nose made abundantly evident. In this state of distress Alec looked over at Uncle Manoah, and his gaze was filled with such an abject plea that Manoah sat up intently and stretched his neck, wrinkled and scaly like the bark of a tree. He stretched his neck and craned it in all directions. Apparently he grasped what had happened, for he knew Alec well. And he said, "Alec, you don't have anything to worry about. We'll play a trick on our creditors that'll give them something to think about for the rest of their lives. Just watch!" He got up from the rigging and leaned his massive upper body back into the corner of the boat, waving to the creditors to hurry up. Then he signaled Alec to go and lead them onto the boat in a proper and polite fashion. Alec went up to them trembling and whispered, "Nothing hurts me more than to have to break my promise, friends. It's sad to say, but you can't even count on death these days. It's not my fault."

Then he helped the creditors across the narrow gangway and let them go to the back of the boat, where Uncle Manoah was propped up in the corner. They gathered around him in silent reproach, as if they were expecting an explanation and payment. Alec too approached him at last, his heart filled with fear, but with full confidence in Uncle Manoah's rich store of tricks. He stepped up to him, tapped him on the shoulder, and when he didn't move, he turned him cautiously around. Everyone could see that Uncle Manoah was dead. They saw as well the triumphant smile on his face, and they shifted about uneasily in shame, anxious to be gone. They hurried off the boat in sincere and open flight.

Alec turned to Manoah, filled with praise, and spoke these words: "I've seen a lot of things in my life, Uncle Manoah, but I've never seen anyone play dead so well. The creditors are gone, the danger's past, you can come back to life and have a fresh cup of coffee."

But Manoah, tall and rigid, lay back in the corner without moving. Worried, Handsome Alec quickly felt him all over in shocked awe. And then he realized that Uncle Manoah was really dead. Alec bowed deeply and whispered to him, "Uncle, this is one trick I really wasn't ready for."

A VERY PLEASANT FUNERAL

ᴥ§ My Aunt Arafa died while on a short journey to Poland, to be exact in the snug little market town of Wszscinsk on the Narew River. She was a heavy, full-bodied woman, my aunt, wtih powerful shoulders and a captain's reddened hands. She was unusually strong as well, and used to giving orders. She hadn't shown any sign during the trip that she was planning to die. On the contrary she made a few crude jokes now and then, constantly ate more than the combined total consumed by both my cousins, the Urmoneits, who were traveling with her, and threw almost every host she dealt with into a tizzy.

My aunt died with a curse on her lips, right in the back of the carriage, while the cousins were sitting up front on the coachman's seat, shy and unsuspecting. They weren't even surprised when things got quiet behind them and the crude jokes ceased, along with the orders. They had no idea how lucky they were, the two of them. Well, finally they had to stop to water the horses, and when they went to help their aunt down so she could stretch her legs, the reddened captain's hands dangled toward them, as limp as limp could be, and on top of that their aunt's face was so peaceful that the cousins began to suspect something, as most people would.

They began first of all by checking everything according to rule. They thumped her chest, listened to her heart, held a downy chicken feather under her nose, murmured a few magic formulas, massaged her. But their aunt reacted like most dead people, she wasn't in the

110

least interested. Upon which Bogdan, one of the cousins, spoke up and said: "I think we've got a problem here. We left, as you recall, with an aunt who walked and talked. But you'll notice this one isn't making a peep. She's more or less gone."

"She's gone all right," said the other. "But unfortunately she's still sitting in the carriage. And unless I'm greatly mistaken, the way things stand she's not likely to get out again on her own."

"We'll have to report this," said Bogdan. "Shall we try the police?"

"Not on your life," cried the other quickly, and raised his hands in shock at the thought. "If we report it they'll investigate Auntie, and they'll investigate us. They may even suspect us. And with the laws about corpses in Poland, it may be winter before we get her home."

"I don't suppose that makes much difference to Auntie," said Bogdan.

"It does to us, though," replied the other Urmoneit. "Just take a look at Auntie. Doesn't she look like she's sleeping? Let's just keep going, and if anyone stops us and starts asking questions, we'll just tell them to hold it down, we've got a lady asleep."

So my cousins watered the horses and rolled on at an easy pace to the border. Of course they timed it so that they arrived at the barrier in the middle of the night, and then things went like this: Bogdan sprang out lightly and went back to his aunt, put pillows around her and puffed them up nicely, and just as he finished the border guard came out. The guard was a slim, leathery fellow who eyed my cousins, eyed the carriage and horses, and generally snooped about in a bored manner. Well, then he saw their aunt, climbed right up to her and said, "And may I ask who the dead lady is?" Upon which the cousins replied in a tactful chorus, "It's Arafa Gutz, our maternal aunt."

"Maternal, paternal," said the guard, "why the devil is she so quiet?"

"Because she's sleeping, word of honor. And may we ask you, Pan Captain, to keep it down around a sleeping lady?"

"Fine," said the guard, "everything's all right then, but what guarantee do I have that your maternal aunt isn't, for example, among the dearly departed?"

"If she had departed," the cousins said, "she couldn't be sleeping here, and she's sleeping here now." The guard thought this over, and since the logic of it appealed to him, he let the carriage pass on.

The Urmoneit cousins traveled through the night and arrived the next morning in a little village called Kulkaken. As you can imagine they were more than a little hungry by this time. They'd been starving long enough, my cousins had, and so they stopped the carriage in front of an inn and went inside to strengthen themselves for the remainder of the journey. They devoted themselves to the task with a will: bacon, eggs, smoked ham, cabbage soup, honey, onion cake, and canned pears, to which they added a huge pot of coffee. Spent most of the morning eating, they did, and when they went back outside—well, what do you think had happened? Their horses were gone. And with the horses, the carriage. And with the carriage, their auntie.

Well, the cousins raced all around the inn like, say, wild whisk brooms, whisking back and forth in their search, yelling and cursing, but what they didn't manage to find was the carriage with their aunt.

After they had searched until they were tired and hungry, they went back into the inn and ate some more. After they had eaten, Bogdan was smiling again. He smiled for a long time, and then he said, "Well, there's some consolation in all this. Just think about the fellow who stole our carriage. He must have had a big shock. Think how his hands must have trembled when he found out Auntie was dead."

They consoled one another, laughed about the thief, and, as you might imagine, started out rather late for Suleyken. They cut across the meadows to shorten the trip, walked along the railroad embankment, and could soon see the lights of Suleyken. They saw a few men, too, they did, and couldn't believe what they heard from them. It seems that Aunt Arafa had returned around coffee-time that afternoon. She was lying asleep in the back of the coach. And she looked dead to the world.

The Urmoneits, bright as they were, figured out immediately that the horses had become bored in Kulkaken. Got tired of waiting and just took off by themselves. "You'll see," said Bogdan, "the horses will be in the stable." And they hurried home worriedly.

They had hardly arrived in the courtyard when who should they run into but Glumskopp, an old, toothless servant. He grinned from ear to ear, rubbed his hands, and in his rabbity, nibbling way, announced: "A party, hee hee, we're going to have a party. And there'll be herrings in cream."

"And who's throwing this party?" asked Bogdan.

"The good Lord's throwing the party, hee hee," Glumskopp nibbled out. "He let the old gal die, and knowing Him I'm expecting a very pleasant funeral."

The cousins shoved him aside politely and entered the house of mourning. It smelled of roasts and pastry and smoked meat and who knew what else. But the Urmoneits controlled themselves and proceeded in tandem into the living room. They went straight in and, as the primary mourners, were immediately surrounded by a crowd of people offering their condolences. Hands stretched out to them, mouths curved downward. Their aunt was referred to as a tender, delicate flower. Everyone whispered, copious tears were shed, consolation was offered as needed, and then everyone sat down at the table.

The cousins noticed instruments for a brass band still covered with sheets under the window. Everything was set. Good. But first Bogdan Urmoneit rose and delivered himself of the following: "We should pause for a moment in memory of our dearly departed Aunt Arafa . . . just a bit longer, please . . . hold it . . . all right, that'll do. And now I'd like to know where Auntie is."

"Departed," someone in the band called out.

"No," Bogdan said gravely, "I mean where's her body?"

"Her body's not on view anymore," replied a one-eyed forester. "We laid her mortal remains in a suitable coffin. And to give us a little more room here in the house we've propped the coffin up against the stove. The body has a comfortable place to stand there."

Bogdan nodded. But he nodded absent-mindedly, for he had noticed someone among the mourners who had touched his heart, shall we say, tenderly. And Bogdan's heart started to bloom mightily, to throw out tendrils, to twine itself about the figure of a certain Luise Luschinski, a pale little person with a birdlike, tear-stained face.

Bogdan forgot what was going on around him. He smiled at Luise Luschinski with such overwhelming ardor that the whole crowd noticed. The musicians, of course, always hungry for such things, misunderstood the situation, took out their instruments, and started to play a slow waltz. At the sound of the music Bogdan came to his senses, stopped smiling, and resumed his mourning. But it was too late, far too late. Things were underway.

Happiness drew near on the feet of Luise Luschinski. As if wafted to him by the music, the pale little person was suddenly standing in front of him saying, "This is your waltz, Bogdan Urmoneit."

Upon which Bogdan looked about him uncertainly, and finding consent and even encouragement in the eyes of the mourners, answered, "Gladly. But very slowly, please."

So off they swayed, and as was to be expected, other couples soon followed them. The music got louder, now and then a laugh could be heard, among others Glumskopp's nibbling laugh—in short, the crowd was working up a thirst. Also, of course, an appetite. They endured their hunger and thirst until the one-eyed forester came back out of the kitchen and announced, "Hosanna, the stag is dead."

And so they ate. What did they eat? I'll restrict myself to my own case. Although I was still underage, I downed eight eggs, sunny-side up, with bacon, five meatballs, some hare, a duck neck, a plate of chicken giblets in vinegar, a plate of chopped tripe, half a pig's ear, and a baked apple. Besides that I had baked onions, a roast fish, and late that evening a couple of crayfish that old Glumskopp had caught in the river. As I said, I was underage, and not responsible for my actions.

So first they ate, and when they had finished eating, they started drinking. And drinking led, as it often does, to an incident that can only be described as—but first let me tell you what happened. Edmund Vortz, a tailor, having had his share of drink, maintained in all seriousness that Hindenburg was, in his eyes, about as cultured as a Suleyken hen. A colossal uproar ensued. The one-eyed forester jumped up and hit the tailor in the chest with such force that the offender flew under the table and lay there for some time without showing any signs of life. They had almost forgotten him when he piped up again, claiming that he, Edmund Vortz, would have won a bigger victory at Tannenberg—which brought the one-eyed forester back onto the scene. He knocked the tailor down a second time, but once the latter had regained consciousness, he challenged the forester again. There wasn't a great deal left of the tailor, and there would soon have been even less had not Bogdan put a stop to the fight. "Aunt Arafa," was all he said, and a pensive peace and harmony immediately spread over the gathering. Oh yes, the only word to describe the incident was: serious.

As for the funeral, it was worked in during a pause. Aunt Arafa was given a nice plot beside a Masurian pine tree. The gathering praised the location, spoke movingly over her grave, and went back to the house, where the party swung into full force. It lasted three days, and when it was over, Bogdan gave a little of the leftover food and a full bar of soap to each of the mourners. And everyone who had come seemed willing to overlook the fight, and assured him that it had been, all in all, a very pleasant funeral.

A GRAND DAY IN SCHISSOMIR

They were both barefoot. One of them was leading a goat and the other a calf. They met at the crossroads, and while the goat and calf were taking note of one another in astonishment, the barefoot gentlemen exchanged greetings, offered each other snuff, and decided, without wasting many words, that it was a fine day to go to market. The heaven swelled its blue breast, the grasshoppers were singing their song, and the air was filled with expectancy. After having decided, as we mentioned, that it was a fine day, together they sprinkled the grass at the side of the road, and took another pinch of snuff. Then Herr Plew called his goat and Herr Jegelka his calf. They looped their ropes around the animals' necks and started out briskly for Schissomir, the animals trailing behind. Schissomir, a friendly little market town, was six miles away, and they wanted to be on their way. Six miles isn't exactly a stroll, of course, particularly with a goat and calf in tow, and so the two men eventually began to curse, which no one will hold against them. They each cursed according to his mood, Herr Jegelka more than his neighbor, since his calf was just beginning to discover the world and proved to be particularly stubborn, wanting to go here and there, suddenly taking a special interest in a gleaming puddle, or eyeing his fellow traveler, the goat. The goat was an old one, and much more manageable.

"This isn't so easy," said Jegelka. "God knows Napoleon wouldn't have made it out of Russia so fast if he'd had this calf in tow."

"Presumably Napoleon would have handled it differently," Plew replied. "If I know him, he would have ordered someone to carry a stubborn calf like that."

"Yes, he was certainly one for making it easy on himself," Jegelka conceded.

So they walked on, reproaching Napoleon for this and that. Finally they got around to talking about prices. Jegelka, whose hand was already red from tugging on the rope, declared, "Considering the trip to the market, I mean with the calf along, I've already got more invested in this than the calf's worth. I'm not going to sell it except at top dollar. I'm not going to bargain, and I won't lower my price one penny."

"I can see your point," said Plew, "but it's different with my goat. It's already old, and practically milked dry. It's only worth what it weighs. I'll just be happy if somebody takes it off my hands. I can tell you that, seeing as how we're from the same village."

"Yes, you can tell me," said Jegelka. "Well, let's see what happens."

They were in the friendly market town of Schissomir before noon. The air was filled with sights and sounds. The people were merrily bustling about with straw on their boots, cracking whips, laughing, eating greasy bacon, peering into horses' mouths, and pinching piglets on the back, producing a storm of high-pitched squeals. Fat women had their skirts tugged at, kids were bawling, bulls were bellowing. A goose got into a herd of sheep, sending a few sheep careening among the cows, which sent a few cows off on a tear down the dusty lane between the market stands. When one huge fellow finally caught the goose, it flapped and honked so wildly in his hands that he got scared and held it tighter, with the result that the goose died, which in turn brought the sharp-tongued owner into the picture. In short, it was a grand day in the friendly little market town of Schissomir.

Plew and his goat, and Jegelka with his calf, were soon surrounded by several interested buyers. They argued and laughed, felt the goat's udder, peered into the corner of the calf's eye and its ears, and suddenly a short, stocky livestock-dealer pulled out an envelope, counted out some money, and gave it to Plew. The man wrapped the rope leisurely around his wrist and led the goat away. Plew counted his money happily, and then went over to his village neighbor Jegelka and said, "Hosanna! I sold the goat. If you hurry we still have time to treat ourselves to one before we head home."

"I could have got rid of the calf long ago," said Jegelka. "But it was a hard journey, and I'm not about to let them talk me down. There's no need to rattle the change in your pocket, neighbor. It doesn't impress me. Go ahead and treat yourself if you want. I'm staying here until someone pays me enough to cover the calf and the trip. If I don't find anyone, I'll take the calf home."

"Fine," said Plew, "I'll come back here a little later. It's a long road home, neighbor, and it'll be more pleasant with two of us."

Plew went to treat himself. Then he strolled along the dusty lane between the market stands, staring at anything he thought worthy of a stare, exchanging greetings, carefully wiping the soles of his boots when fate led him too close to the cows, and in general enjoying himself in his own fashion. By the time he got back to Jegelka the livestock market was closed, but the calf was still unsold. "Looks like bad luck is dogging you," said Plew.

"It's not bad luck," said Jegelka, "I just don't want to sell the calf for less than my price. Now the market's closed. I'll have to take it back home. As far as I'm concerned we can go."

They started out together, one leading his calf, the other joyfully clinking the coins in his pocket. He couldn't stop talking about how lucky he had been to sell his goat, which after all, looking at it realistically, was only good for slaughter. Plew pointed this out so often that Jegelka finally began to get angry, because he knew very well his neighbor was trying to needle him. So he kept quiet and thought about what he should do.

Suddenly, Jegelka stopped with his calf, called Plew back, and pointed at the ground. There sat a frog, green and blinking, a handsome shining fellow.

"Just take a look at this frog, neighbor," said Jegelka. "Do you see it?"

"Sure, I see it," said Plew.

"Good," said Jegelka, "then I'll make you an offer, neighbor, one you're bound to want to take me up on. You've been fortunate enough to sell your goat. You have money. If you want, you can keep your money and take my calf home, too. All you have to do is eat this frog."

"Eat it?" Plew said to make sure.

"Eat it!" said Jegelka emphatically. "When the frog disappears down your throat, you can lead my calf away."

"That's a generous offer indeed, neighbor," said Plew, "and I'm going to take you up on it. I'll eat the frog and then you give me your calf."

Having said this, Plew bent over, grabbed the frog, closed his eyes, and bit it in two, while Jegelka watched with a look of odd satisfaction.

"Keep it up, neighbor," he said, "I've seen you swallow the first half. Now for the legs."

"Just give me a minute, please," said Plew, upset and with his eyes rolling. "I've got to give my stomach time to get used to this stuff. Can't we walk on along the road a bit? I'll eat the other half pretty soon."

"Sure," said Jegelka, "that's fine with me." They walked along together in silence, and the further they walked, the sicker Plew became, and the more certain he was that he'd never be able to get down the second half of the frog. He tried desperately to think of some way out of his predicament. Meanwhile, however, he remained the picture of confidence and high spirits, so that Jegelka, who now only owned half his calf, began to worry.

All at once Plew stopped unexpectedly, held out the remaining frog half to his neighbor, and said, "Well, neighbor, how about it? Seeing as how we're from the same village, we shouldn't be taking each other's property. If you'll eat the rest of this frog, I'll give up my claim, and you can keep your calf."

"Now that's right neighborly of you," said Jegelka happily. And he ate the second half of the frog, gagging it down with his stomach lurching. Now the calf behind him was all his again. "It looks like I'm bringing something home from the market after all," he said with a grimace.

They continued on into the village, lost in thought, and when they parted ways at the crossroads, Jegelka said, "Well, neighbor, it was a fine day at the market. But I still can't figure out why we ate that frog."

WHEN THE CIRCUS CAME TO TOWN

◄§ I can't recall the exact name of the circus anymore, but it must have been something like "Anita Schiebukat's Traveling Show." An event of the first magnitude of course, this circus, you could tell that by the fact that the kids of Suleyken were given the day off from school, work ceased in the fields, and there wasn't a house in town where anything else was being talked about but this self-same circus. All of which doesn't mean it was a particularly big one. In any case it moved onto the meadow belonging to the fire brigade, set up a little tent, and parked its wagons neatly nearby.

Everything went quickly and quietly, and before the population of Suleyken could turn around, they were invited by Anita Schiebukat's Traveling Show to attend the first performance. A band played tunes intended to lure the customers in, an old elephant was led about, all sorts of highly auspicious noises were in the air, and the little tent was quickly filled. The audience brought along preserves, pickled cucumbers, jacketed potatoes, and smoked fish. They exchanged greetings, strolled for a while in the meadow, and then, chatting with one another in small groups, they entered the show tent.

Fine. And then Anita Schiebukat, a powerful, well-nourished woman, greeted the audience most personably, said just the right things to flatter them, and then disappeared to suitable applause. But before she disappeared she cried out, "Let the circus begin!" and with that things were underway.

The first person to appear in the ring was a morose, half-naked man, who stopped, scowled darkly around the arena, stretched, and opened a small chest. What did the little chest contain? What else?— knives, long, sharp, and admittedly dangerous.

And what did this half-naked, menacing oddball do but pick up one, two, three, five of those knives, and call for Anita Schiebukat in a shrill voice. And lo and behold, the well-nourished lady came out and stood with her back against a wall of wooden boards. And then it happened: this fellow flung his knives right at Anita Schiebukat. All five ripped into the wood, but thank God not a one hit her. The Suleyken audience moaned in terror, hid their faces in their hands, whimpered, and emitted small cries of fright.

But that wasn't the end of it. This half-naked, sweaty fellow pulled the knives out of the wood, stepped back a few paces, and started hurling them at her again, as rough as could be.

Well, a sense of the limits of the permissible had finally been awakened in the breasts of a few Suleyken men. And that sense was awakened most fully in the huge fisherman Valentin Zoppek. He stood up from his bench, stepped into the ring, went calmly up to the man with the knives, and said, "This lady said so many nice things to us. Why the devil are you throwing knives at her? I'm warning you, one more knife and you'll have to deal with me. We don't throw knives at people around here. Am I right?"

"Right," murmured the Suleyken audience.

Anita Schiebukat came up breathing heavily, asked what was going on, quickly saw what the score was, and ordered the half-naked man to get behind the curtain—which he did, accompanied by the grumbling of the crowd. He wouldn't have been allowed to get off so easily had it not been for the carefree smile that Anita Schiebukat immediately beamed toward the audience, which quickly quieted them down.

With this same smile she then introduced a sly little hunchbacked man in a frock coat and top hat who hopped into the arena, threw kisses to the audience, and seemed to expect applause before he had done anything at all. All at once, however, he reached up into the Suleyken air so rapidly that no one could follow him and a bouquet of sweet-scented lilacs appeared in his hand. Sounds of astonishment ran through the little tent. In a burst of spontaneous enthusiasm they tossed him pickled cucumbers, which he nimbly caught on the fly, and herring, and not a few hearts. He calmly gathered them all in.

Then he set up a table, placed a box on top, and placing himself inside the box, locked it from within. All I can say is that all at once the box fell apart and the sly little hunchbacked man was gone. Zappka the mailman and Junior Urmoneit were so worried they were about to jump into the ring, when the little magician, heaven only knows how, appeared up on the balcony with the band, blowing a trumpet, and then lowered himself down a rope to thundering applause. Encouraged by the extended applause, the magician surprised everyone by stepping to the edge of the ring, reaching inside the vest of my uncle, Stanislaw Griegull, and pulling out a—all right, who wants to guess what it was? A rabbit, of course, full of life and kicking. The Suleykers were struck dumb by this, and my uncle, word of honor, got up and began removing his clothes one piece at a time. He was hoping to find more rabbits, of course, or even a nice plump duck, or a chicken fluttering out of his underwear. But nothing of the kind happened. So my uncle re-dressed during an expectant pause which would have soon been followed by applause had Stanislaw Griegull not suddenly spoken up. He turned toward the magician and said, "I see that the rabbit has disappeared behind the curtain. It's my property, however. As everyone could see, it makes its home on my body. Therefore I demand the immediate restitution of said rabbit."

At this point the silence became, shall we say, oppressive. The audience was swayed for a moment, and the magician eyed the speaker in some consternation. But he soon got a grip on himself, went up to my uncle, and said, "What sort of rabbit makes a habit of living under a man's vest? As everyone could see, it was just a magic trick, a bit of what you might call flimflam."

"Makes no difference," my uncle said, "the rabbit lived under my vest, it was kicking around, it was alive. So I demand restitution. It's my property." Then my uncle glanced over at the local gendarme, and when the Law in the person of Schneppat nodded, he added in a stubborn voice, "And please make it snappy." So Stanislaw Griegull received the rabbit, placed it on his lap, and the performance continued without further ado.

Continued how? A washtub was now carried in, and lying within it, surliness personified, was a fat old seal who answered to the name of Rachull the Insatiable. Hanging on the washtub was a large sign bearing the words, "Please don't muck about with the seal"—which seemed to be their way of saying not to tease or mistreat it. But no one in the audience had the slightest intention of doing anything of the kind. They restricted themselves to applauding the seal, who apparently had nothing against this. At any rate he didn't object to being carried out again without ever having left the tub.

As soon as he was gone, the well-nourished Anita Schiebukat stepped into the arena again, gave my uncle an odd look, and announced, "Our next attraction is a man named Bosniak. He eats iron bars for breakfast and drinks twelve liters of milk each evening. His strength knows no bounds. Anyone who can stay in the ring with him for two minutes without being thrown off his feet will receive a refund on the price of his ticket and three marks twenty to boot!"

She stepped aside and this fellow Bosniak rolled in. The benches trembled at his tread. He bared his teeth, stood on his small head, and in general behaved in a way intended to assure us of his extraordinary ferocity. No one dared take up his challenge.

No one?

Yes, there, someone in the back was raising his hand, only he was so thin that people tended to look right past him. Who was putting himself on the line with such incomprehensible foolhardiness? My uncle the cobbler, Karl Kuckuck. The Suleykers seemed paralyzed as he pushed his way past them. Their gaze followed him in a last melancholy farewell, but there was no one to talk him out of it.

So he skipped into the ring, regarded Bosniak with gentle pity, and said, "All right, I'm ready." The huge small-headed man immediately stormed at him, spread his arms, snorted, and locked his arms together, but Karl Kuckuck had ducked away at once and was now located behind the chewer of iron bars. The latter, believing that he had the cobbler in his grasp, squeezed so hard that tears came to his eyes—but he was only squeezing himself. Well, this happened a few more times—after all, how could anyone catch hold of a piece of cobbler's thread like my uncle?—and in the end this Bosniak was so exhausted that he sat down panting on the ground and had to be brought to his senses with a pail of water. Meanwhile Karl Kuckuck made his way to the ticket booth, accepted the money he had coming, and wended his way home with his family.

As far as I recall, that's more or less how things went in Suleyken with Anita Schiebukat's Traveling Show. And as we were later to learn, it was a long time before another circus visited our village. We assumed this was because they were afraid to appear before such a sophisticated audience.

THE TRIP TO OLETZKO

It's often the case, ladies and gentlemen, that even a small deficiency can lead to a trip—for example being short one kilo of nails. A man in Suleyken by the name of Amadeus Loch, whose farmlands stretched out near Goronzä Gora, or Hot Mountain, found himself in exactly this predicament. He needed enough nails to build a shed, and so this Loch went to his wife one day and spoke more or less as follows: "It seems, my dear, that we're about a kilo short on nails. I'll have to make a trip to Oletzko. And to make it more enjoyable, you might just as well come along. The preparations will be the same, and one shouldn't travel abroad alone."

Thus spoke Amadeus Loch, and went forth, and when he was gone, his wife, née Popp, lined up all the necessities for the trip on the bench beside the fireplace.

As far as food goes, the bench contained the following: bacon, flat cakes, pickled cucumbers, a pot of cabbage, dried pears, a basket of eggs, grilled fish, onions, a loaf of round bread, and a rabbit stew. Then, while Amadeus was getting the wagon ready, she laid out a jacket, rubber galoshes, blankets, towels, and wrist warmers. And after she had dug out her four petticoats to put on under her things, she hurried over to her brother, Paul Popp, and delivered herself of the following:

"Amadeus and me are short of nails by about a kilo and have to go abroad. Tomorrow, or the day after, we're taking a trip to Oletzko. And one shouldn't travel abroad alone. Since I'd miss you all terribly, it would be nice if you could come along. It would make the trip easier for me."

With that she departed, and after a brief discussion, the Popp household set about preparing for the journey. Preserves were opened, salted meat was laid out, herring was grilled, a chicken was slaughtered and cooked, bread was baked, and a pair of wool stockings was quickly finished in a whirlwind of knitting needles. In addition, the horses were given new shoes, the harness was repaired, and the dog's rope lengthened. After the most pressing preparations had been completed, Paul Popp himself hurried to his brother-in-law, Adolf Abromeit, who had never shown the world anything but his large, red ears. And he spoke to him as follows: "We're forced by fate to take a trip abroad. And the fact is, Adolf Abromeit, that no one ever feels comfortable abroad—starting with cats and finishing with horses. So I'd appreciate it if you'd come along with us; it would make the trip a little pleasanter."

Adolf Abromeit, a nervous fellow by constitution, raced from the cellar to the attic, from the attic to the barn, from the barn to the stable to the kitchen, and when he had finally gathered a few things together, he ran across the fields to his uncle, the mailman Hugo Zappka, and said: "There's been an accident. A big fire in fact. We have to go abroad, to Oletzko. We need you with us, Uncle. Because of the cats and horses."

And with that he ran back.

Hugo Zappka, the mailman, took the day's mail, sorted it neatly into stacks, brought the books more or less into balance, and sat down to write out his last will and testament. Then he made all his arrangements for the trip and went to see my grandfather, Hamilkar Schass, who went in turn to my Uncle Kuckuck, who went to Ludwig Karnickel, who went to the Urmoneits, and little by little the whole village of Suleyken, without further ado, was ready to accompany one of its citizens on a trip abroad.

You can get some idea of the imposing number in the party when I mention that Amadeus Loch's wagon was about to enter Striegeldorf when the last of the group, the rather sullen Bondzio, was just setting out from Suleyken.

So they were underway, and from what we heard, the following things, among others, took place on the trip: two children were born, old Logau lost his wooden leg, a quarrel broke out between the cobbler Karl Kuckuck and the fisherman Valentin Zoppek, the woodcutter Gritzan went so far as to speak two whole sentences, a wild aurochs was sighted, which turned out later to have been a cow, the legendary beetfields of Schissomir were inspected, the trip was interrupted to watch the famous Kulkaker Fusiliers do their drill, and, of course, a kilo of nails was purchased in Oletzko.

According to further reports the group returned after a considerable time and dispersed in mutual agreement that it's pleasanter not to have to travel alone when you go abroad.

A LOVE STORY

◄§ Joseph Waldemar Gritzan, a tall, taciturn woodcutter, had been stricken by love. And it wasn't just a skinny arrow lodged in his back, but, in keeping with his line of work, a full-sized woodsman's ax. The ax hit him the moment he saw Katharina Knack, an unusually healthy, rosy-faced young girl, washing clothes. She was down on her pretty knees by the side of the stream, bending over, a stray hair or two in her flushed face, while her imposing arms dealt splendidly with the wash. At that moment, as we've said, Joseph Gritzan was walking by, and the ax was in his back before he knew what hit him.

As a consequence he didn't go into the woods, but instead wound up around five in the morning at the pastor's house in Suleyken. He roused the man from his bed by drumming at the door, and said, "Pastor, I've got a notion to get married. So I'd like a certificate of baptism."

The pastor, rudely awakened from sweet dreams, looked at Joseph Gritzan somewhat less than graciously and said, "My son, if love won't let you sleep, at least let others do so. Come back after breakfast. But if you have time, you can dig up the garden. The spade's in the stable."

The woodcutter looked quickly over toward the stable and said, "When I've dug up the garden, can I have a certificate of baptism?"

"Everything will be taken care of in due course," said the pastor, and took his leave.

Joseph Gritzan, encouraged by these words, went to work with the spade so energetically that the garden was dug up in no time. Then, after conferring again with the pastor, he placed wire rings in the pigs' noses, milked a cow, picked two red-currant bushes clean, slaughtered a goose, and chopped a mountain of firewood.

Just as he was starting to repair the shed, the pastor called him inside, filled out the certificate of baptism, and handed it to Joseph Waldemar Gritzan along with various gentle admonitions. He folded the document slowly and carefully, wrapped it inside a page from the Masurian calendar, and put it away safely somewhere within the area of his massive chest. Offered his thanks of course, as was to be expected, and headed for the spot on the stream where love's tender ax had struck him.

Katharina Knack still didn't know the state he was in, nor did she have any idea how much he had already set secretly in motion. She knelt by the stream singing, pummeling and kneading the wash, from time to time allowing herself a view of her wholesome face in the river.

Joseph embraced her rosy form—with his eyes, of course—gasped for breath, swallowed and choked a while, and then, after he had finished swallowing, went up the small wooden dock where she was kneeling. He had thought long and hard about what he should say to her, and now that he was standing beside her, he said it: "Scoot over."

It was certainly an unambiguous sentence. Katharina quickly made room for him on the dock, and he sat down beside her without another word. They sat there for, oh, maybe half an hour, being quite proper and saying nothing. They watched the river, and the woods on the opposite bank, observed the little smelt boring into the bottom of the stream, sending up small murky clouds, and occasionally looked at the ducks drifting along. All at once Joseph Gritzan spoke up: "The strawberries'll be ready soon. N' the blueberries in the woods." The young girl wasn't prepared for this speech, and jumped nervously before answering, "Yes."

And then they sat there as quietly as hens, looking out across the meadow, gazing over at the woods, peering up at the sun once in a while, or scratching their feet or necks.

Then, after an appropriate length of time, another unusual thing happened. Joseph Gritzan reached into his pocket, took out something wrapped, and said to Katharina Knack, "Want some likrish?"

She nodded, and the woodcutter unwrapped two sticks of licorice, gave one to her, and watched her sucking it. She seemed to like it. She was in high spirits, but not so high that she actually said anything. She dangled her legs in the water, made little waves, and looked him in the face now and then. He didn't take his shoes off.

Thus far everything had progressed in an orderly fashion. But all at once, as usually happens in such situations, old lady Guschke stepped out of her house and yelled, "Katinka, what's holding up the wash?"

Whereupon the young girl sprang up in confusion, grabbed the bucket, and was about to disappear without more ado, as if the licorice stick had meant nothing. However, Joseph Gritzan had, thank God, already searched through the broad plains of his chest and found the certificate of baptism, which he now unwrapped carefully, waving the girl back to him.

"D'you read?" he said.

She nodded quickly.

He handed her the certificate and stood up. He watched her face as she read, his whole body trembling.

"Katinka!" yelled old Guschke, "Katinka, have the ducks eaten the wash?"

"Read it all," the woodcutter said insistently. God knows, the fellow was already blocking her way.

Katharina Knack immersed herself more and more in the certificate, forgot the world and wash, and stood there like, let's say, a dreamy calf.

"Bring the wash, bring the wash," old Guschke began to chide again.

"Read it all," Joseph Gritzan insisted, and he was so excited that he didn't even stop to wonder why he was talking so much.

Suddenly old Guschke shot out of the gooseberry bushes, a fast-moving, well-endowed woman, came right up to Katharina Knack, and demanded, "The wash, Katinka!" And giving the woodcutter her tartar's look, she added, "She's supposed to be washing clothes, for heaven's sake!"

Oh, the wonder of love, especially of the Masurian variety. The dreamy, rosy-cheeked young girl lifted her chin, showed the certificate of baptism to old Guschke, and said, "It's signed and sealed. What a beautiful baptismal certificate. I'm going to get married." Old

Guschke was stunned at first, but then she laughed and said, "Mercy! mercy! all the things that come in the wash. While it was soaking we didn't know a thing. And now that it's ready to iron, look what's happened."

Meanwhile Joseph Gritzan had pulled something out of his pocket again. He held it out to the young girl. "Want some more likrish?"

BOLLERUP

AN EVERYDAY LEG

꿈 In Bollerup, neighbor, the wind doesn't let anything stop it. It comes in fresh from the Baltic, setting the foamy caps spinning on the waves, then piles up against the steep, eroded cliffs of the coast, is shunted aside, squeezes through the channel, and has a clear run to the village. No hedge or lovely wood stands in its way. It attacks with vigor, seeming to confuse the sloping fields of rye with the sea. It stirs up the blades, tries to put them to flight, to flatten them into waves and make a little foam dance randomly upon the ears. And if it doesn't manage to do that, at least it sets the ryefield itself in un-expected motion—making it duck, flinging it about, giving it a good thrashing, forcing it to flow uphill, and myriad similar effects.

Whenever I visit Bollerup I take time to watch the wind in the fields of grain, to see what experiments it has in mind, what new ideas it wants to try, like making shadows, or fooling the eye so that at times it seems you could cross the field in a rowboat.

The last time I was sitting on the cairn, watching the wind, Jens Otto Dorsch was in the midst of mowing the field. He's a grand-nephew of my brother-in-law and has the same name, Feddersen, but since almost everyone in Bollerup is named Feddersen, they've agreed to various nicknames so that they can tell one another apart when the need arises, an idea which makes sense to me. So Jens Otto Dorsch was sitting on the tip-seat of his mower—he's always refused to buy a combine—morose, his mind a blank, mowing the rippling field from the outside in, round and round, impoverishing the wind each time, so to speak, by leaving it only bare stubble. He mowed along the slope toward the coast, then parallel to the beach for a stretch, looking like a rider moving through gentle waves of bright, muddy water. Then he turned sharply and came back up the slope toward the woods, neither singing nor whistling, although it was almost quitting time. The only interest he betrayed was an indifferent desire to mow down the field, stealing it from the wind. Thus, without being asked, he offered the people of Bollerup ample justification for their choice of his nickname, Dorsch—the Codfish.

I can't remember how many times he had gone around the field, nor how long he had been at it. At any rate the rough right-angle turns were becoming tighter and tighter, and he still hadn't stopped. Nor had he spoken a word to his horses or to himself, when to my surprise, the rattling of the sharp-toothed blades, made of the finest steel, suddenly ceased. I jumped up and scrambled up on the age-old stone parapet the prehistoric people had placed atop their burial mound. I wanted to find out exactly why Jens Otto Dorsch had interrupted his work. In fact he had now descended from the reaper and was walking around it. It looked like a huge, damaged insect with its long rakes, tilted knifeboards, and all its swivel-mounted, retractable rods and bars.

The Codfish circled the machine, checking it here and there, morosely, reproachfully, cocking his head to listen, rapping on it, until finally, leaning over the machine, he seemed to have found the problem. Something was caught in the knifeboard, in the sharp-toothed shearing blades. Something was stuck, a stone, a stick of wood, perhaps an entire branch. In order to free it, he had to step onto the running board and let himself down into the open machine-work. His feet touched ground, and I saw him reach with both hands for the obstruction. He pulled on it, tugged at it sharply, and drew forth from the blades, which I repeat were made of the finest steel, the prong of a branch as thick as his arm. The blades hadn't been able to cut through it because the branch was too elastic, providing no resistance.

Well that's fine so far, and I'd prefer to stop there, because if it had been up to me, I would have had Jens Otto Dorsch get back up on the machine, start up the horses, and continue reaping for all time. But the story insists upon the fact that he stood there a bit longer in the open machinery, tugging at the branch, scratching his head, for all I know in bewilderment, as we sometimes read about country people doing.

At any rate I still see him busy there, see him out of one eye at least, while the other eye has long since recognized Lothar Emmendinger, a delicatessen owner from Kiel, who had set himself the task of freeing Bollerup from the tyranny of the rabbits. This respectable Sunday hunter emerged from the forest with his rifle in readiness, glancing around nervously, raising and lowering his gun, apparently spotting rabbits everywhere, when I could see none. He was blind to the pleasures of the sunset and the play of the wind in the rye. Suddenly he ran out into the field, lifted his gun, and fired. Yes, he fired a shot and took off running toward the coast, borne on the wings of his excitement, as if he were after the fleeing rabbit, seeking to save itself on the beach, I suppose, or perhaps even in the water.

I still couldn't see any rabbit, although I have to admit that the shot was not without effect. As you will recall, Jens Otto Dorsch was standing within the open machinery of his mower. His horses, two brown Holsteiners of gentle disposition, stood hitched before it, and when the shot went off they reacted as they felt they had a right to—they bolted. The horses started up in panic, startled and frightened, pulling with all the strength that fear apparently provides, and went rushing off in an unnatural, hampered gallop across the field. The wheels of the reaper began to turn, the rakes began to rake, the knifeboards came into play, and the sharp-toothed blades began their work.

Jens Otto Dorsch could do nothing to stop all this, and as the machinery engaged with full force, he was simply flung out the back like, say, a particularly heavy, loosely bound bale of hay. He fell onto the field and lay there without moving. But during his fall I noticed, with the sharp eyesight my relatives have often praised, that Jens Otto was strangely foreshortened. One of his legs in particular seemed not quite up to its proper length, a fact I quickly ascribed to the quality of the blades in question. At any rate the morose fellow lay motionless on the stubble, and that made me more or less lose my head. I was so anxious to get help for the foreshortened Codfish, professional help, that I raced along the worn path to Bollerup, where, however, I found no one. It was like a ghost town. And so I knocked at the house of Wilhelm Feddersen, the Ax. They called him the Ax in Bollerup because he split up everything he came in contact with. I told him quickly what I'd seen, and it was only when I'd finished that I noticed he was lying bathed in sweat under a heavy blanket, suffering from a high fever, and totally indifferent to everything.

Angry with myself, I ran on to Fedder Feddersen, the Lighthouse, and told him about the accident. Not content with that, I also broke the news to Jörn, Gudrun, and Lars Feddersen, known respectively according to their characteristics as the Sea Robin, the Crow, and the Jackrabbit. They proceeded in the aforementioned order to the rye-field to help the foreshortened Codfish. I was the last to arrive.

I arrived, emerged from the forest, and saw the Codfish sitting on the tip-seat of his mower, morose, his mind a blank, as always. That threw me so totally that I gathered up my courage, came closer, and raised my eyes, I'd like to be able to say calmly, to the shortened leg. I saw at once that the left leg was approximately half its normal length, but at the same time I noticed the missing half carefully hanging from a hook on the side of the wagon, tied on with a shoestring.

It was a wooden leg. It swung back and forth in a gentle rhythm. I looked up at Jens Otto Dorsch questioningly, bewildered and confused, and he said, "The blades got my everyday leg. If it'd happened while I was in my Sunday best, I'd have really been mad! My Sunday leg back home is made of oak. But, hey, this one was only pine!"

BREAKING THE SILENCE

෪§ There were two families in Bollerup, neighbor, who hadn't spoken with one another for two hundred years, in spite of the fact that their fields lay side by side, their children went to the same school, and their dead were buried in the same churchyard. Both families were named, as you'll already have guessed, Feddersen, but for the purposes of clarity we'll call one the East Feddersens and the other the West Feddersens, as did the people of Bollerup.

These two families had never exchanged a word because they regarded each other as, how should I put it, scum, stinkers, ragtag and bobtail among other things. They hated and despised each other so deeply, perfectly, and eternally that both sides had long since decided to change their name. The only reason this hadn't happened yet was because each felt the other should do so first. So they were both still named Feddersen, and when they wanted to specify the odious members of the other family, they turned to zoology, calling them wolves, toads, conger eels, vipers, and now and then spotted polecats. It was no longer possible to ascertain the exact origin of this two-hundred-year-old hatred, with its accompanying silence. One ancient fellow said it had to do with a wagon wheel that disappeared, others spoke of plundered chicken roosts. There was also talk of a damaged picket fence.

But I don't think the cause makes much difference. What's of interest is how both families did all they could to give a permanent form to the expression of their hatred. To give only one example: whenever one family would mention their foes, any small children who happened to be present would immediately make throat-slitting gestures. My brother-in-law even claims that babes in arms, if present, would change color, although I consider this reading too much into things. It is indisputable, however, that when forced into contact, members of both families would clench their fists and look the other way, or automatically hiss contemptuously. Fine. No one will be particularly surprised at all this, everyone's familiar with similar situations.

It may occasion some surprise, however, when I serve notice that one stormy evening the hostile silence was to be broken—but let me tell it all in proper order.

One evening, after two hundred years of silence, the heads of both families, Friedrich Feddersen von East and Leo Feddersen von West, had gone out in their boats to pull up their eel baskets. Many of the farmers in Bollerup with fields near the shore, among them Friedrich and Leo Feddersen, catch a lot of fish on the side. So as I was saying, they both pushed off from shore at the same time, made their way to their baskets across a dull, lusterless sea, beneath a dark, low, and equally motionless evening sky, the sort of sky that brings out the silver eels. It was oppressively hot and humid; their heads were squeezed by the pressure. It wasn't the sort of day that made you feel carefree. The men, who had long since seen each other, both acted as if they were totally alone on the Baltic. They rowed with short, choppy strokes to the line of poles from which the baskets were hanging. They tied their boats securely, pulled up the baskets, undid the cords, and carefully released the eels into the bottoms of their boats. Meanwhile the evening delivered on the promise it had held out for some time to the knowledgeable: it burst.

A storm gathered quickly over the Baltic, something changed in the sky, strong winds began to buffet and stir the water. Waves arose, and before both men knew it, they were overtaken by a heavy rain and the shore withdrew into the darkness. The current and the waves combined to demand of the men every ounce of strength and rowing skill they possessed. They rowed and rowed, were driven back, rowed on again—we needn't make it easy on them. It's within our power to leave these two deeply hostile men plying away as long as we want. We can set the wind's resistance against them, we can make the elements roar to our heart's content, there are no limits to our power.

But at some point we have to move the story along, and that means the boats of the two deadly enemies have to be pushed toward one another by the current, the wind, and the carefully planned waves. They have to emerge from the tumult to find themselves face to face. For so it was: without either man having intended it, their boats were brought together, appearing simultaneously on the crest of the same wave, came shall we say crashing together, failed to withstand the impact, and capsized.

Neither man could swim. They did what all nonswimmers do in such situations: they grabbed on to one another, held on tight, and wouldn't let go for anything. They sank together, swallowed water together, bobbed back to the surface together, and were seized in their desperate embrace by a long wave that carried them several meters toward the shore. Whoever wants can tell the story of how they coughed and sputtered, whirled about and would not let go, as wave after wave took them nearer to the shore. We'll content ourselves with noting that they could suddenly touch bottom, and how, together, they pulled themselves from the suction of the sea and waded toward the shore, which they eventually reached, joyful and still clinging to one another. They sat down together, exhausted, arm in arm, and according to tradition, Friedrich spoke the following words, after two hundred years of silence: "Too bad about the eels." To which Leo is said to have replied, "Yes, too bad about the eels." Then each of them reached into a jacket pocket, pulled out a broad, flat bottle of rum, and exchanged a few more words, namely, "Prost, Friedrich," and "Prost, Leo."

So now we have to let a little time pass and allow the flasks to empty, a period during which it seems worthy of mention that the men exchanged bottles. They warmed themselves, clapped their arms, and gazed silently at the Baltic, which was making every effort to appear agitated. Then they laughed, threw their empty bottles into the sea, and walked arm in arm across the cliffs, through the forest to Bollerup. It's not known whether they broke out in song, but it is certain that they walked arm in arm as far as the village square, where all at once they broke apart and measured each other with surprised looks, at which it's said their jaws hardened and their lips compressed. And suddenly Leo Feddersen hissed, "Toad," and Friedrich hissed back, "You spotted polecat"—upon which both of them felt the proper thing to do was to head east and west respectively.

Since that time a beautiful, tragic silence has again reigned between the two families, and they are once more bound by two hundred years of hate. And that's how the people of Bollerup, who don't set much store in seeking causes, are used to having things.

HOME BUTCHERING

~§ In Bollerup, neighbor, it used to be the case that every second person knew the art of home butchering: where the hammer had to hit the ox, how to bleed the animal properly, how to handle the meat knife, how to saw the bones—all that, as I say, was part of common knowledge, something you grew up with. Every second lad past confirmation knew the influence of bile on the quality of the meat. He was as familiar with cleaning the stomach as with the location of the bladder and how to extract bone marrow. That's just how it was. It would be easier to believe that half the numerous Feddersen clan couldn't add, wait patiently, or keep quiet than to believe that they didn't know anything about butchering.

But as I say, that used to be the case, back when a certain Michael, who later called himself Mike Feddersen, emigrated to America, to Chicago, where he made it so big that by the turn of the century a slaughterhouse bore his name. Today all this self-evident knowledge has disappeared. Bleeding and cutting up are no longer numbered among the basic skills; all the fine knowledge concerning the location of the bladder and the use of intestines has been lost. The last person who knew all this was Kai Peter Feddersen, known as Peter Hambone, who developed ptomaine poisoning and died after a surprisingly short stay in the hospital.

Whoever wants to slaughter an animal in Bollerup today, whether he likes it or not, has to call in a butcher from the city. But since this man, contrary to the Bollerup custom, insists on being paid in cash, no one has his butchering done at home anymore.

There was one person of course, the blacksmith Uwe Johannes Feddersen, called Pincers, who wasn't satisfied with this situation, and insisted on doing his butchering at home. But since he had neither the necessary knowledge, nor the inclination to pay a city butcher, he had to stop and think things over. He spent several months thinking about the various possibilities, brooding about it at work, on the beach, in the peat bog, and discussing it daily with his wife, née Feddersen. The question was how they could, on their own, and at no expense, go about butchering their prize sow, which was too fat to actually win a decent prize.

Pincers, who was known in Bollerup as somewhat of an oddball, was bound to think of something some day, and, as my brother-in-law's grandniece reported to me, the blacksmith suddenly interrupted his work one afternoon, rushed in to his wife, and announced, "This weekend we're going to slaughter the pig." His wife replied, "Fine with me." That's what she always said at first, and usually repeated it several times, "Fine with me." Uwe Johannes Feddersen stood there smiling, hammering the ideas straight in his head, so to speak, and after he'd managed to do this, he explained, "They're cutting peat in the bog now. The prisoners are out there cutting peat under guard. I'll bet there's some murderers among them."

"Fine with me," said his wife, at which the blacksmith continued with, shall we say, appropriate excitement. "We'll get us a prisoner. He'll be an expert and all we'll have to do is feed him." "They got all sorts of guards watching the murderers out there while they're cutting peat, and the guards have guns," said his wife. The blacksmith was ready for this objection and countered it with the observation, "Then one of them will have to escape. To our house. To Bollerup. When he's here, we'll start butchering. It seems to me," Pincers continued, "that you could go out to the bog and talk one of them into escaping." "Fine with me," said the blacksmith's wife.

So she put on a kerchief, took a basket and a knife, and walked out onto the soft meadows, looking just like an eager mushroom hunter. The marsh birds didn't even scatter in alarm when she appeared.

Ute-Marie drew nearer to the peat bog, stooped harmlessly now and again, drew closer to the guards, and began talking with them, for all I know, about poisonous and nonpoisonous mushrooms, which would have made sense. She had a long conversation with them, while keeping an eye on the men in striped clothes who were working. Moist squares of peat flew through the air, wheelbarrows squeaked along springy planks, and stacks, even turf-brown towers, of peat squares were erected by dirty hands. A heavy, bald man who used his peat-cutter with precision drew Ute-Marie's attention almost forcibly. Every thrust, every slice, betrayed an exact knowledge of the correct degree of force and a calculating eye, which may have led the blacksmith's wife to think something like, "Fine with me—he's my man." She wanted to catch his attention, but the guards signaled it was time to quit, and Ute-Marie had to return to gathering mushrooms.

Fine. And since I'm growing a bit impatient myself, I'll just mention that she had to go mushroom hunting six more times before she was able to make the man cutting peat understand what it was she wanted. He had no desire to escape. All he wanted was to spend the rest of his days cutting peat. Ute-Marie was reduced to portraying herself as a young widow. God knows, she may even have mentioned ham, clear Schnapps, and carefree nights before she could move him to put down his peat-cutter. At any rate he finally promised he would escape the first time there was enough fog.

Upon this the woman removed her bright kerchief, returned home, and, together with the blacksmith, began to prepare things for the slaughter. They arranged tubs, buckets, and pails, laid out knives and a saw, remembered the hammer, and filled the biggest kettle with water. As a precaution, they also brought down one of the blacksmith's old suits from the attic.

According to my brother-in-law, it was only two days until the fog arrived, allowing the story to continue. You are free to imagine, then, how a shadow detached itself from the wine-red barracks and disappeared into the swirling fog without heeding the challenge of the sentry, to whom he seemed simply an elf king, slipping hurriedly through billowing strips of white muslin to the moor and across the meadow. The blacksmith and his wife were lying fully dressed in bed when they heard a shy tapping on the window. At this the blacksmith quietly withdrew, for he was in total agreement that his wife should present the picture of a young widow. The tapping was repeated, and then the wife, frightened and confused you might say, let in the heavy, bald-headed escapee. He closed the window, then the door, without saying a word—at which point both of them are lost to the story, at least until morning.

They emerged the next morning, were greeted by Uwe Johannes, who introduced himself as his wife's brother, and after a good country breakfast they dropped by the stall, as if by accident, where the sow was rubbing her scaly, bacony mass against the wood.

While the escapee was trying unsuccessfully to scratch the pig, the blacksmith, according to report, locked the door and armed himself with a flat crowbar, which until that moment had been lying with its tip in the fire beneath the dangling water kettle. The blacksmith pointed the crowbar calmly toward a bench on which the slaughtering tools were laid out and said equally calmly to the escapee, "You've eaten and slept. Now get started."

The bald-headed man looked bewildered, and perhaps a bit concerned as well, as the blacksmith continued, "You're going to butcher the sow, and I advise you to do a good job. Get going."

The escapee retreated from the hot crowbar until he came to the whitewashed wall. Then he said: "Me? Butcher? I'm supposed to slaughter the pig?" "You," said the blacksmith, "and no one else. You know about these things. Why do you think we brought you here? Now get started." There wasn't any window to leap out of, and in a voice filled with frightened protest, the escapee asked, "Why me? I've never hurt anyone. And certainly not an animal." "Get going," said the blacksmith, "all you have to do is what you've done to plenty of others. And here it's okay." "It may come as a surprise to you," said the escapee, "but I can't stand the sight of blood." The blacksmith came up to him slowly, the heated tip of the crowbar held at chest level. "Don't try to talk your way out of it," he said roughly, "we know why you were sent to the peat bog." "Please," cried the escapee, "please, I'm not what you think I am. I can't do what you ask."

"Get going," the blacksmith ordered, "go on, get going!" He waved the hot metal tip in front of the escapee's face, brooking no contradiction. He guided him sideways, forcing him to climb over the worn wooden slats into the pen, which the sow had every right to claim as her own. But she didn't attack him. Instead, she trotted into a corner, looked at him from reddish, perhaps even grinning, eyes that were almost closed with fat, and waited.

"The hammer," demanded the blacksmith. The escapee appeared not to have heard the order. He straightened up and grabbed his throat, breathing rapidly and with difficulty. His face was a sickly white, and, appropriately enough, covered with a fine layer of perspiration. The sow lowered her head, rooted about in the dung with her snout, and playfully produced an uneven furrow. Uwe Johannes sat on the side of the pen, repeated his order, and had to sit by and witness the sow work her way up to the escapee, examine his shoes, and rub herself against his knees.

"Start!" yelled the blacksmith. "I can't," the escapee said softly, "I just can't do it. And if you don't let me go I'll turn you in."

"Ha," said the blacksmith, or words to that effect, "we can't tell anyone what went on here. We have to keep that to ourselves. Now get started." He slid down off the side of the pen, forced the bald-headed man to take hold of the hammer, lift it, and, at least in imagined anticipation, bring it down stout-heartedly. But things didn't get that far.

For now the escapee was reduced to simply gasping for air. He went completely white and repeated in a weak voice that he was incapable of hurting a living thing. Then he swayed dangerously and dropped the hammer on the ground. The hammer wasn't the only thing to hit the floor. Soon thereafter the escapee collapsed as well, limp as could be, and the sow trotted up to him and poked him in the side with her snout.

How, I ask you, were the blacksmith and Ute-Marie to know that the fellow could faint anytime he wanted? Indeed, those brief, convincing fainting spells had been the basis of his amazing career as a thief. There was no way they could know, and so they carried the unconscious prisoner into their bedroom, threw him across the bed, and withdrew into the kitchen to wait for him to regain consciousness. And while they were waiting, they thought of new paths which would lead to butchering, even considering further ways of employing force. Then they heard the standard rustling sounds which generally announce something unpleasant. They rushed into the bedroom. Of course it was empty. In spite of an extensive search, they couldn't find the man, which led the blacksmith to believe that he must not be there, that he had flown the coop, and was gone.

And the woman who teaches school in Bollerup maintains that he didn't leave alone. The box with the Feddersen savings had taken wing along with him, and was never seen again. For obvious reasons, they couldn't even report it missing. After all that, it will surely come as no surprise that when Ute-Marie saw the prisoner out on the bog the very next day, cutting peat with precision, she didn't bother casting any encouraging glances his way.

FRESH FISH

&‍§ Well, neighbor, what else could Thorsten Feddersen, the fish-monger, do after all the other merchants in Bollerup had decided to go in search of even the most distant customer with the help of mechanized transportation?

Exactly. As did Oscar Feddersen the baker and Laue Feddersen the butcher, he too rolled through the sprawling village one day in a little red delivery truck, slowly, his window open, relying on the white lettering which offered fresh fish. Now the Bollerupers were already praised for their perseverence, but none was more persistent than this gloomy fellow Thorsten Feddersen. He simply never gave up anything until it was irretrievably lost, be it a fishing net torn away by a storm, an unsold fish, or a hesitant customer.

So he rolled along the shady village lane, offering fish here and there—horn pike with greenish bones, pale eelpouts, pink-eyed herring—and was not at all disturbed, or didn't seem to be, when the Bollerupers glanced once at the bright green enameled bed of his truck and waved him on: nothing today, we don't need any fish today. He closed the doors without a word and drove on to the next courtyard, where he found only the farm dog at home, and then, undiscouraged, on to the prehistoric burial mound, with the sun now shining and the air sparkling around him. Back beyond the mound, in freely chosen isolation, lived Jens Otto Feddersen, the Codfish. The fishmonger knocked on his door. He had decided that no matter what, the Codfish was going to be his first customer.

Upon seeing the fish, which weren't exactly gleaming, even under the sun, the Codfish shook his head, as Thorsten Feddersen had anticipated: he still had a pig's neck to finish off, and then maybe he could talk about fish. In case he didn't believe him, he was prepared to show him the pig's neck. Thorsten Feddersen took a look at the pig's neck and departed with hardly a word. He didn't sound hopeless when, having arrived back home, and in the midst of carrying the fish into the cellar, he said to his wife, you've got to break customers down, to conquer them, and the best thing to do is start with one who'll spread the word.

No wonder that two days later the red delivery truck turned once more into the unpaved courtyard of Jens Otto Feddersen. There it sat, its easily read lettering taking effect. The words spoke for themselves, guaranteeing that the fish were not only fresh, but had been caught locally. Knowing Thorsten Feddersen, I'm sure he realized in advance that he still wouldn't be unloading any fish there. He simply stood beside his truck waiting, giving the Codfish to understand by this peculiar conduct the extent of his frightening persistence. He not only took a look at the pickled meat that prevented the Codfish from buying fish this time, he also tasted a piece. And while he was tasting it he stole a look in the larder to see what was there, estimated how many future meals were still on hand, and mentally set the date for his return.

"Now," said the fishmonger to his wife, "it's time for the first sale." And in the certainty of his belief he immediately weighed out a few fish—one package of red-eyed herring, and another of horn pike, for after all the effort he'd put into selling them, he felt Jens Otto Feddersen should buy both frying fish and fish to pickle in laurel leaves.

No one who knows Bollerup will be surprised to hear that this time the Codfish came out of his house the instant the delivery truck entered the courtyard, and without asking a single question took the two packages exactly as if he had ordered them. And no one would have thought to call it a case of coercion.

That day Thorsten Feddersen drove home more rapidly than normal. "Things are underway," he said to his wife. "Now you'll see. Things will take off on their own."

On his next selling trip, he loaded twice as many fish as normal into the truck. He decided to start with the most distant customers, and so he began with Jens Otto Feddersen. The Codfish received him impatiently, and seemed almost offended. He refused even to glance at the cases of fish. The longer he was silent, the clearer it became that he was deeply annoyed about something. That put the fishmonger at such a loss that he finally asked, "Didn't I give you a good price on the fish?" "The price was right," said the Codfish, "but the fish were old, smelly, and tasteless."

I can just picture the fishmonger drawing back in shock, waving his hands before him in denial, and having thought a moment, explaining, "Is that my fault? I offered them to you three times. If you'd bought them a week ago they would have been fresh! Why blame me just because you took so long to make up your mind?" The Codfish turned aside deflated, if not surprised. He paused, thinking it over, letting the peculiar Bollerup logic of the fishmonger's explanation sink in, then ended up buying fresh herring and eelpouts. Still struck by the logic of it, he told others about his experience buying fish, with the following result: from then on whenever Thorsten Feddersen's truck rolled into a courtyard the customers ran out to meet him. They wanted to get their fish while they were still fresh.

A VERY SENSITIVE DOG

ᴇᴋ The greatest loss suffered by Bollerup last fall, neighbor, was the multitude of geese, hens, and turkeys who left their feathers at the base of the cliffs in front of a freshly dug network of tunnels. These gave every sign of being inhabited by a family of foxes that seemed to enjoy a positively Oriental supply of relatives and descendants. The feathered population of the village was disappearing so rapidly, and the mountain of bones and feathers in front of the main entrance to the burrow grew so provocatively, that Ole Feddersen, a grand-uncle of my brother-in-law, took his double-barrel shotgun from the rack, provided himself with shells, and invited me along to witness the fox family's demise.

I accepted the invitation with some curiosity, told Ole Feddersen's four brothers to meet us at the fox lair, and, under a weak sun, with a cool wind in our faces, we proceeded toward the shore. Although the wind was right, we didn't see a single fox. No fire-red pelt flashed by, no damp, pointed muzzle emerged from a burrow, no fox cubs were wrestling over a goose wing, as might have been expected. The foxes, who seemed to consider it their natural right to enjoy the Bollerup fowls, appeared on this occasion to have moved, say to Asserballe.

Ole Feddersen sat down on a boulder, not at all surprised. "Sometimes," he said, "they can even catch a scent against the wind. But that won't help them."

"Maybe we can pour water in the tunnels," I said. "They don't like water."

"We'll put something else in the tunnels," said Ole. "A visitor. We'll send down a visitor."

"A dog?"

"A dog," said Ole in almost visionary enthusiasm. "A dog like you've never seen before. Very valuable, very sensitive, and so small he can force his way through the tightest tunnel. I've rented him by the hour. It's Thimsen's dog, from Steenaspe. I don't want to talk, but the dog's worth the money."

After a while Ole's brothers arrived, quiet, lanky men, and two of them carried guns. They sat down on the boulder, looked at their feet, as was their habit, and waited. I sat on the boulder too, and reckoned there was room for eight more beside me. We entertained ourselves by watching the Baltic wash over the pebbles, depositing worthless seaweed upon the beach. From time to time I looked over at the silent foxhole.

Fine. And now I have to leave us sitting on the boulder for a long while, since Thimsen from Steenaspe was taking his time, letting us wait. But finally we saw him coming along the edge of the cliffs: a flat-chested man with a crooked neck, in high rubber boots. He carried a rucksack on his back. He greeted us in proper fashion, and when asked about the dog, removed his rucksack carefully, opened it, and let us get a good look inside. And there it was: at the bottom of the fur-lined rucksack sat the valuable little dog, shivering, looking at us with troubled eyes. In the presence of this sensitive creature one of Ole's brothers found his voice again and asked in astonishment, "What's the fur lining for?"

"For warmth," Thimsen said promptly.

"Can't he get warm running?"

"This dog is so sensitive that he can only leave the rucksack for six minutes at the most. Then he has to go back in, for warmth. Unless he's warm he can't give a quality performance."

"Well let's see some quality performance then," said Ole Feddersen.

We walked over to the fox family's network of tunnels and divided up. Each of us stood at a difference entrance. I heard the men loading their weapons. Then Thimsen lifted the valuable animal out of the rucksack, stroked it, talked to it gently, perhaps building up its courage, and pushed it cautiously into the main entrance. The dog disappeared down into the darkness with a rustling sound, a disturber of the vulpine peace. We stood there frozen, you might say, in expectation, holding our breaths, in total readiness. Thimsen took out his pocketwatch and observed the motion of the second hand.

Any moment now, I thought, a fire-red body will fly out of the burrow, be hit by a blast of buckshot in mid-leap, and receive his just reward for all the missing geese, hens, and turkeys. He'll lie on the ground, quivering a bit perhaps. But nothing happened. Nor did any growling or barking come from the burrow, no matter how closely I listened at the main entrance. Nothing moved but the second hand, and all at once Thimsen said, "Three minutes. Anton's been down three minutes now."

No one answered. No one seemed to have heard his remark, and you can imagine why. In a certain sense the story demands that I intentionally draw it out, stopping the clock at this point, perhaps to describe the movement of the shadows, or the architecture of the fox lair, at any rate shifting attention from the watchfulness with which the men await the results of Anton's subterranean efforts. On the contrary, I'm skipping two minutes ahead to when Thimsen says in concern, "Another sixty seconds and he'll have to come up. He has to warm himself up in the rucksack."

I bent down close to the main entrance and listened, but still there was nothing to be heard. Thimsen opened the rucksack and began warming up the fur in advance by hand, rubbing and stroking it. Ole Feddersen held his gun motionless, ready to shoot. "Now," Thimsen yelled suddenly, "that's six minutes. He's got to get into the rucksack." He knelt down at the main entrance, pushed me aside, and yelled urgently, "Anton! Come on out, Anton! Right now! Forget the fox!" Is anyone surprised that no reply issued from beneath the earth? The valuable little dog didn't stir.

The danger increased, and each of us would gladly have kept the minutes from passing. An expression of open despair appeared on Thimsen's face. He dashed back and forth in agitation, pressed his hands to his head, lifted his eyes, no doubt to the heavens. Anton, the sensitive, rented dog, neither appeared nor forced the foxes to bolt before our guns. It was easy to see why a man like Thimsen would begin a series of gentle lamentations, and I must say they closely resembled curses. Eight, ten, fourteen minutes passed. Anton was long overdue.

His fate was sealed. What had he done with the foxes, or what had they done with him?

I listened again, for the last time, at the main entrance. And this time I really did hear something, a frantic digging and scratching, accompanied by an excited whining. I waved Thimsen over quickly to listen. He did, and then announced in helpless rage, "They're burying him alive. The foxes are burying my Anton alive in their labyrinth."

"Anton's still alive?" I asked.

"He'll stay barely alive like that," said Thimsen.

"Barely alive's not quite enough for a fox hunt," said Ole Feddersen.

"We've got to help him," said Thimsen, "we've got to dig him out."

This decision was reached at the eighteen-minute mark, at a point where Anton, the valuable dog, should have been warmed up three times over. I was sent to Bollerup to fetch spades, which leaves me in a position to describe my journey there and back, but not to say anything about what the men did while they were waiting. I hurried. I brought back two spades to the fox lair and was not surprised to have them grabbed from my hands and put to use with, let's say, frantic energy. The network of fox tunnels was exhumed in a rage of total destruction, with Thimsen throwing himself to the ground every few moments to listen. He could hear nothing. "A corpse then," he cried out, "if I can't have Anton alive, I'll carry Anton home dead."

How long did we dig? I don't know exactly. I only know that our work was accompanied by cries of admiration, for none of us had ever seen the artful labyrinth of a series of fox tunnels from within. It must have taken us at least two hours to finally uncover the long escape tunnel the foxes had dug, its exit concealed behind a large bush. There was no doubt in our minds where the foxes had gone, but we couldn't figure out what had happened to Anton, the valuable dog—at first anyway.

We later learned that Anton was already waiting for his master, this fellow Thimsen, in Steenaspe. Since the sensitive dog would have had to have been warmed twenty times over in the meantime, rumor has it that he was shivering terribly—which caused Thimsen to raise his hourly rental rate after the fact. And since Ole Feddersen refused to pay the difference, a court case ensued that's still going on to this day.

THE VILLAGE POETESS

᷍ Even in Bollerup, neighbor, there are events no one dares miss, not least among them a reading by Alma Bruhn-Feddersen. No sooner had the great village poetess announced a willingness to read from her collected, but as yet unpublished, works, than the tickets were sold out. She had tarried so long in self-imposed and slightly threatening silence that the inhabitants of Bollerup were eager to learn why she had chosen to emerge from her gloomy isolation into the spotlight of public attention.

The evening's reading was set for a fall weekend. The leaves whirled in the wind, and in the distance, dogs set up a melancholy howl. Two hours before it was to start, the crowd began streaming into the large hall in the Mühlenkrug tavern. Not even a sheriff's sale could have brought so many people together. They came resolutely up the side paths in single file, skipped along the sandy lanes, flowed together on Main Street, and poured toward the millpond, building up almost threateningly in front of the Mühlenkrug, where Main Street intersected with the second most important road in the village.

Of course Lars, Jörn, and Wilhelm Feddersen were there, and naturally Doctor Dibbersen, and the Codfish wearing his Sunday leg, and I even spotted two fishermen from Kluckholm, who had sailed over from their treeless isle. Impressive as was the number of spectators attracted by Alma Bruhn-Feddersen, their behaivor was even more striking. They filed in solemnly and expectantly, with shy reverence. There was no noisy exchange of greetings, not a single out-of-place remark,

the whole mood quiet and subdued—you know what it's like sometimes.

An hour before the reading was to begin, the large hall in the
Mühlenkrug was not only full, but overflowing. They sat on the floor,
leaned against the window sills and radiators, crowded together in the
aisles, yet no one seemed to mind or become upset. All eyes were focused on the raised platform with its chair and table. It was a very low,
hand-carved chair behind a folding table covered with a blue-and-white
checked cloth. There was also an old settee and a vase with asters, the
favorite flowers of the village poetess. A yellow poster hung in the
background at about eye-level, with black lyres in the top corners. It
repeated what everyone knew: for the first time in several years, Alma
Bruhn-Feddersen will read from her collected works.

So, since there is little to be heard from the audience apart from
murmuring, whispering, and here and there a few quiet words, we can
skip the waiting period beneath the faded garlands and refocus our attention just as the great village poetess steps onto the platform.

She was not the first person to appear. The hand that felt its way
along the curtain, pushing it out, taking so long to find the opening,
belonged to Linchen Madsen, a pale, frightened woman who served as
Alma Bruhn-Feddersen's housekeeper. Imperious, with the face of a
grumpy Saint Bernard, the poetess stepped onto the stage, a gigantic
black crocheted cloak draped about her pear-shaped body, her manuscript in one hand and an ivory-handled cane in the other. She shoved
her way roughly past Linchen Madsen, banged her cane once on the
floor, and looked reproachfully at the audience, which inevitably produced a feeling of guilt in several of them. They hunched up their
shoulders and hung their heads. The fact that the applause was so restrained was entirely due to the respect in which the poetess was held
by the audience.

Then she whacked her cane down upon the table and seated herself
in the low chair. Now I could see that she wore black woolen stockings
and high-topped laced boots. Her jowls wobbled with every rapid jerk
of her head.

All at once she reached behind her, fumbled about, and pulled from
a secret pocket in her dress a few meters of brick-red handkerchief with
white stripes. She blew her nose carefully, but with such power that the
lights in the room flickered. Then she opened her manuscript and

looked pensively for a moment at the ceiling. Just at this moment, as she was gathering her forces, someone else dared to blow his nose, namely my distant cousin Frietjoff Feddersen. The village poetess slammed her manuscript shut and stared out angrily at the mischief-maker, who tried to excuse himself by shrugging his shoulders several times. Her gaze became so increasingly unpleasant and demanding that Frietjoff Feddersen was obliged to stand up and not only apologize for the interruption, but also to stammer out an explanation of when and where he caught cold. Namely, at night, while he had been stumbling around the kitchen in his bare feet getting a drink.

The village poetess nodded, and held her hand out palm upward as if to say, you see, that's how such things happen. Then she opened her manuscript and concentrated anew. She had just drawn a few deep trial breaths, when a disturbance arose from one of the low windows. There were the sounds of cursing, eager tapping, and finally even bits of a protest song, at which point there was really nothing left for Alma Bruhn-Feddersen to do but slam her manuscript shut again in anger. She made a sign to the two fishermen from Kluckholm, who got up and went into the garden, at which the noise suddenly ceased. The troublemaker, who was soon led in by his long arms and pulled in front of the platform, was none other than Sven Feddersen. He was drunk. He had evidently had so much of the red-currant wine he had inherited that his legs couldn't agree on which way to go. Nevertheless, he insisted on staying for the reading.

A fiery glare from the poetess sufficed to wipe the self-satisfied grin from the drunken man's face. It was replaced by a sweet-sour smile, his grandiloquent gestures subsided, and, while still in the clutches of the Kluckholmers, he too soon decided that an apology was in order. Now the poetess ordered them to bring Sven Feddersen up on the stage. As he stood trembling before her, she used him as a living ex-ample of the deleterious effects of alcohol. She pointed to his head with her handsome black cane and spoke of "softening of the brain," indicated the "turbidity" of the eye, and by the time she had reached his liver the crowd was beginning to ask questions. As always in Bol-lerup, a thorough discussion ensued, and by the end of the exchange Sven Feddersen had sobered up and was allowed to go sit down in the middle aisle, followed by the reproachful eyes of the audience.

Alma Bruhn-Feddersen adjusted her clothing, opened her manuscript, and ran a thumb that tolerated no resistance diagonally across the paper to smooth it. Then she tuned up with a few rattling sounds which recalled an anchor chain being raised with a winch. To this she added a brief but energetic series of lip exercises. A turn of the head back toward Linchen Madsen, who was sitting on the settee in a manner which can only be described as well-behaved, and then the poetess delivered herself of what had come to her during her self-imposed isolation.

I remember it well. First she ran Bollerup through all four seasons, with everything we're accustomed to expect from them. She draped winter over the village, shrouded it in white, tossed a few stray crows into the sky, let the frozen reeds rustle and the stove crackle—supposedly a fiery knight riding through the kitchen. Then she staged a winter storm with the customary local snow flurries, actually cried out, "Whooo! Oooo!" and sent a gale whistling about the farmhouses. The riverbanks, as she put it, froze "in icy white," and the old willows turned suddenly gray. That last bit sounded familiar to me. When she came to the "little injured doe," digging for grass in the snow with damaged hoofs—she made our church bells ring out faintly at this point—an old woman next to me sighed and wrapped her arms around herself as if she were freezing.

She didn't need to shiver long, for the baton had already been passed on to a dappled spring. The melting snow-waters inevitably tinkled merrily over hill and dale into a welcoming Baltic Sea. A breeze passed through the reeds, and this time they resembled spears. In meadows and fields, in the "quick-set hedge," in the forests, not only a "cheerful pulse" but a positively "wild tumult" reigned. All boded well and summer could not be far behind. She drew it, bottle-green, into the hall with strong strokes of her oar.

She placed a sleeping wanderer in the midst of rye and green clover, with seemingly friendly insects humming about him. Next, after what I assume must have been a warm rain, the fields gave off a freshly spiced steam. She set "little red ponies grazing" before our eyes, a billowing sail which illuminated a bay, dragonflies, softly rustling woods of course, and an oppressive heat that she likened to a sitting hen. Alma Bruhn-Feddersen's cherries glowed redly and proudly, and throughout Bollerup the "joyous swish of the sickle" could be heard. With that she was ready to turn things over to autumn.

Harvest time arrived with falling acorns and "chubby turnips," bringing us gifts of "golden apples." She hung an early morning fog around a farmhouse and piled up crates of silver mackerel. As for our fall weather, at one point a herd of horse-clouds galloped across the sky, then later "hardly a breath stirred in the treetops." That seemed familiar to me too. What else did she do with fall? She had stubble singing, "all is over, all is over," she lit a potato fire, and for final good measure she decided to "follow in dreams the wandering birds and their brighter fate."

Alma Bruhn-Feddersen straightened up abruptly and called over Linchen Madsen. The housekeeper opened a small tin box, which I could see was filled with large pills. The poetess took one and swallowed it without water.

Why was there no applause? Was the audience too intimidated? Or were they perhaps too deeply moved? Most of them gazed at the floor, presumably examining the grooves between the boards, a few twirled key-chains, others massaged their fingers and wrists, and I saw one of them—Thimsen from Steenaspe—examining his teeth in a mirror.

The poetess now announced three shorter samples of her work, first of all "The Blacksmith's Dream." It was based on the notion that each of us would like to be transformed into the thing he loves, and so one evening the blacksmith found himself turned into an anvil upon which the whole world hammered. Most of the audience didn't know how to take this dream and showed little reaction. But then she read, "The Great Eel Hunt," and suddenly a finger shot up, with a rigid insistence impossible to overlook. Nevertheless, Alma Bruhn-Feddersen paid no attention. First her third sample had to be thrown into the pot, one she called "The Gaze of Sick Animals," which concerned an obsessed veterinarian and opened with the line, "Who gallops so late through rain and wind . . ." As she was reading it in a dark, growling singsong, fingers suddenly started flying up everywhere, snapping, waving, not to be ignored.

She had barely finished reading when, without being asked, one of the Kluckholmer fishermen stood up and said he had a correction to make. He'd heard her say something about the seven prongs of an eelspear. That wasn't right, because eelspears always have four prongs. He requested that she change that. Moreover he wished to point out that spring was the best season for mackerel. Alma Bruhn-Feddersen looked at him annoyedly and asked, "Are facts all you've got in your head? One prong too many and you can't understand poetry!"

And another thing, Jens Otto Feddersen, the Codfish, said, speaking up. "You said this evening that at a certain time the 'joyous swish of the sickle' is to be heard throughout Bollerup. I've never managed to hear sickles swishing, and I doubt if anyone else has either, for the simple reason that there aren't any sickles in Bollerup anymore. I request that you change that." Now Alma Bruhn-Feddersen could barely control her anger. "Where," she said, "where is anyone so simple-minded as to take the word sickle literally? Sickles are well-known tools of Death, and the like, that's what he harvests with, for God's sake!"

The audience was divided on this point; some applauded and others shook their heads gravely. The poetess bore this patiently. But she almost lost her composure when a certain Mogens Feddersen, a former forest ranger, requested permission to speak. He claimed to know for a fact that only stags, goats, and sheep dig in the snow for grass. No doe would, and certainly not an injured one. Could she possibly substitute a stag for the doe?

With a dismissive gesture of contempt, the poetess replied, "You've been a forest ranger for twenty-five years and you still don't know a thing. You can't depict the suffering of animals in winter by talking about a stag, you have to show a slender, helpless doe." "But a doe never digs in the snow." "Then they'll dig there from now on," said the poetess, "and everyone will just have to get use to it, including you."

She was staring grimly at her text and had leafed back and forth through it a few times, when, with typical tardiness, the blacksmith Uwe Johannes Feddersen, known as Pincers, stood up. At one point she had mentioned him personally, he said, about what his dreams might be, and just to avoid any misunderstanding, he would like to make clear that he had never in his life dreamed of an anvil. If he dreamed at all, it was about shellfish, codfish, pike, and occasionally loaches. He herewith rejected any other sort of dream.

I simply can't describe the look Alma Bruhn-Feddersen aimed at the blacksmith, composed as it was of indignation, outrage, contempt, and surly arrogance. She examined him for a long time, and then said something that would have been better left unsaid. With curled lip she stated, "Your remarks, Uwe, show me that I'm totally correct. Only someone who's received his daily allowance of hammer blows on the bean could talk like you do. So you must be an anvil after all. But you can draw consolation from the fact that there are plenty like you in Bollerup."

As the blacksmith sat down to ponder this, protests erupted everywhere, threats flew toward the platform, and fists shook beneath the garlands. Very slowly, her lips still curled, the poetess gathered together her manuscripts and handed them to Linchen Madsen. "Hey," the Codfish suddenly yelled, "we paid to get in. We've still got twenty minutes coming, or are we going to get our money back?" The poetess slammed her cane down on the table so hard that it produced instant silence. Then she cut a second swath through this rather uneasy silence: "You're all too interested in facts. Poetry is simply wasted on you. As far as I'm concerned you can all have your money back and choke to death on your facts." She disappeared behind the curtain without another word, and was followed with an insulted shrug of the shoulders by Linchen Madsen.

Since that day the great village poetess has been living once more in self-imposed silence, and I must admit that her fame has not diminished, but instead is quietly and steadily increasing.

German Lessons

HEILMANN

꧁ Midway through that winter he arrived on a bicycle and a mission, following the ice-packed groove of a sleigh. This effectively prevented him from looking up, forcing him instead to keep a steady eye on the rut he had chosen, for every time he raised his head the rim of a wheel would immediately scrape against the icy walls of the narrow channel, the handlebars would pull to one side, and when he jerked them back, the front wheel would twist at an angle to the groove, jam fast, and— wrapped as he was in his long uniform coat and with his old rifle across his back—he would be hard pressed to jump off in time. He came alone up the village road past the school, offering anything but a convincing threat. The impression he gave as he passed before the smoke-colored cottages of our village in that gray February twilight was that of a desperate and sullen man forced to follow a groove which had already placed more demands on his attention, strength, and agility than he could handle.

We could see him drawing nearer from our classroom windows and thought we could hear his groans and curses, the maledictions he directed specifically at the runner-wide groove and the damnable fate which forced him to follow it. It was Heinrich Bielek. We recognized him immediately, with the quick, sure instinct with which one recognizes someone from one's own village, even in the snow-gray twilight, even if he's wearing a uniform with an old rifle across his back: Heinrich Bielek, sick, with bristling white hair—though not so sick that they were willing to dispense with his services. Of course they couldn't

165

use him—or "deploy" him, to use a favorite word of theirs—in just any way they wanted, but he wore their uniform, increased their number, and gave them the security of a reserve.

We watched him struggling past the schoolyard and assumed he had long since reached the other end of the village and was on his way to Schalussen or wherever the frozen sleigh track and his orders might be taking him, when two men brought him through the hall, carried him into the teachers' room, and deposited him on a sofa. As I was later to learn, they laid his rifle across a scratched-up leather armchair, opened his coat, and watched a while as he doubled up, threw himself onto his side after a few tries, and pressed both hands flat against his stomach without uttering a sound. But before they could offer to fetch the doctor from Drugallen, he straightened out again and calmed them down with a gesture. It was just an overdue case of the cramps. He'd been expecting an attack the night before, and he knew the course it took so well that he expected to handle the pain on his own.

So it was probably more the thought of the bluish, ice-packed sleigh track than the pain that kept him on the sofa in the teachers' room, next to a wall filled with cracks and beneath the photograph of a uniformed man with pince-nez who looked down upon him calmly and impartially. Although he seemed to be feeling better, he made no attempt to rise, but instead passed out cigarettes, without smoking himself, and returned the frighteningly impartial gaze of the man in the photograph, whom he would have taken for a teacher if he hadn't known better. But Heinrich Bielek knew him so well that he even understood the fear this man inspired, or was said to inspire.

When he had finally decided that his stomach cramps were not going to allow him to continue following the sleigh track, he removed the ill-fitting coat of his uniform, rolled it up, and pushed it under his head for a pillow, sizing up both men through his acorn-shaped eyes. He didn't ask about his bicycle, a further sign that he had no intention of continuing his journey. Instead he acquainted the men with his mission, thus exposing them both to the unwelcome pressure of helping the man who lay stretched out before them.

By taking them into his confidence—one of them was Feustel, the retired preacher, a bachelor who smelled of tobacco and onions—he left them no other choice but to send for a boy before they were even asked. They called the youngster into the teachers' room and had him approach the sofa where Heinrich Bielek was lying. Although they knew his mission, they left it to the man on the sofa to convey the orders to the boy, and as Bielek began to speak, their faces showed a lively and concerned interest, as if they were hearing all this for the first time. The boy, Bernhard Gummer, with his thick neck and hanging head—we were all familiar with his gentle, friendly imbecility—stared at the old rifle lying across the leather armchair and betrayed by neither nod nor look whether he had understood a single word about the mission and how it was to be carried out, a state of affairs which led Feustel to lay his hand on the boy's shoulder and ask him to repeat slowly what he had just heard.

The boy did not disappoint them. Without lifting his head he repeated that he was to go to Schalussen, to Wilhelm Heilmann, the scrap-metal dealer, to bring him here to the school, into the teachers' room, to the man in the uniform, to Heinrich Bielek. If he didn't come, they would go that same day to get him. It was urgent. The former rector straightened up with satisfaction, and Bernhard Gummer carefully pulled on his coat, put on his earmuffs, and listened for a moment as if he were a wireless operator receiving faint signals through his earphones. Then he donned his mittens, which were tied to a string, and shuffled out of the school.

The boy knew the way, he lived in Schalussen himself, and he also knew—we all knew—Wilhelm Heilmann's cottage and the sheds and the dump behind the sheds where a hill of rusty iron lay: old bicycle frames, pieces of tin, reddish-brown tangles of wire, empty pump casings, thrown horseshoes and banged-up kettles, with dandelions or deadnettles shooting up through the gaps in summer. This hill seemed to us more a landmark of the Heilmann home than stock in trade from which they lived, for it never flattened or shrank, we never saw it loaded on trucks, never even saw it sorted, like peas, into good and bad piles. It simply lay there season after season, generation after generation, a hill of uselessness. And yet they must have made a living from it, mysteriously and shrewdly. Whole families of them had put their trust in old iron, nourished themselves with its help, had grown up and passed the rust-red hill on as an inheritance to the next Heilmanns, who apparently neither increased nor diminished it, but instead seemed intent only on preserving it intact. Our grandfathers, our fathers, and we: generations of our village plundered the back of the hill when we needed a few groschen, went around to the front, and sold it back to the Heilmanns, who purchased what they had already owned three times, upon which our people would witness the rubbish sail back onto the hill, so that it no longer had its former shape, yet kept its same volume, thus giving it that strange sense of permanence. Although Wilhelm Heilmann lived alone, we had no doubt that one day a new Heilmann would appear from somewhere to take possession of that hill of old iron—take it and watch over it like the last piece of firewood on which his life depended.

From what I heard, the boy found Heilmann reading in bed that morning. He was not surprised to discover that the old man was lying fully dressed beneath the heavy covers. He went up to him, sat down on the edge of the bed, pushed up his earmuffs, and stated his mission. After he had finished, and saw that the old man was neither surprised nor defensive and afraid, he advised him to hide or to lock himself up in the cottage, and if not that, then at least to buy a gun, since the other man was carrying one. But Wilhelm Heilmann, the last man of the Hebrew faith in our forlorn little corner of Masuria, gave a sour smile, the smile of an inevitable certainty which could and must be borne, threw back the covers, and stood up. He had been lying in bed with his boots on. The boy went into the kitchen, sat down on a stool, broke off a piece of gray leavened flatbread, and started to eat it. He didn't have to wait long, for the old man had simply exchanged his reading spectacles for his work glasses and was already standing in the dark kitchen, urging the boy to lead the way.

The old man looked neither toward the whitewashed cottage, which he left behind unlocked, nor at the snow-covered hill beneath which the rusty heritage of the Heilmanns lay, but went ahead of the boy, following the sleigh track, the frozen snow crackling beneath his feet. Once, by the weeping willow, which was glazed with ice, the boy caught up with him and pointed toward the dark, seemingly impenetrable forest wall, pointed wordlessly, his gesture and his entire attitude expressing but a single intense urge. Wilhelm Heilmann smiled sourly and shook his head. Perhaps he knew that he was the last in our small corner, that he had simply been forgotten or spared, more likely forgotten, a fact which forced him to wait implacably until the moment arrived when it was his turn as well. Now that the boy had come for him he was reconciled to it, something had gone out in him:

his curiosity, the despair he had found himself prey to as they had been led off one after the other. Often enough they had passed by his cottage and his mound of iron on their way through Schalussen without threatening him or even putting him on notice, something which, more and more, he had secretly awaited. It was two years before they turned their attentive cruelty upon him, not as if they had suddenly remembered him, but as if he were an object they had stored carefully away and were now bringing forth. Wilhelm Heilmann was ready for that— never for a moment had he given in to the weakness of hope.

Wearing his knee-length, earth-brown greatcoat, he preceded the boy through the lane of smoke-colored cottages to the school he himself had attended, walked up the path strewn with ashes and tiny cinder crumbs, discovered the bicycle and paused beside it, nodding with a smile and thrusting his hands deep into his pockets. Bernhard Gummer came up beside him, changed his expression, and drew near the old man. The boy's protruding lips moved, whispering something unclearly, urgently. Then he turned around and disappeared into the school without looking back.

The old man waited until he heard the sound of hobnailed boots in the corridor, then pushed himself away from the wall with his back and stepped toward the uniformed man who carried a rifle in one hand and was buttoning up his coat with the other. "Ready, Wilhelm?" "Ready, Heinrich." Wilhelm Heilmann had nothing else to say, and nothing seemed to him important enough that he wanted to know about it. The knowledge he carried within himself like smuggled goods exceeded anything he could ever learn from Heinrich Bielek, and so he simply went out to the road with him, turned with him, and gave a little wave back at the school, walked beside him through our village with the sure and self-evident manner of a man who knows and shares the path and plans of the other. They went past the village common and crossed the old wooden bridge, whose rails still bore the scars of the harvest wagons that had passed that autumn. An icy wind met them in the open field, cutting into their faces. Wilhelm Heilmann felt his eyelid beginning to twitch. A snow-covered sign pointed in the direction of Korczymmen, fourteen kilometers away, on the border. The wind raced straight toward them across the snow, forcing a painful chill into their lungs, and they lowered their heads and leaned into it. "Not the friendliest weather," said Heinrich

Bielek. "It'll be better once we're in the woods," said Wilhelm Heilmann. A sleigh with muffled figures came toward them. They stepped
aside, hands waved at them, and they returned the greeting without
knowing to whom they were waving. The tinkling of the sleigh-bells
faded into a valley.

As they reached the spot where the forest began to enclose the road,
Heinrich Bielek felt as though a hot bullet had struck him in the stomach. It hit him so unexpectedly, with such total force, that he pressed
both hands to his body, let his bicycle fall, and dropped to his knees in
the snow. The cap fell from his head. The protective band was shoved
up out of his collar. The rifle-strap pulled across his chest. Wilhelm
Heilmann looked down at him blankly, and as he felt the old man's
quick, suspicious glance, he lifted the bicycle and held it fast in both
hands—like a burden he neither wished nor dared to drop at any price,
a silent demonstration that he had no intention, either now or later, of
taking advantage of such an opportunity. It was neither depression nor
weakness which was revealed in this moment, but a decision to forgo
any action which might alter what he had so often expected, experienced, and lived through in nights of listening and dreaming. He held
the bicycle tightly and didn't dare rub his twitching eyelid, just stood
and looked at the uniformed man in the snow, who now struggled
onto all fours, paused for a long time as if gathering the necessary
strength to rise to his feet, then brought his hands together and pushed
himself erect in one motion. He stood there a moment anxiously, not
quite believing he was up, then turned and said tersely: "All right, let's
go, Wilhelm."

They followed the fresh tracks of the sleigh through our ancient
forest, sheltered from the icy wind which raced through the tops of the
pines, shaking from the branches great clumps of snow which drifted
down to earth among the trunks like powdered dust. Far ahead, by the
side of the road, felled tree trunks were lying in piles. The yellowish
gleam of their sawn faces led the way to where the path disappeared.
Wilhelm Heilmann was pushing the bicycle, and the other man had
unslung his rifle and was carrying it in his hand. They walked along
together, making an effort to walk side by side, even when the route
made it difficult, even when they had to watch each other out of the
corners of their eyes, not so much in fear or mistrust, but from a de-

sire to advance together, to be pulled along by each other's steps. A distant thunder rolled over them like a winter storm. Heinrich Bielek lifted his head, listened without stopping, and said softly: "Heavy artillery." Wilhelm Heilmann looked upward blankly in response— with the same lack of expression with which he had flung old scrap iron onto his hill.

The woods thinned out. They walked past the frozen marshlands and up the hill into the forest once more. It opened to receive them with the same willingness with which it had closed behind them, and as they reached the dilapidated wooden observation tower, snow began to fall. The path divided, and a second sign pointed toward Korczymmen, eleven kilometers. They followed the sign without a word, as if they had long since settled on a common goal.

Wilhelm Heilmann thought about the man who was taking him in, or more properly, passing him on, remembered his one-eyed father, the cottage in which the Bieleks lived, hard-working and dexterous broommakers, whose most visible wealth was a horde of dirty children that swarmed through the birch forests in the springtime to cut the small elastic shoots. He thought of young Heinrich Bielek, who had sat in the arms of the trees to pluck lime blossoms for tea, who went barefoot until late in October, and who, at a wedding, had disappeared under the coach in which the bride was sitting. He even remembered that special talent Heinrich had, one that had always amazed him: the ability to drop a pocketknife blade-first into his lap in such a way that he never received the slightest cut. Suddenly Wilhelm Heilmann became aware that he was going too fast, or that the man beside him was walking more slowly. He didn't stop, but simply tried to adjust his pace to that of his companion. When this proved unsuccessful, so that he had again moved into the lead, he finally did stop and, turning around, saw that Heinrich Bielek was no longer behind him in the sleigh tracks, but was stomping off to the side through the deep snow toward the trees, using the stock of his rifle as a support. He immediately lifted the bicycle and turned around, even before the order to do so reached him, following the trail which led through the snow to a hut made of spruce logs, like the ones our foresters build for themselves in the summer. The door was only wired shut. They pulled the wire apart and stepped inside. Four straw mattresses lay on the bare floor. No window, no stove, just a shelf on which stood tarnished aluminum cups. Notches had been cut in the doorpost; snow lay in one corner.

Heinrich Bielek lowered himself onto one of the straw mattresses, stretched out with a moan, and pointed to the mattress next to him, where Wilhelm Heilmann, having brought the bicycle into the hut, sat down, then took off his glasses and polished them carefully on the sleeve of his greatcoat. Having done this, he stood up and went to the door intending to shut it. Hearing a weak order he turned around and saw that Heinrich Bielek was pointing the barrel of the rifle at him from his mattress, saw how he struggled to keep the barrel on him, turning with him as he slowly walked through the room back to his mattress. The door stayed open. Sudden small gusts of wind hurled the snow in. A cold draft streamed over them.

Pain held Heinrich Bielek in its powerful grip, pressing him into the straw mattress. He thrashed about with his legs, tossing his head from side to side, while never forgetting the man who sat next to him quietly watching. He was so far from forgetting him that he turned over suddenly and stared at him with his eyes opened wide, frightened and defensive. The effect of the pain was such that Heilmann now appeared to him monstrously enlarged and, in all his physical superiority, so intent on flight that he already saw him running away, the earth-brown greatcoat flitting here and there among the trunks, behind the pine trees, where even a bullet could not reach him, and Heinrich Bielek thought, "Don't do it, Wilhelm, don't you do it."

Then he felt his buckle being undone and his coat opened, or rather he felt the sudden relief much more than the individual actions that caused it. He let go of the rifle, pressed his hands flat on his stomach, and after a while felt the cramps loosen their grip and recede, freeing him so noticeably that he sat up with his back against the hewn logs of the wall. At one point, while Wilhelm Heilmann was rubbing his eyes, he pulled the rifle over to him again and laid it across his lap.

They sat opposite one another in silence, and, for no longer than it takes to draw a breath, they both had the impression that their senses were playing tricks on them. Neither looked at the other, neither one said a word. They seemed instead to be perceiving each other by means of their listening, motionless bodies, seemed to be acting in concert with these bodies as well, and when one of them arose, the other rose almost as quickly, stood there with the same indecisiveness, began to move with the same hesitation. After some time, when it had stopped snowing, they stepped from the hut together, stepped out into the open without fear and without hope. Wilhelm Heilmann pushed the bicycle, not thinking about the missed opportunity, nor turning his thoughts back to those minutes in which he could have left the hut unnoticed and without risk, or could have done what the total defenselessness of the other suggested. He let Heinrich Bielek lead the way. They went on through the woods toward Korczymmen.

Before reaching the border village, which Wilhelm Heilmann knew but hadn't visited in years, they turned off the main road and followed a path stamped out in the snow until they reached the clumpy, frozen ramparts of the trench which ran through the middle of the forest. They heard the sounds of picks and shovels, and the rattle of clods of earth being thrown against the trunks of trees.

They saw women in scarves and old men working in the bottom of the trench, and saw children by the walls shoving out stones, roots, and hard clumps of earth. Wilhelm Heilmann nodded to them as he passed. A long way ahead of them a machine gun fired, and then they heard a few individual pistol shots. Guards were posted behind the ramparts. At a gesture, Wilhelm Heilmann leaned the bicycle against a tree and continued without pause in the direction from which the shots had come. A young, broad-faced man came toward them, his gun held diagonally across his chest. He stepped between them. He ordered Heinrich Bielek to go back. When he turned around, he saw that the man in the earth-brown greatcoat, the man he was supposed to be leading, was already silently walking ahead.

THE PUNISHMENT

๏ No, nothing to eat for me, Christine, just a schnapps will do. Where is he? At the boardinghouse, I took him back there myself when it was all over. Our court physician gave him a shot to calm him down, but it didn't help. He was shaking the whole trip, poor old guy. What's that? Of course he'll calm down, but tomorrow he'll start all over again. You know Father, he'll want to challenge his acquittal, he'll come to my office dragging a new catalogue of his offenses along with him, he'll drive the whole state attorney's office crazy trying to convince them that they should prosecute him. An indictment! That's the only thing he lives for, to be indicted for having failed to render aid, for knowing collusion, or just for being in the war. You know he's made a real art of it. He's succeeded in transforming his whole life into one long chain of omissions and commissions. You mustn't underestimate an old public health officer, even if he does seem slightly off. Yes, it's a mania. He collects grounds for his own prosecution the way other people collect oil paintings or beer mugs.

The plan? You mean our plan? Of course we carried it out, just as Olaf, Günter, and I had agreed. I can't expect my colleagues to keep spending time on my father's imaginary offenses forever, so we made a plan, and we thought it wasn't bad either. And at first—I'll have another schnapps—everything went just as we'd hoped. Thanks.

You should have seen how Father looked when he appeared before the court; pleased, dressed in black, with an aster in his buttonhole, if you can imagine. I can't help it, he looked like an elderly bridegroom, one of those dissolute types always ready to wink back. The way he strode across the square! Swinging his cane and even striking the lampposts lightly as he passed. For all I know he was even whistling, at any rate we were looking from the window at what seemed to be a happy man, hurrying to his trial.

Suspicious? No, he wasn't suspicious, Christine, he thought the action being brought against him was a reward for his stubborn persistence. He never realized it was a fake trial, one we hoped would cure him of his mania, of the pathological introspection that was getting on everyone's nerves. We wanted to get him off our backs, so we worked out the plan in our office and agreed to carry it through. Olaf, Dieter, and Günter did it for me as a favor. Well, you know them, they wanted to help me out. And they were just as bewildered as I was when they saw how happy Father was, and his relaxed self-satisfaction as he greeted Adam Kuhl at the top of the stairs.

Adam Kuhl? He was born in Marggrabowa too, like Father, they've known each other since childhood. Kuhl worked for the post office, but now he was acting as a witness for the prosecution. Just imagine, Father not only dug him up, he even helped refresh his memory. In order to get a trial, he furnished his own witness for the prosecution. We noticed that he gave something to Adam Kuhl as he greeted him. Everything, his gestures, the way he treated the man who was to bear witness against him, testified to his gratitude. He took him gingerly by the arm, and, as they entered the justice building side by side, heads bowed toward each other and smiling, you might have taken them for accomplices who were up to something. That's true, we were in the same mood.

You mean where did the trial take place? Not the courtroom, we just used the large magistrate's hearing room, where it wasn't so noticeable that we lacked an audience. But Father was so wrapped up that he didn't seem to miss one. He'd got his trial, and you should've seen how eagerly he placed himself in the dock, and how promptly he answered the questions put to him by Olaf concerning his personal background. Olaf had taken over the prosecution, I served as his assistant, Dieter played the judge, and Günter acted as the public defender. The entire collective experience of the state attorney's office didn't prepare us for an accused man like my father. He gave at least three answers to every question directed to him, not only willingly, but obsessed by a desire to provide the court with a picture of his very being, and you could tell immediately how methodically determined he was to expose himself. He actually managed to tinge each and every detail with self-accusation. No, Christine, he wasn't trying to establish any mitigating circumstances in accusing himself. From the very first I had the feeling that he wanted to be convicted. You should have heard how he described his professional career. His doctoral dissertation was supposedly written by a colleague, he was expelled from the Albertina as an advanced student for performing an illegal operation, he had finally managed to gain a position as a public health officer by denouncing his predecessor. That's how he began.

You mean is it all true? Yes, I'm afraid it is, Christine. At first, the way he was standing there, twisting and turning, and trying to get us to believe him, made us look at each other in amusement. We thought we knew what he was up to. But we soon realized that we were wrong, and that everything he brought up against himself was more or less the truth. By more or less I mean that it corresponded to his own subjective truth. The joy he showed in destroying his own reputation! The impatience with which he offered his offenses to the court! Whenever Olaf spoke, Father would shake his head, or make clear by gestures of protest that he didn't agree with his prosecutor. He felt that he was not being sufficiently exposed, not clearly enough marked as a criminal, and sometimes he simply couldn't hold back, he would jump up and start talking, not only strengthening the accusations and enlarging upon them, but reproaching the court. Why? Because he hadn't been indicted even earlier. In his opinion he had presented the court with more than sufficient grounds for an indictment in the past.

You're right, Christine, there were some serious faults in the catalogue he trotted out for us, but they were so universal, true of so many people, that we paid no attention to them. What were we supposed to do? For instance, he wanted to be convicted because he took part in the war, and could swear that he had shared responsibility for the deaths of two or three enemy soldiers. What sort of law were we supposed to apply in that case? We dismissed it as a soldier's duty to obey an order. Yes, that's right, this time he did give us something specific and concrete, something we'd decided to pursue because he'd managed to find a witness for the prosecution, Adam Kuhl.

Yes, I'll have another glass, but just half a one, please. Thanks. So picture it, the large magistrate's hearing room, Father eager and happy in the dock, to his right Adam Kuhl in what is serving as the witness-box, the sham judge before them. I should point out that he wasn't at all disturbed to see me as the assistant attorney. I thought all along he would be satisfied with a district attorney. And then, after the questions about his personal background, came the charges. Father nodded vigorously and approvingly as Olaf accused him of having played into the hands of those in power at the time. And he looked over at Adam Kuhl, encouraging him to confirm the charge. I'm coming to that, Christine. Olaf recalled the final weeks of the war, when everything was obviously lost, and there was only one thing to do, save yourself and others. Of course that wasn't how it was seen by those whose power was coming to an end. They demanded a final uprising, a final resistance, a final draft. Adam Kuhl was to be part of this final round of the draft, to be called the Volkssturm. But Adam Kuhl didn't want to go. He couldn't see the point in running risks at the last minute, and in order to avoid the draft he had to pretend. What? That's what I'm going to tell you. He claimed his vision was getting worse every day. He said that he not only had trouble telling people apart, he could hardly even recognize them, and therefore he wanted to be declared unfit for service.

The malingerer was sent to a doctor, the public health officer, who was supposed to confirm the disability officially. Of course that's how it turned out, Christine, Father was one of the last doctors still around. All the others were gone. So anyway, Adam Kuhl appeared before Father, who examined him and pretended to believe Kuhl's claims, but he did so only in order to gain his confidence. I wanted him to bask in security, Father told our court, because that would make it easier to turn him in. What's that? Just hold on.

First you've got to imagine the scene. Kuhl, the witness for the prosecution, is trying to make everything seem innocuous. He says that things could have been a lot worse, and the main thing is that everything turned out well in the end. At which point the accused gets angry and warns the witness not to trifle with the proceedings. He practically demands that the witness attack him properly, and old Kuhl is forced to admit sadly that Father did all sorts of things: he struck a match in front of the malingerer's eyes, he had him walk through a low doorway, a sure test. At any rate he set a number of traps for him and finally he managed to denounce Adam Kuhl. Father caught him picking up his pension and counting out the money. Kuhl told our court: the doctor finally saw through me and denounced me, as he had to. And Father, jumping up: I could have covered up for the witness. I didn't do it. I denounced him and turned him in. They assigned him to a penal regiment after at first having sentenced him to death.

Christine, you should have seen how the accused, to his own disadvantage, kept correcting the witness. Kuhl actually said at one point that the doctor was only doing his duty. This upset Father so much that he told Adam Kuhl in no uncertain terms that in so blindly fulfilling the one demanded of him, he had failed a much higher duty. No, things weren't over so quickly for Adam Kuhl. His regiment was captured, and he spent more than four years in a prisoner-of-war camp by the Arctic Ocean. The heart disease he brought back with him is no ruse. Father took full responsibility for everything the witness suffered. He declared himself guilty as charged and asked to be convicted, requesting the court to take his other crimes into account in the sentencing as well. You're right, Father was harsher than any prosecuting attorney, and when Günter tried to rise to his defense, Father not only squirmed uncomfortably, but kept interrupting him too. You've never seen the like of it, the way he argued against his own defense attorney! Father had to be warned several times. The enmity with which he stared at Günter from time to time was in no way make-believe. That's the right word, merciless; he was merciless in his struggle to receive the punishment he thought was appropriate. The more critical the matter seemed, the more serious his case appeared, the greater his satisfaction.

That's right, Christine, then the court withdrew to confer. We went into a room next door, smoked, watched Father and Adam Kuhl go to the window and hold a whispered conversation. It looked as if Father was reprimanding his chief prosecution witness. We didn't need to confer. We had given him his trial, and we assumed we'd made him happy.

The verdict? You're as impatient as Father. He couldn't wait to hear the verdict either. You should have seen him jump up from his seat when the court returned, eager to hear the words he thought he'd earned. He practically bent forward to meet them and remained rigid with expectation until we were seated again and Dieter stood up to deliver the verdict. No, it wasn't in writing. Dieter had just jotted down a few notes during the trial, that's all he needed. Father looked hopefully at Adam Kuhl, then at Dieter. He seemed absolutely certain that his guilt had been proved definitively and that the court would now confirm it officially.

Dieter isn't responsible for what happened, certainly not. His verdict was based on convincing arguments. I was even surprised at how detailed it was. He described once again the situation at the end of the war, mentioned the laws pertaining to special groups, as well as military law, and was forced to come to the conclusion that in such a situation malingerers had to be punished. At that point Father had already pricked up his ears and started making his gestures of protest. And when Dieter not only praised Father's actions, but portrayed them in such a way that anyone could understand them, he approached the judge's bench and protested under his breath. What's that? That's right, when the acquittal came, Father lost control. The same man whose self-restraint you've always so admired seized Dieter's hands and demanded to know how he could justify such a verdict. Dieter had determined that during the period in question, Father had not been conscious of any wrongdoing, and therefore had to be acquitted by the court, given the lack of any contrary evidence of course.

And this fellow Adam Kuhl? When the acquittal was announced, he actually went up to Father and congratulated him. Do you know what he said? See, Doctor, that's what I always thought, now we can still be friends. Father? He didn't notice Kuhl's outstretched hand, it seemed he didn't even hear his congratulations. Father fell to his knees and begged the court to change its verdict. I saw he was having trouble breathing. He was so agitated that I called in the court physician, who gave him a shot to calm him down. Like I said, I took him back to the boardinghouse myself.

Is that the doorbell? Don't open it, he may be back already, he may already have new evidence against himself. What do you think? What else? We'd have to acquit him. Even if Olaf, Dieter, and Günter were willing to go through the whole thing a second time, Christine, I'm afraid we'd just have to acquit him again.

THE WAVES OF LAKE BALATON

෫ৡ The swim in Lake Balaton doesn't refresh him either. He crouches down, submerges himself up to his neck, shuts his eyes against the glitter of the shifting, barren emptiness. The lake's too smooth, Judith, he says, the water warms up too fast. The small woman with the freckles pushes off from the sandy bottom, bobs up and down, slaps the surface of the water with her palms, splashing him with spray. Two more buses just arrived, she says, maybe it's them—can you see, Berti? The man stands up, peers over at the new, gray-white hotel among the old trees, and reports, those aren't German buses, Judith.

As he's opening the trunk of his car, his swimsuit still dripping wet, the hotel manager walks by, a stocky man with blue-black hair, muttering softly to himself, whispering words which sound like the fading echo of an argument. The manager has already passed by when he realizes the man in the swimsuit is his West German guest and turns back in a short arc to offer his help. Together they carry the towels, inflatable rubber mattresses, thick bathrobes, cork sandals, a travel-kit, leather bag, and several illustrated magazines down to the beach, beneath the half-shade of an old tree whose roots, exposed by erosion, look edible. He looks like a good day, the hotel manager says, the lake he's nice too. Want a cigarette? the guest asks.

Smoking, stretched out on the rubber mattress, he looks out toward his wife, who turns and makes her way back to the beach against the water's resistance, a sparkling wave parting before the bow of her lean stomach. The near shore blinds him, the distant coastline beyond the

artificial harbor dissolves in a pale carp-blue. Before stepping out of
the water, his wife slips two fingers under the elastic of her swimsuit
and mechanically pulls it further down over her thighs. Just two Aus-
trian buses, he says, while she peels off her suit under the cover of her
sea-green Turkish bathrobe, first unhooking the top, then working the
bottom down and sliding it off onto the sand with her foot. Nobody
can come all the way from Stralsund and expect to arrive on schedule,
she says. It all takes away from our time together, he replies. Now instead of three days to talk we'll really have just two and a half.

The man leafs through a magazine, flips a few pages with his head
up, listening. There's a hill on the tree-lined road along the shore
where almost all the drivers have to shift gears. Irritated, he asks, do
you smell that too? That's the local gasoline, as wretched as their
matches. Don't tell me you can't smell it. You know what the man at
the gas station said when I pointed out the low octane to him? He said,
we won't be able to offer an octane as high as yours until communism
triumphs. Figure that one out, Judith.

In spite of her bathing cap, the fringe of her hair has become wet.
Sighing, she looks in her oval pocket mirror, trying to make her hair
lie flat, to control it, to force it into its accustomed shape, her feet
buried in the warm sand.

Seemingly impatient, he jerks open the leather bag, digs around,
sifts through the contents, and pulls out a packet filled with photographs of various sizes. He doesn't want to look at them, he just wants
to make sure that the ones he cares most about were packed too. One
of them is a photo with turned-up corners, apparently taken from an
album, everything in sepia. Look here, Judith, this is Trudi and me on
what they called a Dutch cart, she must have been about seven back
then. Doesn't she have an old, knowing face? I suppose she won't look
much different now at forty.

She holds the pocket mirror at an angle, no longer looking at herself,
but observing instead the couple standing beside their car, who now
nod to one another in apparent confirmation. Judith realizes that she
has been recognized by a long-legged woman with deep, disapproving
furrows in her forehead. The woman is trying to pull her companion,
a seemingly listless fellow in a polo shirt, along with her to the beach.
He lets himself be dragged along reluctantly, lagging behind, content
to leave the first words to her. Now Judith lowers her mirror, turns to

her husband, who is lying propped up beside her, and says hastily, I'm afraid we have visitors, Berti. And when her husband has finally turned around, it can't be, Berti, do you know who it is? Miss "inner rhythm" herself. Mrs. Schuster-Pirchala, my masseuse from Bremen. Oh, call them over, says Berti.

After greeting one another with a familiarity typical of such meetings abroad, with Judith not hesitating to add the "Doctor" to her husband's name, they move from their spot on the beach to a green outdoor garden table from which the enamel paint is gradually peeling away in strips. It's more pleasant sitting here, Judith says, and we may even be able to get a cup of coffee. Mrs. Schuster-Pirchala, engaged in a peculiarly relaxed battle against the insects, "they prefer me because my blood is so sweet," laughs skeptically. She's been in this country for three weeks now, she knows that not even an angry eye can convince a waiter here to do anything more than he feels like doing. We're on our way home, she says. My husband fulfilled a boyhood dream; he finally got to see the wild horses of Pusta, didn't you Erich?

If they only had color here, says Berti, peeling strips of crumpled enamel from the table and flicking them into the water. Paint can conceal so much, but evidently they've settled once and for all on gray. He leans forward to read the license tag on a bus that is crunching across the gravel parking lot in a complicated maneuver. Are they here? asks Judith, and he replies, another "A." After a moment, casually, as if he thinks he owes an explanation to his compatriots, he adds, we're about to celebrate a reunion—with my sister and her husband. Because there was no other way to do it, we agreed to meet here at Lake Balaton. They're coming on the bus from Stralsund. Isn't that in East Germany? asks Mrs. Schuster-Pirchala, and manages to attract a waiter to the table with a wave of her hand. It turns out he's willing to serve them coffee, but not here by the lake. They'll have to "sit on the terrace in the sun" as he says. The masseuse and her husband feel the need for coffee, they take their leave, they'll surely see each other again at supper. Then one behind the other they walk up the gentle, sun-sprinkled slope to the hotel.

Lying once again on the air mattress, Judith picks up the packet of photographs, spilling out a few smaller packets wrapped in rubber bands. Look out, Berti says, don't get them all mixed up. She takes the rubber band off one series, riffles through them like playing cards, looks closely at one, thumbs on through them, and unexpectedly flips back through them again. I'm going to have a hard time saying *du* to Trudi, she says suddenly. It's easier in a letter, but when she's standing in front of me . . . and it will be even harder with Reimund. The only thing I know about him is that he outfits ships and signs his name in a sloping, narrow hand. You'll see, says Berti, he's a great guy. After all, my sister gave up her studies and became a kindergarten teacher for him. But why in all these years has he never done more than sign his name to a letter, the woman asks softly, and carefully assembles a selection of photos, as if by comparing them she might gain the information she needs. She compares them with each other, uncovering new ones, shoving others together, and then she asks, have you ever noticed that over the years Trudi's never sent us a single picture where she's smiling? Does she have to smile? asks the man, and the woman replies, talking her way through them, not here in the garden, not in front of the lighthouse—I take it this is a lighthouse with that round green cap—not even here on the steamer, which I assume Reimund fitted out. I don't know, Berti, I feel like we're meeting foreign relations. The ever-present, vague suffering in Trudi's face does not escape her, the slightly defensive look she has each time she's being photographed. The man shuts his magazine, taps a cigarette from the pack, grins to himself, and says, next you'll be concluding that Reimund doesn't own a tie, since he's not wearing one in any of the pictures. If you're going to be that way about it, says Judith, I think your sister's husband looks disguised in all these photographs: an intellectual who's fallen among the proletariat and is trying to dress like them. That's enough now, says Dr. Thape, I'd rather know what's written on the stone plaques in front of these trees, the freshly planted ones. I can tell you that, Berti, it's the names and occupations of the people who have been asked to plant the trees: poets, cosmonauts, Politburo members on their way through. None of your colleagues, no patent attorneys.

An old-fashioned excursion steamer, sprinkled with faded rust spots, pushes off from the pier and leaves amidst a volley of self-important blasts from the steam-whistle by its smokestack.

Judith is startled when the band begins to play. The musicians have taken their places in the wooden bandstand shell behind the trees and are playing for an "open air dance." They start with "Blue Moon." The couples glide decorously across the round wooden dance floor.

Take a look at the men, Judith says, every one of them with an open collar like your brother-in-law Reimund. Do you think he dances too? My God, Judith, how should I know? I know as little about him as you do, just his signature and the little flourish he always adds at the end of his name. And we haven't come here to dance anyway. Irritated, he adds, you'll see, the first day will go by without a chance to talk. Then we'll only have two days left, because by Monday evening . . . you'll have to be in Vienna, Judith finishes his sentence. After thirteen years, he says, a lot of things build up that need to be talked out.

Although she would like to remain lying in the shifting shadows of the old tree, she helps him carry the beach gear to the car and accompanies him to the reception desk in the spacious, expensively furnished hotel lobby. The young women in close-fitting blue uniforms, selected not just for their linguistic abilities and beauty, but apparently for the particularly impressive lethargy with which they move as well, spend a good deal of time exchanging glances to decide who should wait on the West German guest. Listen, says Dr. Thape, I'd like to ask a favor: in case the bus from Stralsund arrives, would you please let us know? We'll be in our room. The young woman gives a cautious nod. On the stairs, Judith says, you do realize she didn't even ask for our room number?

She rinses her bathing suit, wrings it out, and hangs it beneath the window to dry. She positions herself so that she can look out across the small, lively harbor, while her husband pulls an easy chair into a position from which he can observe a stretch of the shore road, recognizable only as a gray-black, shining band, and the driveway up to the hotel. He leafs absent-mindedly through a magazine, turning the pages sharply, so that each time it sounds like the weak but precise crack of a whip. Under the influence of a grievance which is growing steadily, and which he does not as yet wish to name, he feels annoyed about everything; his questions are too filled with implied reproach.

What are you doing there anyway, he asks, although his wife has been sitting perfectly still, almost without moving. I'm puzzled by Trudi, says Judith. When she holds her head at an angle, it's almost impossible to see the scar on her cheek. But she seems to insist on turning it toward the photographer, every time. That's Trudi for you, says the man, she doesn't want to leave anyone in doubt about her. What do you think she said the first time she told us about Reimund? It was a few days before I left, while Mother was still alive. We were sitting listening to the radio, because Mother enjoyed that so, folksongs from the East mostly. Then Trudi came in, much later than normal for her. She had met Reimund. She said something like, I'm sorry I'm so late, I met a man named Reimund, he spent two years in prison for misuse of public property, ship material, since then he's been rehabilitated, a man you can talk to. That's funny, says Judith, in the photos he doesn't look at all like someone you could talk to. Just see how somber your brother-in-law is here, how silent and grim, here, by the garden fence, and the way his eyebrows grow together. Now hold on a minute, Judith, what sort of an impression would I have of you if I had to rely on those pictures you wouldn't even allow to be developed? At least you couldn't say I looked like a communist. Is that what you think he looks like, asks the man, and then almost accusingly, what does a communist look like then? If you know, you're the only one who does.

He shoves the magazines away with a flick of his wrist; they skid across the table and fall to the floor. Come on, Judith, let's go have a drink. They go down to the restaurant, are attracted to the heavy flowerpots near a column, while a young waiter follows them lazily. They have barely seated themselves when he asks in a confidential tone, as if offering them some new experience, whiskey? Would you like two whiskeys? Dr. Thape orders a bottle of wine, and adds, something from the nearest vineyard. Oh, Berti, look there! Those two again? Miss "inner rhythm"—and how she's got herself up! Mrs. Schuster-Pirchala and her husband enter the restaurant. She's in a pink evening suit with a belt of overlapping gold leaves; her husband, a head shorter than she, wears white trousers with a wine-red club jacket, embroidered near the heart with a huge coat of arms. Let's hope they don't see us, says Judith. But it's too late, the masseuse wriggles her fingers in a joyful sign of recognition and prods her indifferent husband in the appropriate direction, toward the flowerpots. I hope you don't mind if we join you.

Mr. Schuster or Pirchala stares into his wineglass with such concentration that it seems he's looking at something that occupies his entire attention, and he's still doing so, almost as if he's in pain, when the three Gypsy musicians next pass their table. The masseuse smiles at them, slides a worn banknote under the fiddler's sash, and is granted her choice of a tune. All these people, my dear doctor, she says later, have retained their inner rhythm, and that's what counts. That's why they're able to wring joy even from communism. She looks annoyedly at her husband, who is sitting there slumped down in bad posture. The coat of arms reminds Judith of a hunter's target: here's an excellent spot for a shoulder shot. Erich sits up, straightens the small of his back, and smiles resignedly. In a moment she'll be asking him to say something about the inner rhythm of the men who tend the wild horses of Pusta, with whom they sat by campfires singing and drinking coffee. Suddenly Dr. Thape jumps up and cries out, that must be them, Judith, it's them!

He hurries with rolling shoulders to the entrance, where the flow of a new regiment of guests has backed up. Red, tired faces regard the restaurant with a mixture of skepticism and curiosity, a milieu to which they are now condemned, one they will have to get used to. They hesitate for a long time, not daring to sit down at empty tables of their own accord, since no maitre d' or tour guide has shown up to tell them where to sit. There they are, Judith says quietly, my sister-in-law and her husband. And the masseuse asks, how long has it been since you've seen one another, Mrs. Thape? Actually we've never seen one another, except in photographs, it's our first time. The woman in the old-fashioned hat? asks Mrs. Schuster-Pirchala. Beside the man with the open collar, Judith confirms.

Dr. Thape embraces his sister warmly, almost like a wrestler about to try a new throw, and then embraces more circumspectly his brother-in-law, who seems to stiffen slightly, as if to say with a good-natured smile, if we must; I hope things go well.

Judith stands awaiting the relatives at the table. She takes both of Trudi's hands in greeting and lightly grazes her cheek. Reimund in his open collar receives a limp handshake. And these, Judith says with sweet sourness, are people from Bremen we know quite well, whom we've met here by chance, Mr. and Mrs. Schuster-Pirchala. They shake hands across the table. Now, how shall we do this, says Dr. Thape, hoping that the inner rhythm of the Bremen contingent will lead them to withdraw, we only have five chairs here. Pull up one from the next table, says the masseuse, and turns her most open-hearted smile, for no visible reason, on Reimund. You must be thirsty, says Judith, and hungry too, you must be exhausted after such a long trip. Berti, look after them right away. It's all right, says Trudi, it was just a little hot toward the end. Trudi takes off her hat, shakes out her hair, pulls her wrinkled dress over her knees, and gives a small wave to an older couple who are apparently traveling with their group. Well, she says, so here we are, a little late, but that wasn't our fault. What do you say, Reimund, asks Dr. Thape, what would you like to take the edge off your thirst? We always have the same thing, says Reimund, a beer for Trudi and two beers for me, sweet and simple. He inspects the woman he doesn't know, her gold-leaf belt, her purse shot through with golden thread. He senses that she wants to win the right to a question with her smile, and to stop her, he asks, are you staying long in Hungary? We're on our way home, says Mrs. Schuster-Pirchala, and then continues, without being asked, to tell how her husband managed to fulfill a boyhood dream.

Dr. Thape is not at all pleased that the first taste of their reunion is tainted by the presence of this outside couple. He urges his wife to do something by repeated surreptitious signals, to which she answers only with an irresolute shrug of her shoulders. At any rate it is clear to her that her husband holds her responsible for the unwelcome presence of these people, and since there's nothing she can do about it now, she turns away and looks toward Trudi. I hear you come from the D.D.R., says Mrs. Schuster-Pirchala, how are things in East Germany these days, in general? Reimund, at a loss, looks over at Trudi, who tactfully runs her outstretched forefinger down the side of her beer glass, and then he says, from the way you ask, I gather you'd like to know if we still have almond cake; I can personally attest to the fact that we do. I'm afraid, Dr. Thape says impatiently, that if we order something to eat now, we really won't have enough room for six people at the table. Let's just scoot closer together then, says the masseuse, my husband and I will only be ordering vegetarian plates, so we'll hardly take up any room at all. Reimund and I can go over and join the group we traveled with while we eat, says Trudi. What you do think, Berti? It looks like it might come to that, says Berti, ill-temperedly signaling the waiter to take their order.

And how is Father? Dr. Thape asks across the table. Trudi looks at her brother for a long time, as if this is an unusually difficult question for her to answer. I don't know, she says quietly. Sometimes I have the feeling that he's aged greatly, but at other times—particularly from some of the stands he takes—he seems to be getting younger. He sends his greetings. The conversation pauses, and Mrs. Schuster-Pirchala says, that's typical of a lot of older men, at a certain stage they begin to pay almost exaggerated attention to how they stand. He's taken up Mother's main enthusiasm, says Reimund, you've never seen anyone so taken with listening to the radio. We have to turn it off after he falls asleep.

The waiter has made a mistake. He's brought five carp soups, although only four people ordered it. He looks worriedly at the extra bowl, on the steaming surface of which a smoothly rounded fishbone gleams. You can just take that back to the kitchen, my good man, says Mrs. Schuster-Pirchala, upon which Judith declares tersely, leave it here, I'll eat it. You can give it to me, says Dr. Thape, Trudi can tell you that I've loved soup ever since I was a boy, isn't that right Trudi? I gather you don't care for soup, Mr. Schuster-Chinchilla? asks Dr. Thape, and the man in the wine-red jacket stiffens and says with a smile, I had enough soup in the army to last me a lifetime. By the way, my name is just Schuster. But you won't mind if we enjoy our soup in front of you I hope, asks Dr. Thape, controlling his animosity with an effort. Go right ahead, says Mr. Schuster, motioning for them to start, go right ahead, it doesn't bother me at all. The masseuse gives a signal to the fiddler, the man nods, he understands. But before his group arrives, swaying and bending, she asks, things are getting better there as far as goods for the people go, aren't they? I mean in the D.D.R. Trudi acts as if she didn't hear the question, and Reimund spoons up his carp soup with carefully portrayed pleasure. It's not until the masseuse says, we hear that things get a little tight there from time to time, that Reimund replies, it's going to get a little tight right here at the table by the time the main course arrives. Well we certainly won't be crowding you, says Mrs. Schuster-Pirchala, we're just having a teeny-weeny vegetarian plate. For God's sake, says Dr. Thape, I feel a breeze here. What do you say, Judith, shall we move to another table? The big table in the corner is free, says Mrs. Schuster-Pirchala, it'll seat eight people easily.

Trudi smiles, bows her head patiently, opens her purse, finds the old, pale-green case immediately, and has Mr. Schuster pass it on to her brother. Father sent this for you, she says, he insisted on it. Looks like a watch to me, Mrs. Schuster-Pirchala observes, and now they all look on while Dr. Thape opens the case and lifts out a pocketwatch.

What did I tell you, says the masseuse, probably hasn't been wound either. Trudi watches her brother's reaction closely, sees how surprised and touched he is, and his restrained joy in front of them. She adds by way of apology, that's all, we didn't bring anything else for you, we didn't presume to bring anything else after Judith's letter. What do you mean, says Judith, what letter? You wrote once that you had everything you needed and that we shouldn't send you anything, Trudi says quietly. You thought the things we had—no, you didn't say they were of poor quality, but we don't want to talk about that now. The watch is running, says Dr. Thape, it's running fine, and the chain is thin enough to slip right through my buttonhole. The musicians abruptly begin playing behind him, and he jumps as if he has received a surprise injection, shuts his eyes in torment, and holds his hands over both ears as if to protect them. Reimund says something to him, but he doesn't hear it.

A carp head with an insulted expression lies abandoned in Reimund's bowl, and, to Trudi's entertainment, he sticks a toothpick in its mouth, tips his head at an angle, and announces, hygiene, the first step on the road to revolution. We shouldn't overdo hygiene, says Mrs. Schuster-Pirchala, most people don't realize how vitally important the body's flora are. At this Dr. Thape squeezes the watchcase convulsively, leans back, and says in a threatening undertone to the masseuse, you seem to have something to say about everything. Mrs. Schuster-Pirchala is startled, she looks at her husband disconcertedly. She says, I don't know what you're getting so upset about, hygiene really is . . . Dr. Thape interrupts her irritatedly, brushes Judith's hand from his forearm, taps the watchcase on the table, and says in a strained voice, you might as well know once and for all that I haven't come all the way from Bremen to hear your views on the body's flora. In case you haven't noticed, I've come, we've come, for a reunion after a long separation. A family gathering if that's all right with you. Berti, says Judith, drawing it out soothingly, and Mrs. Schuster-Pirchala, protesting almost painfully, I've never ever been attacked like that, out of a clear blue sky! We were having such a good time, and all at once you come at me like that! It's looks like we're in the way here, Erich. Let's go. Please, says Judith trying to smooth things over, my husband didn't mean it that way, not like it sounded anyway, did you, Berti? Mrs. Schuster-Pirchala, grimly preparing to depart: that's all we need, to be told we're not wanted, that we're disturbing a family gathering, are you ready Erich? The acquaintances from Bremen leave without saying goodbye and look for a table as far away as possible. Forgive me, says Dr. Thape, but I just couldn't stand it anymore. You were too rough, says Judith, you could have let them know more gently. But I tried, says Berti angrily, I kept trying to let your masseuse know that someone was out of place here. Stop quarreling kids, says Reimund, licking his lips in a show of anticipation, here comes the main dish, an original Hungarian shepherd's goulash.

Now Dr. Thape lifts his head, his face gleaming with perspiration, and looks straight at Trudi, lifting his glass to her. Now that we're by ourselves, he says, I'd like to drink to our reunion again. The waiter interrupts him shyly, asking what he should do with the two vegetarian plates. Not eat here? he asks, and Dr. Thape replies brusquely, over there, see, at the table by the entrance—they're waiting for the stuff. Good food and music, says Reimund in drawn-out pleasure, as long as they have those, Hungary's always worth a trip.

Judith excuses herself to go to the powder room. She has to pass by the table at which the couple from Bremen are now sitting before their vegetarian plates. Trudi watches her sister-in-law approach the table and say something quickly to them, probably trying to patch things up. You know, Berti says, I've looked forward to this reunion for so long that I was already counting the hours you were late. And then these interlopers push their way in. Prague was the problem, says Reimund, the reason we were so late was that a young girl acted up during a stopover in Prague—you know. She met some thoughtless West German there who presumably wanted to bring her out, that's what they said on the bus. But you can understand why, says Berti, and Reimund, shrugging his shoulders, I don't know. For example, says Trudi, Father still can't understand why you left back then. He says you abandoned us. Berti tries to reply, but the Gypsy band at the next table, playing with well-rehearsed enthusiasm, soon proves more than a match for his voice, and he waves his hand in resignation.

Everyone takes plum brandy with their coffee here. Even Judith lets herself be talked into it. She's settled into an all too polite silence, although she seems to be pleasantly surprised by Reimund. Now, Trudi, take your time and tell me all about it—how are things at home? Trudi looks at her brother, lifts her shoulders, at a loss, prevented either by the wealth or banality of the possibilities from selecting quickly from her experience. Well, Berti, what can I say? The house is still standing, Father's in good health, for the past few years a teacher from Riga, a friendly old woman who never raises the blinds, has been living in your room. Reimund holds his empty glass up to the waiter for a refill. Then he strokes Trudi's scarred cheek happily and begs her pardon for having interrupted. Now if I had to answer a general question like that, he says, I'd start with the things that count. To the question, how's it going? I'd just say, we can't get replacement parts. And then substantiate that in detail. We've been waiting for a year and a half for a new gutter for the house, and seventeen weeks for a bathroom water faucet. Four months ago I was promised primer—you know, to paint the outside of the house, and I've been waiting so long for an extension ladder that I'm ready to build one myself. That gives you enough to go on, enough to congratulate yourself on having made the right choice about where to spend your time. Well, Berti says, on the other hand you do have much lower rents.

They decide, or, more precisely, Dr. Thape suggests, that they should go up to their room. We can talk more easily there. No one will disturb us, and we'll be all to ourselves. That is, if you can be away from your group that long, Trudi. He picks up the bill, asks for a receipt, and leaves an usually large tip to encourage the waiter to bring two bottles of wine up to the room. Berti takes Trudi's arm, Reimund does the same with Judith, and they stroll along the rows of tables toward the exit. The couple from Bremen deliberately turn their backs to them.

Look, Trudi, says Reimund, not only is this room twice as big as ours, but it also has a desk, a balcony, and easy chairs for guests. Why don't our socialist friends treat us this well? He discovers the bathing suit under the window and says, I see you've already been in Lake Balaton. It's a strange lake, you know why? There's no other body of water in the world in which the relation between the waves and the wind is so disproportionate. The waves are much higher than you would expect given the average strength of the wind.

Judith lets the suitcase fall closed behind her and steps before them with two small packages in their original boxes. She says: we've brought you gifts, just little things. This is for you, Reimund, and the square one is for Trudi. As they shake their heads in disapproval,

Berti says, we just had to do it. The sight of the massive white-gold cufflinks moves Reimund to say, well, Trudi, now you'll have to buy me a shirt I can wear with them. But his wife doesn't turn to him, she's staring motionless at the bracelet with the inlaid watch and sparkling gems, as if she's thinking what possible justification there could be for her to accept such a gift. Oh, Berti, I don't know what to say.

All three lamps in the room are on. Berti passes the photographs around, and Judith explains to her brother-in-law the location and type of house they have in a Bremen suburb. And you have to remember that less than twenty years ago this was all just pastureland. It's wonderful to sit out on the terrace evenings and watch the lighted ships pass by on the Weser, so close you'd think they were gliding across the meadows. Some of them, says Berti, may even be ships you've outfitted. Then he shows their relatives a new series of photos. Here you can see the inside of the house, my workshop, the southern exposure in the living room, Judith's bedroom and her own private room beyond it. And you have workers to do all that, don't you, asks Reimund. Judith does it, Berti says, she hangs wallpaper, paints, builds bookcases—the electrical system's the only thing she doesn't trust herself with. That's just what Trudi does at our place, Reimund says. While Judith is pouring wine, she says, now you've got to show us your pictures, and Trudi replies, pictures? We didn't bring any pictures along.

Judith regards her sister-in-law over her glass, searching, surprised, trying perhaps to figure out what forces her to admit Trudi's superiority. She examines her clothes: the buckle shoes, the olive dress, wrinkled by the trip, the pendant on her lapel, with what seems to be a Hanseatic schooner in full sail. Suddenly she says something completely different from what she originally intended to say. I'm glad you liked the things we sent you from time to time, Trudi—even if they were used. They were nice things, Trudi says, things we had a hard time getting, even the Red Cross was amazed.

Reimund has no objection to Berti's ordering another bottle of wine. He signals his agreement with a why-not gesture, and follows up on a previous remark. You're mistaken there—no one today, anywhere, can choose pure freedom, just a bureaucracy that's more or less easy to get along with. The bureaucracy that decides which replacement parts you're going to get, what chance you have to move up the ladder, how many organizations you have to belong to in order to earn their trust. I tell you, give us a better bureaucracy and exports will rise under socialism. And I tell you, Reimund, even after five generations people will never stop longing for the important small freedoms socialism denies them. But we're not out to convince one another, so let's leave politics out of it.

The waiter doesn't seem to understand the scolding Dr. Thape gives him for delivering the new bottle so listlessly. He dismisses him without a look, his head lowered, and without handing him a tip. Still in a bad mood, he asks Judith whether she has the flash ready. If it's all right with you, he says, we'd like to take a few pictures. Individually, in couples, switching around, they photograph one another in the room. The sudden glare of the flash is so strong that Judith is worried she'll have her eyes closed in every picture. Afterward Dr. Thape says, at least we've got those. And then, just to know, he asks how long Trudi and Reimund are going to stay in Hungary. Two weeks? Unfortunately, he says, I have to be back in Vienna again by Monday evening.

They toast each other. And now, Trudi, says Dr. Thape, tell me what little Sonja is doing, the champion swimmer, and Ralf, and Bruno next door. Trudi smiles. Sonja? she asks—her youngest daughter holds all the records for the backstroke. Sonja married Bruno, who, as far as I know, became a judge. And Ralf—he drowned trying to cross the Baltic in a canoe. Bruno a judge? Dr. Thape asks skeptically, and Trudi replies, why not? Why shouldn't he be? Oh well, says Berti, we were together in school, and I spent a lot of time at his house. His father was always in trouble with the police. Sure, says Trudi, but his father had those troubles at the right time.

Reimund yawns, reaches for his jacket with the coarse herringbone pattern. That's how it is, he says, the color of things rubs off on us, objects, ideas, conditions, one way or another, each according to where he lives. He begs their pardon for having yawned and reminds them that he and Trudi sat in a hot bus for nine hours today. He lifts his collar above his jacket with self-assurance and smooths it flat. Dear, dear Reimund, I don't entirely agree with you, says Berti, maybe conditions rub off on those who are pale, or colorless, but not on people who, so to speak, have their own primary color all along.

In the hall outside they discuss with lowered voices when to meet for breakfast. Reimund holds out for nine o'clock, warning them that he's totally useless before nine, so they leave it at that, shake hands, and wave one last time.

Berti smokes his last cigarette in tense silence as he undresses. Judith sits on her side of the double bed, looking forward as always to a joint summation of the past day, or at least its most important events. After a while she says, one thing for sure, I can't show myself at Mrs. Schuster-Pirchala's again, after all that's happened. Pichalla or Chinchilla, Berti says relieved, and pausing for a moment, you'll find ten others to work you over. But why did she have to wind up here of all places, a woman with the sensitivity of a steamroller? I still think you should have handled her differently, says Judith. Differently? A woman who pushes her way into a family reunion? Who immediately starts talking and blathers on as if she belongs there? Maybe she has relatives herself over there, says Judith. I just can't understand, Berti says, how you can stick up for that pink pain in the neck, she ruined my mood for the whole evening. You were the one who said to call them over, says Judith, when I saw them by the lake.

They lie side by side in bed, as if carefully placed there, right hands behind their heads, staring at the ceiling, with only the night light on. The fact is, says Judith, I just can't get close to Trudi. And you heard how she let me know, merely in passing, that she gave away all the things I sent her—sometimes without your knowledge—that she just gave them all to the Red Cross? That can't be, says Berti, I didn't get that at all. That's typical of Trudi, but we'll have a word about that tomorrow. You'll have to take her watch down to her at breakfast, she promptly forgot her gift, even though Reimund didn't forget his. I like Reimund, Judith says slowly, what about you? —He never even asked me what I do, says Berti.

Dr. Thape in a flowered sports shirt, and Judith in faded but ironed shorts, descend the stairs, murmuring greetings, veering to the reception desk where recent newspapers and magazines lie, prior to entering the restaurant. A laughing youth in a roomy porter's uniform, seemingly unaware of the impression he makes in it, hands Dr. Thape a letter. Judith looks over from the postcard stand and sees her husband tearing open the envelope. He reads the letter, lets it sink, reads it again, and then looks around for her in bewilderment. She comes over to him and asks, is it from Vienna, do we have to leave? It's from

Trudi, he says, here, read it, you won't believe it. Upset and contemptuous at the same time, he says, they were given a chance, early this morning, their only chance, to see the last wild horses of Pusta. Just an excursion they say, but unfortunately they won't be back till Monday evening. Judith reads the letter, then slowly lifts her head and says, it's just an excuse, Berti, nothing but an excuse. Something went wrong, I don't know what happened, but something went wrong. Come on, let's go into the restaurant, and we can talk it over while we're having breakfast.

THE END OF A WAR

⋙ As our minesweeper glided through the straits at reduced speed, they merely glanced at us and turned away. They looked up from their fishingboats, from their lighters, from the rotting wooden docks, quickly and indifferently, or so it seemed, and then immediately turned aside and continued stacking their crates of cod and mackerel, scrubbing their decks, spreading their nets, or ducking their heads to light their last shreds of tobacco. They had a way of looking right through us when we passed them on the crooked streets of the little harbor town, and now they noted our departure with an equal lack of interest, exchanging no gestures, making no comments, paying no particular attention. Occasionally they even turned their backs to us as we glided past, our forward gun uncovered, just working harder, almost embitteredly. They seemed to have already accustomed themselves to the MX 12, a gray minesweeper. They put up with the commanding silhouette before the whitewashed, boxy building of the harbor commandant by ignoring it—as did most of those in that quiet Danish harbor where we were stationed during the final months of the war.

The shore receded, the straits widened, the sea gulls hovered over the afterdeck in the weak breeze, as always. We passed the jetty, the white laquered lighthouse gleaming in the sun, and the crumbling fortress in which a deranged king once spent his final years. The gentle wake from our bow lapped upon the stones, lifted the little boats tied there, and set them rocking. None of our guns was manned.

Further out at sea, presumably protected in the lee of the islands,

196

a homeless armada lay at anchor: old freighters, repair ships, tugs, and barges. They had fled from the harbors now lost in the east, and had managed to save themselves by heading west on their last reserves of oil and coal, one by one, or in slow-moving convoys, crossing a dangerous Baltic Sea sprinkled with floating debris. They had been lying for weeks in holding positions, but they had not received permission to enter any of the few remaining harbors, whose docks were filled with warships.

The wind didn't pick up, and a fine haze lay over the sea as we passed the immense wreck of a former troop transport ship which lay grounded, tilting only slightly, at the very edge of the channel. The gentle surf washed across the rusty platforms of the antiaircraft guns, broke high upon the superstructure in slaps of spray, fell back, and flowed away in foaming rivulets. Sea gulls, lined up like a coded signal, sat upon the spars, casting themselves off from time to time, one by one, in brief wheeling flight, only to return quickly to their perches. We continued at reduced speed.

The commander called a few of us to the bridge. Looking out to sea as if lost in thought, he informed us of our mission, speaking now loudly, now softly, at times falling into dialect. Our orders were to head for Courland where a division of the army was cut off but still fighting, having dug in with their backs to the Baltic Sea, although all was lost. We're going to Libau, the commander said. We'll take wounded on board in the harbor and transport them to Kiel. Fleet commander's orders. He buttoned the jacket of his uniform over his turtleneck sweater, cast a glance at the chief quartermaster, and stood there a while as if expecting something, a question or a protest, but neither the quartermaster nor anyone else said a word. They simply waited in stubborn silence, as if demanding some further commentary on this news. The commander gave the order to man the double-barreled guns.

Standing at the helm, I heard them discussing what course to take. Since the ports in Pomerania and East Prussia had been lost, there was no longer any escort to the east we could join. We would have to try and make it on our own, staying far away from the coast in order to avoid being spotted by their planes. The commander favored a northeast course, past Swedish Gotland. He suggested that we continue traveling in Swedish territorial waters so that when we headed back southeast we would be crossing the Baltic Sea by night. We'll never make it, Tim, the quartermaster said. The commander replied, hesitantly, and as always, a bit dismissively: I've never been in Libau, this may be my last chance. They both came from the same little town in Friesland. Before the war they ran fish trawlers, and both were captains.

We were moving along at marching speed on a course that the commander had settled upon and marked out himself. The sea was rippling. A torpedo boat passed us at high speed. Through the glass we could see bandaged soldiers in all the gangways. In the end, the commander said, they're all used as hospital ships. The sky was clear; condensation trails dissolved high above us. Two empty rubber dinghies floated on the water, wobbling in our wake. The radioman brought an emergency call to the bridge from a sinking ship, a large yacht named the *Cap Beliza*. She'd hit a mine. Bending over the chart, the commander announced the location of the accident. We couldn't go to help them. We were too far away. It's crazy, Tim, the quartermaster said, we'll never make it through to Libau. They exchanged tobacco silently, filled their pipes, and lit them simultaneously. Their planes and submarines are clearing out everything east of Bornholm, the quartermaster said. We have our orders, said the commander, they're waiting for us in Courland.

We stopped. The life raft floated along the ship's side, a line was thrown down, and one of the two barefoot soldiers caught it and tied it around a wooden crossbar. They had no weapons, and their possessions were wrapped in a section of canvas tent that they wanted lifted on board before they left the raft themselves. They needed help as they tried to climb the steps that had been lowered over the side, and they had to be supported on their way to the cabins. We had just started up again when several planes flew in from the west, low over the water. They came at us as if flung from the horizon, and their gleaming propellers seemed to revolve and then reverse themselves in a slow whir as they do in films. Our alarm horn was still blaring and croaking as the bullets began to strike the water, throwing up violent fountains, sawing their way across our deck, across the bridge, and the forward portion of the ship, flinging one man forward into the tip of the bridge. Our double-barreled guns swung around and fired tracer bullets whose lines of flight sailed off above the planes. They only came by once. The dead signalman was tied up in a sailcloth—not sewn in, but only tied—and, loaded down with two weights, dropped over the stern into the sea.

The quartermaster talked with the two barefoot soldiers. They were military staff members who had left a Pomeranian harbor on board an armed tugboat. During the night the tug had rammed a tanker. They couldn't believe we were on our way to Courland. Their faces were filled with fear. The one who spoke for both of them asked to be set down anywhere on land. They stuck closely together. They were told that since we wouldn't be stopping at any harbors on the way, they would have to remain on board for the whole trip. The one who spoke for both of them said softly, as if to himself: but things are coming to an end, they may already be over.

Even though the lookout was intensified, nothing could be seen. We were running on a northeast course, passing through occasional patches of light fog, weakly penetrated by the sun. The sea remained calm. Almost no wind. Drifting colonies of jellyfish, moving in rhythmic contractions, gave the water a milky sheen. When we plowed through them the water gleamed in thousands of points at the sides of the ship. Once we sighted a flat streamer of smoke with no apparent source on the horizon. Silence, space, emptiness. It seemed as if we were traveling through an unendangered zone, through an expanse which had been spared—at least momentarily. We traveled on full alert. The men sat or stood together at their battle stations, engaged in interminable discussions.

The radioman carried the rumor to the bridge himself. He didn't come right out with it. First he told about the rescue operations underway for the *Cap Beliza*. Four ships, including two destroyers, were at her side. He studied the sprawling charts and calculated our course, then stood smoking for a while in the tip of the bridge. It wasn't until he was about to leave, as he was turning around, that he said, something's going on. Something's in the air for sure. What do you mean? asked the quartermaster. Capitulation, said the radioman. Unless I'm wrong, we're about to surrender.

Ahead to starboard a massive white ship appeared above the line of the horizon. It was a Swedish passenger steamer, blue and yellow on the sides and both smokestacks, running at full speed and self-confidently, under the protection of neutrality. Passengers lay about on the sun deck on lounge chairs, presumably wrapped in camel's-hair blankets, and couples strolled on deck or lounged against the railings, while stewards bearing trays anticipated their every wish.

It wasn't easy keeping my eyes straight ahead, staring out over the helm, as they started to talk again behind me, the quartermaster asking, what will we do, Tim, if it happens? And the commander replied after a pause, don't rack your brains over it, the fleet won't forget us.

"And if we lose contact with them?"

"We know our mission."

"We have more than one mission."

"What do you mean?"

"The ship. The crew. It's over, Tim. They're in Berlin . . . We'll never make it to Courland. Why do you want to risk everything?"

"What do you suggest?"

"Let's head for Kiel. Or toward Flensburg. Returning safely is part of our mission too. The ultimate mission."

"I'm thinking about those poor dogs. They say the whole tongue of land across the bay in Libau is covered with them. Wounded and taken prisoner. Think what it would be like to be wounded and in prison. Ivan's prison."

"If we had any chance at all . . . You know me, Tim. But I'm telling you we couldn't get a single one out. We'll all be in the creek before the coast's in sight. That's what a lot of us think . . ."

"Who are you talking about?"

"The crew. Word's getting around that it's almost over."

"We have to risk it."

"The men think otherwise."

"And you, Bertram?"

"Take them home. That's all I can say, take them home."

The forecastle was filled with off-duty men. Here and there they were playing cards, or one would be lying asleep across a table. Beneath the portholes they were carrying on cautious but agitated conversations; beside the lockers they chewed their lumpy bread and drippings and drank their coffee from aluminum cups. It smelled like oil and paint. A newcomer, a very young fellow in leather overalls, sat alone reading. He read, then closed his eyes and leaned back, both palms upon the stained and spotted book.

Now, in a quiet moment, the vibrations of the ship could be felt everywhere. Suddenly the radioman opened the bulkhead door, stepped slowly inside, and stood motionless. He looked past us, as if he were listening, not to us, and not to the suppressed voices beneath the port-hole, but to some distant signal, a rustling in the air that left him at a loss, not unhappy or in despair, but simply at a loss, and because he stood so still, all attention was soon focused upon him. What's up? cried one. Friedeburg's signed, he said quietly, at Lüneburg, Fleet Admiral von Friedeburg: we've surrended. And then he spoke firmly into the silence: we've surrendered along the entire British front, and in Holland, and here in Denmark. He accepted a cigarette and said, at Montgomery's headquarters in Lüneburg. Then he scanned our faces, urgently, demandingly, asking that we see what this meant, but none of us dared to speak. No one moved. For a long while we just sat there numbly, as if riveted to the spot. The first person to react visibly was Jellinek, our oldest gunner. It was a common rumor aboard the MX 12 that he had been twice demoted during his long career. He pushed off quietly from the bulkhead, walked up to his locker, pulled a bottle of rum from beneath his woolens, and held it up, offering it around. No one joined him, no one reached for his own bottle, everyone turned to look again at the radioman as if he still had something to say, as if he were withholding some information that would affect us and the ship directly. Hardly anyone saw the tears in the newcomer's eyes.

The Baltic Sea lay as if dammed up beneath the sunset. Its colors were fading and running, taking on random shapes and forms. Here and there the water foamed, bubbling and boiling, shot through with schools of mackerel. The commander took tea on the bridge. He cupped the bowl of his pipe out of habit while he smoked, to hide the faint glow of the embers. The officer of the watch switched binoculars, exchanging the day glasses for the heavy night ones. He rotated me-chanically at the waist as he scanned the horizon. There was nothing to report. MX 12 was moving along at marching speed through the lingering darkness—an apparently undetectable target in the vast expanse of the sea.

No one slept, or wanted to sleep. The ship was under a blackout. They sat scattered about the forecastle in the dim glare of the emergency lights and listened to the old gunner, who seemed to know what surrender would mean for the MX 12. It's clear enough, he said, it's standard procedure: you stay put until you surrender the ship; you do no damage to the ship, you don't sink it, and you certainly don't undertake any missions. He raised his head and nodded in the direction of the bridge, shrugging his shoulders resignedly, uncomprehendingly, as if to say: they don't seem to have caught on up there, they probably don't realize we have to reverse course and head back to base. Someone said, that'd be something, if we took a hit now, after we've surrendered—at which the newcomer, who had sat brooding for a long time, said in a strained voice, jump in a lifeboat, bail out if you're wetting your pants. You should hear yourselves. It makes me sick.

A tanker lying deep in the water passed by, running westward in the luminous darkness, and before it was astern the submarine alarm sounded on the MX 12. The tanker changed course immediately and steamed away at full speed, while we headed straight for the spot where the watch had sighted the periscope and its glimmering trail. No one on the bridge could figure out what the commander intended by this maneuver, however, since we had no depth charges on board. Perhaps he thought we could ram the submarine, perhaps he only hoped that our attack would give the tanker a chance to get away. At any rate we cruised the area for some time with guns manned, and it was only after a long search that we resumed course again. Let's make up for lost time, said the commander, that's all we can do now, make up as much time as possible.

We've surrendered, Tim, said the quartermaster.

"It's a partial surrender."

"You know what it means though."

"Whether we surrender the ship tomorrow or the day after tomorrow . . . and if we can take just a handful back west . . . that's the only goal left for the naval war command, to bring our men back to the west . . . to get them out of the east . . ."

"Where do you expect to surrender the ship?"

"Where? In Kiel maybe. Or in Flensburg."

"You've made up your mind then?"

"Yes, we'll go to Courland and pick up our men and then head home."

"You know that all missions are canceled."

"This is our last mission."

"They can prosecute us. You. The crew."

"What's the matter with you, Bertram?"

"Listen, Tim. The men are waiting below. They won't go along with it. The risk—it's not worth it. Not after the surrender."

"And what do they want?"

"They want you to reverse course."

"Are you saying this on their behalf?"

"On their behalf. And on behalf of common sense. But talk with them yourself. After all . . . they only want one thing: to go home."

"Do you realize what that means?"

"They're set on it."

"I'm asking if you realize what that means?"

"It's their right. Now that everything is over."

"What you're planning . . . it can backfire . . . Bertram, I'm re-responsible for the ship. I give the orders here."

Before the second watch came on, they occupied the bridge. They climbed the stairs impatiently and resolutely, with heavy tread, seven or eight men apparently set on resistance, or at least on refusing orders. Things hadn't gone as they'd expected, so now they hung their rifles over their shoulders with the barrels pointing downward and surrounded the commander, who continued smoking calmly in the face of their silence. Two of them pushed the executive officer into the chart room. For a moment or two it seemed as if they had lost their courage, or suddenly realized what was at stake in taking this first step. I stood at the helm and felt their discomfort, and their hesitation. But I also felt, in the lengthening silence, a strange and growing embarrassment, caused no doubt by the presence of a deeply ingrained respect for the commander. But then the gunner and the quartermaster stepped forward. They seemed to have agreed upon their roles. They forced themselves through the tightly packed group of men; then the old gunner looked the commander in the eye and stated the crew's demands in relatively mild terms. His opening sentences still sounded hopeful that the commander would recognize the crew's demands, and would grant them, even if reluctantly. He said, you know we stand by you, Mr. Kaleu. Most of us have been on all the missions. Many of us know how much we owe you, even personally. Now it's over. We have only one request—that you give the order to return. The commander looked at them one after the other, surveying the half-circle of dark visages. He didn't seem to feel threatened. He said: man your stations, now. And, since no one moved: man your stations, I said! He didn't sound upset. His voice was as calm as ever, and it remained normal when, after a moment's pause, he stated: you're refusing a direct order.

The gunner said: We just want to reach home safely. Come back with us, Mr. Kaleu.

After a warning which struck some of them as almost friendly—don't get yourselves in trouble, boys—the commander reminded the men that the MX 12 was on a specific mission and explained that he intended to carry out that mission unless the fleet commander changed his orders.

Everyone realized that this was the last chance he could offer the men occupying the bridge. As if to see how many of them had been moved by his appeal, he stepped toward the chart room, apparently to bring out the executive officer. At a gesture from the gunner, two men blocked his way. All right, said the commander, all right then. General refusal to obey orders at sea: that's mutiny. Go to your rooms, said the gunner, you and the executive officer are under arrest for the remainder of the voyage. Listen to me, said the commander, and listen carefully. I'm still in command here. What you're doing is mutiny. Suddenly, in the midst of the tension and uncertainty, we heard the quartermaster say, I'm removing you from command. To preserve the safety of the ship and its crew, I'm taking over command, with all the consequences. I will bear full responsibility. These sentences were stated with such firm formality that I had to turn around to see for myself that it was really the quartermaster who had spoken. The commander and he were facing each other, their bodies practically touching. They paid no attention to the rifle barrels mechanically raised at them.

Unseen, beneath a veiled moon, the MX 12 reversed course in a smooth sea. The foaming arc of our wake soon faded, and a distant observer might have had the impression that our sudden maneuver was the result of a surprise order or momentary whim, or, since we soon were running in the opposite direction at top speed, that we had given in to panic. Everyone who could remained on deck or on the bridge, where it was more crowded than ever before. Men were shoving and pushing past one another, asking questions and talking things over. I was constantly asked what course we were on. Are we heading for Kiel? Yes, for Kiel. It wasn't joy that stirred within them, that made them crowd in a circle around the quartermaster, who sat impassively in a canvas chair, his shoulders slumped. It wasn't joy.

The quartermaster inspected the contents of his tobacco pouch, pulled out a wad of long strands for himself, resealed the pouch, and passed it to the gunner. Addressing him formally, he said: take this to the commander. The gunner smiled. Don't you recognize me, Bertram? I'm your old friend. The quartermaster said nothing, and seemed not to have heard the question. He filled his pipe and tamped it down without looking up, then held it clamped between his teeth, unlit.

"You have nothing to reproach yourself for," said the gunner, "You had to do it."

"The crew should man their stations," said the quartermaster, "all of them. We'll remain on full alert until Kiel. In a few hours it will be light."

"Fine, Bertram, you can count on us."

"Keep the two dogfaces below deck."

"They know we're heading home. They want to come up and thank you."

"They can keep their thanks to themselves."

"Shall I bring you something to eat? Tea? A sandwich?"

"No. I don't need anything."

"There's something else I wanted to say, Bertram. You've seen my record. You know that I was demoted. Both times for refusing to obey orders. And I would do it again . . . yes, I'd do it again . . ."

"Yes, all right."

"You understand what I'm saying. I can only carry out an order if I understand why it's given. If it can be done responsibly. You have to have the right to question things . . ."

"Anything else?"

"You're thinking about the old man, right? Some men can't jump over their own shadow. But maybe he thinks the same way we do about it. To himself, I mean, secretly."

"Take him the tobacco."

At first the lookout reported a vessel ahead to starboard. Slowly the superstructure raised into sight, the silhouette became recognizable, and soon we knew that it was MX 18, our sister ship. It was running on a west-northwest course, presumably toward the islands. As it came into view, it seemed that we were meeting ourselves. We all watched it, waiting, tense and uneasy, and then a light flashed. It was signaling to us, C to C, commander to commander. Our second signalman lifted the blinker onto the railing of the bridge, ready to answer. They were sending the same query over and over, C to C, only that, constantly, insistently, but we gave no answer.

The signalman looked around at the quartermaster several times, afraid he might have missed an instruction, but the quartermaster simply stood there peering over at the other ship without raising his binoculars.

He let our sister ship's inquiry pass without response, and since our radio shack had also been ordered silent for the moment, we escaped any consequences. No doubt they took us for a shiftless lot, and shook their heads more in puzzlement than in anger.

In the pale of early dawn they brought sandwiches and hot coffee up to the bridge. We ate and drank silently, looking out over the gray, quiet sea, above which the first light of day would soon be breaking. It was not perfectly still, and a patient gaze could see a stirring in the deep, gentle waves that rolled in a certain direction for a short time and then expired. The towering clouds above the horizon kept changing shape, gathering and dividing. The gunner brought the tobacco back to the quartermaster. The commander had refused it.

The fleet had not forgotten us. They sent a radio message that threw the quartermaster into a state of temporary uncertainty. Although I didn't read the text myself, I gathered from the drawn-out deliberations I overheard that the fleet had reconfirmed the mission they believed we were on. Not only that, they instructed us to change course slightly and meet a sister ship, MX 21, opposite Gotland, from which point we were to proceed in tandem toward Courland. They asked for our exact position. While our men were still discussing this, trying to figure out how to answer, they received a second radio message telling them to proceed on their own on the mission. MX 21 had sustained engine damage during an air attack and was now drifting, totally disabled. The quartermaster listened quietly to the suggestions made by the radioman and the gunner. Perhaps he didn't even hear them, and was just nodding from time to time, lost in thought, pretending to pay attention. In any case he eventually sent his own text to the fleet. He reported that in order not to endanger the ship and its crew, it had been necessary to change command. MX 12 would proceed to Kiel and await further orders.

We should have reduced speed. The fish trawlers had set out their nets, small, fog-gray trawlers, all making their way together in the early dawn, seemingly held in place by the thick steel hawsers. We came up on them quickly. No one thought of avoiding the crude armada, upon which scarcely a man was to be seen. All of the trawlers were flying the Danish flag. We ran among them at full speed, far enough away to avoid cutting any nets, but close enough so that their boats rocked in our wake and the bottle-green glass floats on their nets bobbed up and down. This brought one of the fishermen out of his narrow, homemade cabin. He came into view and gestured angrily at us. They can do that now, said the gunner, now they feel free to shake their fists.

The islands came into sight. We wanted to pass them on our starboard side, and then head southward, when a vessel appeared out of the washed-out blue, a flat, low boat that passed the anchored ships at a high rate of speed, one of the new S-boats. The bow rose up out of the water, foam and white spray hid the stern. It was coming our direction. The broad, bubbling path it traced across the quiet sea curved toward us as we shifted course slightly. It almost seemed as if they were seeking a collision. They're after us, the quartermaster said, and gave the signalman a sign to ready himself. We reduced speed, the S-boat circled us once, and then we could see them lift the covers of both torpedo tubes. Their machine guns were unmanned, just the two torpedo tubes were trained on our scarred and dented broadside, with the necessary lead angle. No maneuver could have saved us. They looked us over carefully, taking their time before giving an order, waiting with motors idling, secure in their superiority—or perhaps it only seemed so to us. Finally they gave the order for us to proceed through the straits to our old berth, and we started out again, escorted by the S-boat, which remained behind us on the port side, letting us feel, for all its restraint, the power it could wield. From a distance we no doubt appeared to be traveling under its cover, bearing some important cargo. The gunner put down the binoculars and stood beside the quartermaster.

"We should have kept going, Bertram. I don't believe they even have torpedos."

"That's what you think."

"And even so . . . They wouldn't sink the MX 12. Look over there."

"You don't know their orders. I don't want to risk anything."

"Anyway, they have no right. The surrender has been signed. The rules apply to them as well. According to the law they have to remain at the dock and wait to be handed over. Like us. Like everyone."

"Tell them that."

"Do you really believe they would finish us off?"

"Yes. They're our countrymen. Don't forget that."

"You think we're in for it?"

"They'll give us a reception, our style."

"The crew is on your side."

"We'll see."

"Shall I ask them?"

"What?"

"Ask them, over there on the S-boat. Maybe they haven't heard yet that everything's over. It's possible."

"They're doing their duty. Or what they consider their duty."

A Danish flag hung limply over the crumbling fortress. The flag was flying over the hospital as well, and above the fishermen's market, and even on the damaged dredger, which had lost its bucket chain in a mysterious explosion. They stared from the shore in amazement as we passed through the straits into the harbor. Apparently no one had expected to see the MX 12 come back, turn about as always in the middle of the bay, and dock in front of the commandant's headquarters. Now that we were in the harbor, the commander of our escort manned their rapid-firing guns. They waited until we had put in to dock, then the low, slim boat turned and followed us to the pier.

They were expecting us. We had barely tossed the hawsers over the side when a squad of armed men—naval boots, belts and buckles, rifles on their shoulders—marched out of the shadows of the commandant's office, led by an officer who fulfilled his duty so self-assuredly that it appeared he had practiced every detail in advance. He halted the squad in front of the gangway, marched rapidly on board, walked right past the men without a glance, and proceeded directly to the commander's cabin. With the door still open, he delivered a message in lieu of any type of negotiation, and then accompanied the commander and the executive officer to the gangway.

The commander didn't speak to any of us. He didn't look up at the bridge, nor did he once turn around. He walked toward the whitewashed building oblivious to his surroundings, sunk within himself, offering no thanks to the executive officer, who held the door open for him. After he had disappeared, the officer signaled two marines, and all three of them appeared on the bridge, their faces dark and serious.

You're under arrest, the officer said. And that was all. No explanation, no sign of regret, no questions, just that single sentence that was meant for everyone on the bridge. Exhaustion hit me as we descended. All of us had to hang on to the railings, including the quartermaster. Down on the deck, the crew gathered in front of the gangway, clearing a path for us unwillingly, some of them nodding to us in encouragement, patting us confidently. See you soon, they said, or, keep a cool head, or, we'll soon get this straightened out. They were instructed by the officer to be ready when called upon.

Before we entered the commandant's office, I turned once more and looked back at our ship, then across to the other shore, to the trawlers and lighters, where at this moment the men were no longer working, but instead stood peering at us, spellbound by an event for which they found no explanation.

We were led into what must have been a record office. The dark-stained bookshelves were filled with files, manuals, rolled-up posters, and neatly tied bundles of forms and reports—part of the official history of the little harbor. The doors and windows were fitted with panes of milk glass. The double guard outside could be seen only as blurred silhouettes. One of our group went to a leaky sink and drank from the trickle, and three or four others did the same. After a while we sat on the table and on the floor. I felt a twinging pain in my temples, leaned back against a radiator, and closed my eyes. In spite of my fatigue I couldn't sleep because the gunner kept up a steady stream of talk. He had something to say to everyone, and seemed to think that he had to reassure each of us that everything would soon prove to have been a mistake, the hour had come for the others to give up the ghost. He said: I'll laugh my head off when the door opens and the English commander invites us to tea. He looked puzzled when the signalman asked him in a pained voice to knock it off, and then, when he kept on talking, finally yelled at him, shut your trap, or else! The gunner went to the door and listened, pushed cautiously on the door handle, and was surprised when the door opened. He came to himself quickly, however, when he saw the two guards, and asked them what was going on. One of the guards said: don't mess around, pal, get back in there. The gunner wanted to know if the English had arrived yet, and whether the ships had already been surrendered, to which the guard only replied, shut up and close the door.

At some point they carried in an aluminum stewpot and mess gear. A pale giant in overalls doled out a portion for each of us, glassy noodles cooked in salt pork—how sullenly he served the portions, how hastily, his forehead shining with perspiration. He didn't even pass out the bowls, just slopped them full and left them standing on the table. He was obviously relieved to get away from us. They changed guards while we were eating. We heard their formulaic exchanges behind door and window. The quartermaster ate very little, then gestured tiredly to the rest of us to divide up what remained of his share. The only thing he seemed interested in was the time of day. He stood up several times to look out at the sky.

Conversation started up again as twilight fell. Everyone knew something, or suspected something. They offered up their bits, their suppositions, from every corner, back and forth, in no particular order. One of them said, we haven't heard or seen anything of the crew. Another replied, surrender is surrender. Orders don't mean anything anymore. Listlessly the voices took their turn.

"I'd just like to know what they plan to do with us."
"Surely the whole crew can't be . . ."
"They could at least tell us something from time to time."
"The old man is probably dictating his report."
"They can't pin a mutiny on us."
"Maybe they've already made up their minds up there."
"I'm grabbing a few winks. Wake me if anything important happens."

Suddenly it was still. They sat up straight, listened, heard the sound of heavy trucks stopping outside the window, then rapid steps and a formal greeting at the entrance.

Everyone looked at the quartermaster, who stood in what remained of the light, approached the bookshelves, and rummaged quickly through the files and forms until he found a sheet of paper which was almost blank. He tore it out, took it to the window ledge and, still standing, began to write. He wrote without pause; everything seemed thought out. We had no idea what he was writing, yet each of us had the feeling that it concerned us too, that it involved us, and perhaps that was the reason why no one dared to speak. Large envelopes lay next to the hand towels. The quartermaster emptied one of them, crossed out the address on it, and replaced it with a name in capital letters: the name and rank of the commander. Then he folded the envelope, came over, and sank down beside me in exhaustion.

Here, he said, give this to the commander some time.

Someone yelled out "Attention!" and we all stood up as a young, gray-haired officer entered the room without knocking. He gave a sign for us to be at ease. He stood brooding for a while, then strolled among us, nodding to us, offering us cigarettes from a tin case. I noticed that three fingers were missing from his right hand. He lifted himself up onto the window sill and said, looking down at the floor: I'm your defense counsel. It looks bad, boys. And he added in a slow drawl: the charge is threatening a superior officer, refusal to obey orders, and mutiny.

Suddenly everything became perfectly quiet. Not one of us lifted his cigarette to his lips. The first person to get hold of himself was the gunner. He asked, we've surrendered haven't we? Yes, said the officer, a partial surrender has been signed. Then we can't be indicted, said the gunner, at any rate not by a German military court. The German military court still has specific jurisdiction over members of the German navy, the officer replied. That jurisdiction is clearly still in force and has not been ceded. But surely, said the gunner, we're under British custody now? Yes, said the officer, but that doesn't change anything in terms of judicial control. He gathered us around him, and as he sat almost motionless before us, he had us tell him what happened on board the MX 12.

The migraine continued, it throbbed and burned, and one eye began to water. As we walked down a dreary hall in the presence of the guards, I pressed a handkerchief gently against my eye and temple. A guard barred the way. He made me unfold the handkerchief and shake it out. Then he gave me a heartfelt shove, and I caught up with the others who were walking ahead in a silent row beneath framed prints of old ships. The room into which we were led—it might have been a lecture or dining hall—was poorly illuminated. Guards in steel helmets stood along the walls, armed with machine guns. Benches and stools had been placed on both sides of a large, thick table draped with the military flags of the Reich. There were more benches and stools than were needed. There were eight of us. We marched—we were marching now—across the wooden floor under the orders of a bowlegged boatswain. We stood marking time before the benches, then halted at a sign from him. We weren't allowed to sit down. Then the commander and his executive officer were brought in. They came through the same door we had, walked over to the stools opposite us, and waited expectantly. The commander didn't look at us, or return our gaze. Although we all kept our eyes fixed on him, he didn't turn his head. He simply looked past us, patiently, as if lost in thought. Nor did he seem to notice his executive officer standing next to him.

The naval judge and the others entered through a side door and walked silently to the table. There were six of them, all in uniform, and behind them the defense counsel. When they had taken a seat at the nod of the judge, we were allowed to sit as well. The judge opened the proceedings in a businesslike manner. He was an older man with sunken cheeks and bags beneath his eyes. He spoke haltingly, in a restrained manner, and now and then he would look up and squint toward the lights on the ceiling. At first, as he stated the charges, he showed relatively little interest, but then as he read our names and ranks from the ship's list, he seemed to be gradually overcoming a long-standing weariness. His voice became clearer, and from time to time he accentuated his words by tapping rhythmically on the table top with a silver-point pen. With a precise gesture he turned the proceedings over to an officer who seemed strangely familiar to me—perhaps I had seen his picture in the newspapers, the picture of a bright-eyed man who wore only a single decoration, for highest bravery, and whose dull blond hair was cut quite short. He laid his cap carefully before him on the table. It had no crease or dent, the blue material was stretched as tight as a drum. With the aid of notes he reconstructed the last cruise of the MX 12: time of departure, the announcement of the mission at sea, the rise of a conspiracy, and armed threats against the commander, ending in his removal from command. Finally, discontinuance of the mission and the independent decision to reverse course. When he stated that these events took place while the German people found themselve in a "decisive life-and-death struggle," our defense counsel looked up at him searchingly and then wrote something down hastily on a notepad.

The commander didn't do what they expected. Instead of narrating the events on board in logical sequence, he restricted himself to answering the questions that were put to him—hesitantly, and not turned so much to the highly decorated officer as to the court stenographer, whose face bore a lingering expression of astonishment.

"Would you tell us, please, what your exact orders were?"
"Courland. We were supposed to go to Libau in Courland."
"And what was your mission?"
"We were to pick up wounded soldiers."
"Pick them up?"
"And transport them. To Kiel."

"Was the crew aware of your orders?"

"I informed them as soon as we were at sea."

"So the crew knew your mission?"

"Yes."

"Which course did you want to take?"

"Northeast, along Swedish territorial waters. Later we were to head southeast."

"Did your people know that fighting was still going on in Courland? That an entire army—although cut off—was still resisting bravely?"

"Most of them knew it."

"So they knew that their struggling comrades needed help?"

"MX 12's mission was to pick up the wounded."

"The wounded, yes. Wounded comrades who had been lying for days on the narrow strip of land at Libau. Waiting. Waiting for you to take them home."

"We knew that."

"So, they knew that. And still the crew refused to obey orders. They knew what was at stake, and refused orders. Out of cowardice."

"It wasn't cowardice."

"No? What was it then?"

"I've commanded the MX 12 for two years. I know the men. It wasn't cowardice."

"Then tell us why the crew threatened the commander. Why command was taken from him."

"It was the risk. They probably thought the risk was too high."

"Was that your opinion as well?"

"No."

"It's the superior officer's duty to calculate the risk. He bears the responsibility. Do you agree?"

"Yes."

Suddenly, as the defense counsel asked him to describe what happened on the bridge, the commander looked in our direction. His gaze skimmed across us and settled on the quartermaster, resting there for a long time. They seemed to be exchanging glances, not harshly or in blame, but equally at a loss. And after the defense counsel asked him to describe the events from his own point of view, the commander began by mentioning the rumors that had spread that the war was about to end. He spoke of the mood that these rumors had produced while they were still docked in the harbor, even before they set out to sea. But he pointed out that there had been no breakdown in discipline.

We were underway according to orders, he said. The crew proved themselves during a rescue operation and an aerial attack. The bridge was occupied shortly before the second watch. The men were armed. They demanded that we discontinue the mission and return to Kiel. That was denied. Chief Quartermaster Heimsohn relieved the commander of his duties. He took over command on board. The commander and the executive officer were placed under arrest.

"Lieutenant Commander," said the defense counsel, "did the crew know that a partial surrender had been signed?"

"Yes," said the commander.

"When did they learn of this?"

"We were about ten hours at sea."

"Did you announce the surrender?"

"No."

"But you discussed it with various members of your crew?"

"Yes."

"With whom?"

"With Chief Quartermaster Heimsohn."

"In what sense? Do you remember?"

"We discussed the conditions of surrender."

"The conditions of surrender . . . You are aware that one of the conditions of surrender is a cease-fire?"

"Yes."

"Would you have held to one?"

"I think so."

"Even if you had been attacked? If Soviet planes had attacked the MX 12?"

"I don't know."

"Under the conditions of surrender, however, you would have had to give up any attempt at defending yourself. The MX 12 is under British custody. Moreover, a further condition states that all missions must be discontinued."

"I received my orders from the fleet commander."

"You mean you would have completed your mission in any case? Even if it meant breaking a condition of surrender?"

"You have to stand by something."

"Lieutenant Commander, how well do you know your crew?"

"Most of them were already on board when the MX 12 was stationed in Norway."

"Does that mean that you were prepared to rely upon your men?"

"Yes."

"In every instance?"

"In every instance."

"Did it occur to you that you might be relieved of your command?"

"No. —No."

"How could it happen, do you think? What led to it?"

"I've already said. It was the risk. It seemed too high to most of the men. They thought the MX 12 had no chance to get through to Courland."

"Is it possible that the crew's actions were influenced by the news of the surrender?"

"Absolutely."

"You're certain about that."

"There's no doubt."

"Let me put it another way. Do you think the crew would have followed your orders if the news of surrender hadn't reached them?"

"We went on many missions together, difficult missions."

"Please answer my question."

"I think that if it hadn't been for the surrender, the MX 12 would be on its way to Libau now."

At one point they called for a short adjournment. Those at the table withdrew, while the commander and the executive officer were free to leave the room, although both stayed. They leaned toward each other, whispering, and we were soon whispering to one another as well, seeing what each of us thought—after a moment of strong anticipation when, left alone in the room by the court, we looked over to the other side as if now surely something would be said that didn't concern the others. Nothing was said, not a word, no accusations. We sat across from each other in silence, finally turning to whoever was next to us for his advice, or passing along any idea of our own we thought might be of use. Only the gunner chose not to whisper; he paid no attention to the presence of the guards at the door. He declared in a voice everyone could hear that he did not recognize this military court. He even referred to it as a poor excuse for a court. Since the war was over, if anyone were to dispense justice, it would have to be in the name of the British monarch. Perhaps because no one contradicted him, he asked for permission to speak immediately after the court had returned to the room. He was allowed to have his say. They listened to him in exasperation and astonishment, and for a moment it seemed as if the naval judge was about to cut him off. But he let the gunner finish his speech, and then replied sarcastically, it would have surprised me if a man with your background hadn't raised doubts about the competence of the court.

The lights flickered, and several times they went out briefly. I massaged my temples in the darkness and pressed the handkerchief to my eye; the slight moisture that the cloth retained provided some relief. Each time the lights went out I felt a hand grope for my shoulder, the hand of the quartermaster, who stood next to me and answered in a monotone voice the questions posed by the highly decorated officer, with many pauses, sometimes conscience-stricken. Yes, he said several times, yes, I admit it.

"That's mutiny," said the officer, "General refusal to obey orders on the high seas is mutiny. Do you know what that means?"

"Yes."

"You took it upon yourself to relieve the captain of his command. While on a naval mission. I repeat: on a naval mission. While German soldiers everywhere were fulfilling their ultimate duty, you incited the crew to disobey orders. You made yourself the ringleader of the mutiny."

"At that time we had only one goal: to save the ship and its crew."

"You don't say? You wanted to save the ship and its crew? You wanted to sneak away, to run for it! Let somebody else go to Courland, we want to head home, we're knocking off work."

"The crew was determined to discontinue the mission."

"The entire crew?"

"Almost all of them. The commander knew that."

"So, the commander knew that. And yet he still stuck by his orders.

He was still willing to carry out his mission. He set an example for everyone. He did his duty. Do you think he wanted to sacrifice the MX 12? Do you believe that?"

"No."

"All right then! It's thanks to men like your commander that hundreds of thousands of men were brought to safety—men like him, who were prepared to take a risk, and even to sacrifice themselves."

"We wanted to avoid sacrifices, senseless sacrifices."

"Do you consider yourself a fit judge of what constitutes a senseless sacrifice?"

"Yes."

"So, and because you think so, you stormed the bridge with your gang. And deposed the commander. And placed him under arrest."

"If I hadn't done it, the crew was determined to use force. They had armed themselves without my orders."

"Oh, so we have you to thank that there was no confrontation on board? That no shots were fired? Do I understand you correctly? By relieving the commander of his post, you were preventing bloodshed?"

"I tried to do so. I knew what the consequences were."

"Then you also knew that the commander of a ship in military action has the power of disciplinary action?"

"Yes."

"He would have had the right to shoot you. But he didn't do it. In order to avoid spilling blood, he followed your instructions."

The officer who had taken over the defense apparently knew that the quartermaster had lost his ship twice during the war. He asked where it had happened, and the quartermaster said, the first time at Narvik, the second time while minesweeping in the Bay of Heligoland.

"What happened after you were rescued?" asked the defender.

"After they fished me out," said the quartermaster, "I reported again immediately to the shipboard command."

"How long have you been a member of the crew on the MX 12?"

"Two years."

"How did you get along with the commander?"

"I'd rather not talk about it."

"Would you like to say anything about his abilities as a seaman?"

"It wouldn't be appropriate for me to do so."

"But you respected them?"

"Yes. Always."

"And yet you didn't trust him to get the MX 12 to Courland? And back?"

"No one could have done it. Not even the best seaman."

"How do you know that?"

"I've seen the naval cemeteries at Riga, at Memel, at Swinemünde. We aided several sinking ships. And the emergency signals. We learned from the radio station how many SOS's were coming through. Nothing was getting through east of Bornholm."

"After you had taken command on the MX 12, you received an order from the fleet."

"Yes."

"What was the order?"

"To rendezvous with MX 21."

"Where?"

"Off Gotland."

"For what purpose?"

"To proceed together to Courland."

"You didn't do so?"

"No. MX 21 was attacked and set on fire. By air. It was drifting about, its engines damaged, unable to maneuver."

Finally the naval judge called on me. The others who had testified before me seemed to have heard and seen almost nothing. It was clear from their evasive answers that they were trying hard not to make things worse for the quartermaster. The naval judge looked exhausted now, his skin malarial. He asked me in a tired voice if I, as the man at the helm, had seen and heard as little as the others. I looked over at the commander and said: no. He lifted his head at that and gave me an ironic nod of praise, as if to say: well what do you know? Congratulations!

I was determined to tell everything I knew, and I did so. They got along very well, the commander and the quartermaster. As far as I could tell, they were old friends. . . No, I never heard any threats. . . No, the quartermaster never said that the crew would arm themselves. . . Just concern for the MX 12 and crew. . . The quartermaster most certainly did not order anyone to occupy the bridge. . . Yes, the first time I heard his voice was when it looked like something might be about to happen. Violence. . . I don't recall who placed him under arrest. . . Yes, I still remember the sentence distinctly: I'm taking command of the ship, with all consequences. And he added: I will bear full responsibility. The naval judge listened to me thoughtfully, then suddenly he asked: are you crying, man? No, I said, it's the pain.

They withdrew to confer, and once again we sat across from one another in silence. The commander sat very straight; there was something distant and aloof about his posture. I didn't dare just stand up and hand him the letter the quartermaster had given me. The gunner kept rolling cigarettes and furtively passing them on to us—for later. The quartermaster sat beside me with his eyes closed, as if he were meditating, while the radioman, as I could clearly see, was struggling to keep awake, nodding from time to time and then jerking back upright. We rose automatically as the court returned, and since they remained standing behind the table, so did we. The pain behind my eye and in my temples was pounding and ringing. Suddenly I had the impression that the number of judges had increased, and that wasn't all. Although only the naval judge was speaking, it seemed I heard many garbled voices, enlarging and expanding, tumbling over one another. He was talking about military law, to which everything else must be subordinated, about discipline and obedience and fulfilling one's duty in the hour of need. A frightening historical example was cited by way of warning: mutinous elements on board the largest warships. They had sworn comradeship at sea, comradeship in the chaos of battle, and constant discipline—the iron discipline required for survival. In order to counteract what he feared were signs of a general breakdown of discipline, the fleet admiral had issued certain orders. He ended by quoting them. Therefore, for refusing to obey orders, threatening a superior officer with violence, and armed mutiny while on a naval mission, Chief Quartermaster Heimsohn and Gunner Jellinek are hereby condemned to death. Then in a somewhat softer voice, the sentence must still be ratified.

I looked over at the commander, who stood there in shock. Then he moved his lips as if rehearsing the words, and finally, clearly enough for all to hear, he said, that's insane, that's simply insane. He walked up to the judge's table, determinedly, with labored steps, pointed at the judge and said again, it's insane. That can't be your verdict. The naval judge ignored his remarks and continued listing the prison terms for the rest of us.

We joined the defender in urging the quartermaster and the gunner to submit a petition for leniency, and it was at least midnight when the two finally gave in and sat down together to draw it up, on paper that the defense counsel provided. The quartermaster and the gunner searched for words, sighed, and looked at the defender whenever they found themselves at a loss for a turn of phrase. He sat on the window sill, smoking, and didn't seem willing to help them with the writing itself. The only thing he gave them was the address, which he dictated to them. Then he folded the pleas and stuck them in envelopes he had brought with him. He had nothing to say about the verdict. Perhaps he had nothing he wanted to say. Whenever the signalman or the radioman asked him what he thought about the sentence, he shrugged his shoulders and acted confident: just wait, just wait a while. Before he left, the quartermaster asked me to return the letter he had addressed to the commander. He gave it to the defender at the door, urging him not to forget, seemingly worried, as if a great deal depended on it. As he said goodbye, the defense counsel put his hand on the quartermaster's shoulder. Someone who was trying to sleep in front of the bookcases called out, douse the light, so I turned off the switch and stretched out on the floor. Everyone felt how much there was that needed to be said, but no one wanted to start, and the longer silence reigned in the record office, the more willing we found ourselves to accept that silence.

A guard opened the door cautiously and peered down at us briefly before calling out the two names, not loudly, and not in a tone of command, but almost inquiringly. We all rose and moved toward the door, and our quiet, challenging stance induced the guard to back up into the doorway. Jellinek, he said, Jellinek and Heimsohn. We're supposed to take them on board. What d'you mean, on board? asked one of us, and the guard replied, something's up, important visitors. We looked at each other in bewilderment. A gleam of hope registered on gray faces: on board . . . the petition for leniency. . . They want you on board. . . And we moved out of their way, and milled about, building up this new-found hope in our minds. The pale giant and his assistant brought us bread and marmalade, placed a steaming aluminum pot on the table, and withdrew without a word. No one touched his breakfast. When the salvos were fired—no, not salvos, two machine-gun bursts—the signalman groaned aloud, and someone went down to his knees before the radiator and gagged as if he were about to be sick. We listened. A few of the men had to hang on to something. It's crazy, the signalman said, the pigs—the war's over! It will never be over, the radioman said, the war will never be over for us, for the ones who were in it. That wasn't a sentence, the signalman said, it was murder. Do you hear, murder! The radioman bent over the man kneeling in front of the radiator and looked into his face. Go to the sink, he said, go on over to the sink.

TRANSLATOR'S AFTERWORD

In accepting the 1988 Peace Prize of the German Book Trade, Siegfried Lenz returned to the themes which have permeated his work for over forty years. In the face of a new historicism which attempts to neutralize the past, Lenz argued for the central role of unreconciled human memory and human passion: "For history is never over, its effect always reaches right into the present. It tests us, sets tasks for us, disturbs, reminds, and places obligations upon us, causing us to shudder in the face of the things mankind can do. What is needed in order to capture the spirit, good or evil, of an age, in my opinion, is not a cold and rational flight from human emotion, but a personal involvement prepared to pass judgment. For what is at stake was and always is a human matter. Anyone can locate historical documents, but the spirit of the age can only be grasped by someone who does not turn aside from his own inner self."

What is at stake in the stories of Siegfried Lenz is always a human matter. Whether we laugh or wince in pain, we do so in shared response to our common condition. Nor do we have to be German to feel the force of the lessons Lenz offers. His stories go to the heart of our problematic age.

Siegfried Lenz was born in 1926 in an East Prussian district that is now part of Poland. Drafted into the navy as a teenager near the very end of World War II, he served on submarine combat duty before deserting to Denmark, an experience reflected in the tensions and moral dilemmas of "The End of a War." After subsequent study at the University of Hamburg, he initially embarked on a career as a journalist. An original member of the Gruppe 47, Lenz published his first novel at the age of twenty-seven, but it was not until 1955, and the appearance of a series of simple tales set in his native Masuria, that he attained widespread recognition and popularity. These stories form part of a long tradition in German and Swiss literature that stretches back almost two hundred years, although Lenz's particular blend of humor and vivid characterization is in many respects unmatched in the history of the genre.

Lenz's breakthrough to international fame came with the publication of *Deutschstunde* (*The German Lesson*) in 1968, which was hailed throughout Europe and in America for its sensitive portrayal of the tensions between duty and human values in wartime Germany. A surprise bestseller, it was followed by a series of novels and short stories which have solidified Lenz's reputation as one of the finest living German authors. In 1970, at the invitation of Willy Brandt, he traveled to Warsaw together with Günter Grass to witness the signing of the German-Polish Treaty. Over the past twenty years Lenz has received every major literary prize offered in German-speaking lands.

Although known here primarily as a novelist, in West Germany Lenz is considered a master of the short story as well. The present collection introduces American readers for the first time to the depth and range of his shorter fiction. The stories within each section appear in the order in which they were originally written. The earliest story dates from 1950, while the final story in the collection was first published in 1984. Both the selection and the arrangement of the stories has been made with the author's approval.

Lenz's stories are deceptively simple. In these English versions I have attempted to be true to the carefully nuanced variations in tone which Lenz achieves as he moves from early stories in a style reminiscent of Hemingway, through political parables, to detailed and carefully observed social and psychological studies. I have also tried to preserve the varying levels of diction represented by a surprisingly broad spectrum of narrative perspectives and points of view, ranging from traditional third-person narration to first-person monologues, and from the intentionally naïve oral style of the village tales to the complex triple-narrative of "Fantasy," in which the author offers the reader a metatextual tour de force on truth and fiction.

The source of Lenz's power, however, extends beyond his technical mastery of a particular literary genre. What shines through these stories is a decency and humanity which reverberates deeply in the reader. The kindness, good will, and sympathetic tolerance are unmistakable, tinged with an ironic humor which tempers the sharp edge of social criticism. In story after story, he displays an unflinching eye for the human condition. His portrayal of the young wife in "The Exam" (1969) is typical of an unusual sensitivity, as is the devastating conclusion of "Sixth Birthday" and the case of mutual incomprehension depicted in "The Waves of Lake Balaton." The issues and problems he confronts in such myriad forms are always drawn in their full complexity. Lenz never points a finger which is not simultaneously directed at himself and the reader, at human weakness and human frailty, at human failure. Yet he does not shy away from judgment, and least of all when it comes to the larger questions.

In this sense the stories of Siegfried Lenz continue the crucial task of literature, which he has defined as an attempt "to transform our relationship to the world. Literature is effective when it explains, lays bare, awakens us. By offering alternatives, it challenges us to examine our own lives, in a word, to live with greater clarity. Even when it has been on the defensive, literature has always encouraged us not to give up the dream of better worlds." In accepting the Heinz Galinski Foundation Prize in April 1989, Lenz spoke again of memory and imagination as a "defense against the indifference of history," and announced that he would donate the substantial award he received to a home for the aged in Jerusalem. Then he prepared to depart, as he does each summer, for a small fisherman's cottage on the Danish island of Alsen, where for several years now he has painstakingly produced his stories at a rate of three pages a day.

Breon Mitchell